The Child
at the
Edge of the World

by

Alex Charlton

Grosvenor House
Publishing Limited

This book is published by
Grosvenor House Publishing Ltd
Link House
140 The Broadway, Tolworth, Surrey, KT6 7HT.
www.grosvenorhousepublishing.co.uk

A CIP record for this book
is available from the British Library

ISBN 978-1-80381-943-3

To John, the great facilitator.

With grateful thanks for everything
You do and have done for me and so many others.

It's about time that this was recognised!

With my love

X

Earlier Books by Alex Charlton

The Carousel of Time

Saving Graces

Chapter 1

London in November was probably one of the worst places in the world to live, Cathy Munro reflected, turning up her coat collar and wrapping her blanket scarf more closely around her head and shoulders. It was still pitch black and bitterly cold and Cathy had just finished her hell of a nightshift. She had soothed and healed people who were off their heads on drink or drugs; or old lonely people, desperate for a human voice to break into their world of isolation and silence. Cathy cared. She cared deeply about the human race, about homeless animals, about natural disasters, stray dogs and the ceaseless flood of people who flocked into her hospital's Accident and Emergency department by day and night.

She had recently started training as a Samaritan – a decision that her parents had received in horror, especially when Cathy had confided how challenging she found the trainer's instructions not to get involved with people who needed help.

'But, love, you are flat out being a nursing sister, and it goes against your character *not* to become involved with patients, animals – any living creature that needs your help! You have always given everything you can to anyone who needs it. How are you going to fit in yet another role that drains energy from you? Who actually *gives* you energy in your life?' her harassed mother, Jan, had asked her the previous Sunday, while whisking Yorkshire pudding batter with unnecessary violence.

'You do, lovely Mum!' Cathy gave her mother a hard hug. 'Talking of which, that batter will turn solid or your whisk will break if you beat it for much longer!'

Jan Munro burst out laughing. 'Sorry! You're right. It's your life and your decision. I'll stick to what I do best – cooking!'

Snuggling further into her scarf, Cathy smiled at the memory. She was just coming up to Waterloo Bridge. Only a few minutes now before she caught the Tube, reached home, and could sleep at last.

Idly, Cathy counted the metal uprights supporting the rails of the bridge and tried to remember counting games from her childhood – anything to occupy her tired mind as she determinedly strode along, focussing on the warm, neat flat that she would reach within the next hour. She started to hum under her breath, 'One, two, three, four, five, once I caught a fish alive … six, seven …'

But the next upright was moving, swaying forward and back, towards and away from the black, swirling waters of the Thames far below. Cathy stopped – the childish songs forgotten.

The young woman was tall and wrapped in a black coat. Her hair was long, thick and wavy, and surrounded her head in an unruly cloud, although in the dead pre-dawn November light, it was impossible to tell its colour. Her hands gripped the top rail of the inadequate safety barrier, and her right foot, in a flimsy lace pump, rested on the lowest one. She was rocking to and fro, her eyes fixed on the swirling black river beneath her.

Cathy stopped, nails digging into her palms. She took a deep breath and, drawing on her Samaritan training so far, said softly, 'Hi, can I help you? My name's Cathy.'

The other woman gasped and quickly placed her other foot on the lowest rail. Cathy swallowed down her panic and tried to keep her voice calm and steady, searching for a point of contact. 'You must be cold. Would you like to borrow my scarf? It was a Christmas present.'

'It's pointless. I'm going to be even colder when I'm in the water. Why are you even bothering with me?' Her voice was low and tired.

'Please tell me your name,' Cathy invited. 'If we are going to have a conversation, it's good to know who I'm speaking with.'

'Laura.'

'Laura, please talk to me. It's always good to talk. Please come down. We can go for a coffee – there's a stall over there just opening up.'

The tortured young woman gripped the rail even more tightly, and in the faint grey light of early dawn, Cathy could see her knuckles whiten.

'Why should you care about me? Why should anyone?'

'I do care, Laura. Perhaps if you could share what has brought you to this point, we may be able to work something out – together.'

'Why? That's ridiculous. We've only just met. Why have you taken the trouble to stop on this freezing morning and try to help me?'

3

'Because I'm a human being, just like you. We have that humanity in common. I can see how troubled you are, but at the moment you are only looking straight ahead – at the road you think is the only possible way forward. How about thinking of this night as a crossroads? There are other possibilities: you could turn right, or left. You don't know what opportunities there may be down these other roads.'

Desperate to make some attempt at engaging Laura, Cathy had recalled the words she had heard at a recent Samaritan training session. At the time, she had considered them just too trite and mundane and, even as she spoke, she had no real faith that they would have any impact. Whilst Cathy silently agonised over her clumsy approach, for what seemed like an eternity the woman on the bridge stood poised to jump. But then, almost as if the last vestiges of her energy had finally left her, she appeared to just slide off the rails and subsided on to the pavement, where she sat, holding her head in her hands.

'I can't think of the last time anyone said anything kind to me,' she whispered in a monotone. 'I've been told to move on by the police; to pull myself together by old women, walking their respectable dogs; and jeered at by teenagers who asked me how business was on the streets these days.'

Cathy laid her arm gently across Laura's bony shoulders, astonished at how very slight she was: it seemed as if there was hardly any substance beneath the worn and dirty material of the coat, as she wrapped her warm scarf around the fragile body.

'I just can't face that coffee stall,' Laura murmured, almost inaudibly. 'They would probably tell me to go away because I might put off other customers …'

'Well, we can't stay here,' Cathy said, quietly but firmly. 'Laura, if you can't face people at the coffee stall, please come home with me. I have a warm, safe flat. I have food and hot water. We can talk in privacy there.' Although Cathy's voice was calm and even, her mind teemed with conflicting emotions. She knew what her mother would think of the current situation, and how she would point out the obvious dangers of inviting an unknown, desperate person into her home. She could almost hear the unemotional tones of the Samaritan trainer, warning against 'becoming too involved with any party that approaches you'; and Cathy wondered what protocols would apply, since in this instance she had 'approached the party' herself. Lastly, and perhaps most searchingly of all, Cathy clinically reviewed her own motivation in offering refuge to this vulnerable woman.

Laura was shivering with reaction now and simply nodded without speaking. Cathy helped her to her feet and, as she linked her arm through that of the exhausted woman, she found that she too was shaking. When she had started her Samaritan training, naively, she had thought what an amazing achievement it would be to help save someone's life – but now as the merciless light of dawn showed the dirty clothes and defeated expression of her companion, she realised that there was no room for self-congratulation in this context. This was raw and difficult and heart-breaking.

Chapter 2

'So your mind is made up, Brother Jeremiah?'

The young Franciscan bowed his head and nodded, just once. His well-shaped hands, calloused from the hours he spent in the kitchen garden and orchards of the friary, lay still in his lap, fingers interlaced. As he began to respond to his companion, his only sign of emotion was that he clasped his hands more tightly together.

'He's in my dreams again, Brother Peter. I just can't get away from him. Prayer and work here in the monastery should mean that I have my mind set on my present life of service – or my spiritual future – not on the past, not reliving something I will regret all my life, but can do nothing about. Continuing here would be to live a lie, because I cannot follow the rule of our order. *"The spirit of prayer and devotion to which all temporal things should be subservient"* does not dominate and direct my life as it should.'

'Will you return to your family home?' asked the older man, the Guardian of the friary, whose title indicated the care he had of all friars, visitors and volunteers. 'You have earned a valued place in our community and in our hearts, brother. What will we do without our interpreter of dreams?'

Brother Jeremiah sighed and stood up. 'It's good to know that I have been able to give something back to you all in this place of peace, my sanctuary. Yes. I don't really have a choice. I have to return to the house where I was born – there is nowhere else for me to go but *The Edge of the World*. But I can't imagine that ten years of standing empty on one of the most inhospitable stretches of moorland in North Yorkshire will have done much to increase its charms!'

'Your neighbours must have given up any hope of the farm becoming inhabited again,' Brother Peter commented.

'Almost certainly – and they won't welcome me back with open arms,' the young friar reflected. 'I heard more than one muttered comment along the lines of "Good riddance!" when I said my goodbyes to the town and the dale that had bred me and my father, and his father before him.'

The Guardian nodded, thinking how passionate the young friar became when speaking of the place where he had been born – and how this contrasted with the systematic eradication of emotion that Jem showed in everyday life. 'When you joined our community, you explained that you had rented out the grazing to local farmers, although no one could be persuaded to live in the house and barn.'

'I wonder why not?' mused Jeremiah, very cynically for a monk.

Brother Peter stood up. 'Remember – your adoptive family is always here, Jeremiah. If you wish to return, our door will never be closed to you. Now go with God's blessing … and with mine,' he added quietly as he watched the tall, upright figure leave his study.

Chapter 3

Cathy's tiredness after her twelve-hour shift was forgotten as adrenalin helped her focus all her attention on the woman in front of her. As the raw November day slowly came into being, they sat on either side of the gas fire in the living room, sipping hot tea and eating toast. Gradually she saw some vestige of colour return to Laura's thin, pinched features and thought poignantly how lovely Laura would be if she was clean, fed and warm – such basic human needs.

Cathy did not want to put any pressure on the woman opposite her, and so for some time they sat in silence, each cherishing the comfort of the small flat in different ways, but eventually she asked, 'Would you like to tell me about yourself?'

Laura raised her eyes and looked at Cathy directly for some seconds, before replying, 'Yes, I owe you that.'

'You owe me nothing,' Cathy smiled. 'My mother would tell you that, when I was a girl, I never returned home without some bird or animal in need of love and care!'

Laura attempted to return the smile – and failed – before she murmured, 'Well, I would like to try to explain, but it's hard.' She sat for several minutes, clearly gathering her thoughts and energy. Finally, when she had absorbed the fact that, after months of isolation, someone was prepared to listen to what she was saying, she straightened her shoulders and lifted her head – just a little. 'My name is Laura Jamieson and I am twenty-seven. I was – I am – an artist. Ever since I was a child, I have loved the magic of the natural world – and this was what I painted. But when I left college, I realised that, although people liked to look at my paintings, they didn't often buy them.'

Once Laura had started speaking, it was like the release of a dam. Her thoughts and emotions poured out, sometimes too swiftly to make immediate sense to Cathy – who listened without comment as Laura spoke articulately in a soft, low voice, the shortness of her 'a's telling of her northern origin. Everything about her told its own silent story: the high-end fashion labels on her filthy, worn clothing; her passionate expression; her evident intelligence. Each characteristic utterly at odds with the desperate situation in which Cathy had met her.

'I was invited to exhibit at the *Affordable Art Fair* in Battersea and, as was often the case, my work attracted a lot of interest, although not many paintings sold. In contrast, other artists were selling many more canvasses. Towards the end of the afternoon, a man who had consistently given my paintings his attention during the day spoke to me. He introduced himself as Lewis Devrille, owner of a small chain of art galleries across the South East. We discussed some of the work I had on show, and he confirmed my conviction that the paintings would indeed appeal to a niche market – a narrow and specialised market to which he claimed he had access. He sounded so plausible, Cathy, and

I believed him. Before the exhibition closed, I had agreed to let him try to sell a dozen of my paintings and suggested that we review the situation in three months' time.

'During the following weeks, Lewis telephoned me regularly and then invited me out to dinner. There was a dark charisma about him. The best way to describe it is that I felt that just beneath his charming, sophisticated exterior there bubbled a hidden world of shadows, spellbinding and dangerous. The straightforward issue of Lewis acting as my agent soon became obscured by the complex relationship that was rapidly developing between us. I had dated the usual range of sixth-form friends, and then college students, but had found them limited in experience and, quite frankly, boring. But Lewis was like a chameleon: he changed constantly, and always there lingered about him an edginess, a hint of the forbidden and exotic. Almost against my will I found that I was being drawn further and further into his world. That first dinner led to others, in some of the most sought-after restaurants in London; to cocktails on rooftop bars and a seemingly endless round of experiences which many would describe as luxurious, but to my mind bordered on the decadent.'

Laura looked exhausted. She had gone pale again and her eyes slowly closed. Her painfully thin hands were still clasped around the, now empty, mug.

'More tea?' enquired Cathy, resting her warm hand on her companion's cold ones.

'Yes. Yes please.' Laura's eyes jerked open again.

After the homely routine of kettle-boiling, mug-rinsing and tea-stirring, Laura continued her story, but only after a long pause, during which she examined closely the wholesome, composed face of the woman who had rescued her. 'You look as if you have never come across anything … unpleasant or unnatural in terms of human relationships, Cathy.'

Cathy threw back her head and laughed. 'You're joking!' she retorted. 'I'm a nursing sister in a central London hospital! All manner of natural and unnatural events cross my path. Bodily fluids of the most diverse and disgusting kinds haunt my working hours! I am virtually un-shockable!'

Fleetingly, a faint smile caused Laura's generous mouth to curve upwards softly, but her expression soon became pensive and anxious once more. 'Lewis started to fascinate me,' she continued slowly. 'But I could never anticipate what mood I would catch him in when next I saw him. We became lovers, but always I felt our relationship was on the brink of something dark and dangerous. He started to expect our lovemaking to include things I felt to be repulsive. And there came a night when I knew that what we had experienced together was just pure sensation, with a complete absence of tenderness or love. But what makes me loathe myself more than anything, Cathy, was that the more Lewis drew me into his extreme and sadistic practices, the more ensnared I became.'

Chapter 4

There had been minor changes in the small community clustered along the banks of the river, but Lokisbridge startled Jeremiah by its overall familiarity. As his long, easy stride took him past the grey, stone-built school which he had loved, his feelings were in turmoil; but despite this, he smiled as he saw once again the scuffed, green-painted front door, the outside toilets and the steamed-up windows of the classrooms. Everywhere he looked, superficially things appeared to be the same, but on closer inspection were subtly different. St Mark's Church of England Primary School had been extended since he had been a pupil there: he could just make-out a rectangular building to the rear of the school with a tall, slender, cross-shaped window at the near end – presumably a new hall. What a luxury! He remembered how, together with a handful of his classmates, he had cleared a space for school assembly in the junior classroom. They had pushed back the battered tables and chairs, so that the children could sit facing Miss Wilkins, his charismatic Headteacher. The impact of her assemblies had never left Jeremiah because she had the gift of making the most obscure concepts relevant, and Jem knew that his faith had its roots in that shabby classroom. Looking again at the building that had given him the only colour and comfort that he had known in his young life, Jeremiah reflected that he had never forgotten what she had taught him. He had loved his time there in the bright, lively place which was light-years away from the remote farmhouse that he was forced to call home. It seemed only a few months ago that he had left behind his carefree childhood at the school – but it was nineteen long years, a young lifetime.

There was the sweetshop, allegedly the oldest in the country, which he had visited weekly on his way back home from school. Each Friday morning, he was given his pocket money surreptitiously by his mother and he daydreamed through most of the afternoon lessons, deciding whether his precious pence should be spent on Kit-Kats or Space Dust, Polo mints or a chocolate bar. He laughed quietly to himself as he recalled his intense decision-making process – so naïve, so uncomplicated.

At school, much to his relief, he had been known as Jem, because whatever had possessed his father to name him Jeremiah had always confused and puzzled him. The Walkers had a tradition of using Biblical names for their children – based no doubt on their intense relationship with the chapel – but Jeremiah was unusual even for them. Had his father had a premonition that tragedy would come to the Walker family of *The Edge of the World*, through the actions of their only son?

Jem shivered and slowed his pace slightly as he passed the small stone church and churchyard which lay on the outskirts of Lokisbridge. An indefinable expression, blending sorrow, regret and bitterness, crossed his face as he glanced at the rows of headstones, most with neat pots of flowers, but just a few neglected and overgrown, images of lives forgotten.

Switching his worn backpack, stored under his bed during his years at the friary, to his other shoulder, he started to climb the steep road that led from the bustle of the town up to the silent stretches of the moor which lay, ever-changing like a magic cloak, above Lokisbridge. Jem felt he could close his eyes and still find his way up the narrow, winding road. A broad bend to the left, then a short, very steep incline; a sharp bend to the right and then the drystone boundary wall of *The Edge of the World,* enclosing the fields which had been cultivated by his family for generations. You couldn't see the farmhouse yet: it lay, low and brooding, in the centre of its land, facing the setting sun.

Jem was lithe and fit and the rhythm of his breathing hardly changed as he reached the highest point in the climb to his family home. He paused for several minutes, before turning slowly with, he was shocked to discover, tears in his eyes, to look down across the undulating landscape to the L-shaped range of buildings at the heart of *The Edge of the World*.

Was the emotion regret at lost innocence; sorrow at the repressed life his mother had been forced to live; bitter memories? Wiping his eyes on the back of his hand, Jem gazed steadily at the prospect in front of him.

It was sunset, and a clear, cool spring day. The farmhouse and its attached barn were silhouetted black against the orange-gold of the late-afternoon sky, an outcrop of stone lying immediately to their left, in front of which spread an extensive gorse thicket. From this distance, the farm looked unchanged and Jem could almost believe that his mother would once again have a casserole simmering in the kitchen range, as she had diligently done every afternoon on his return from school – the high spot of her lonely and limited day.

He should have waited until the morning. He had come with a sleeping bag, a single blanket and with matches to light a fire, but with no food or drink to sustain him. So overwhelming had been the impulse to leave the friary and return to the place of his birth, that he knew he had overlooked practicalities.

Jem felt and saw and heard everything with a heightened awareness: the curlew's haunting call; an owl in a small copse away to his left; the imperceptible chill of the evening, descending over the dale and turning field and tree and house to shades of violet and dusky blue. He had forgotten how utterly beautiful it was here.

In the friary, Jem had become used to praising the wonders of creation in general, but in doing so he now realised that he had forgotten the intense excitement that he felt in his guts when he looked at the expanse of the moor and the sharp angles of stone and crag, which surrounded the land which had bred him. He had anticipated the pain and difficulties of returning here to Lokisdale, to this grim, cheerless house, but he had forgotten the impact of the breath-taking loveliness of the place: this, he thought, is the quintessence of beauty. And, for the first time for as long as he could remember, Jem smiled.

Chapter 5

As Cathy drew back the curtains on the unprepossessing grey morning, almost tangibly Laura seemed to gather her strength to continue her story.

'As I was drawn further and further into my relationship with Lewis, I was conscious of becoming distanced from my family. They live in the Yorkshire Dales, in a market town called Lokisbridge – not just down the road I know, but distance had never stopped me spending weekends or even holidays with them, especially my grandfather, Geoff Jamieson. If I told Lewis that I was planning a weekend back home, his jaw would tighten, and he would point out with exaggerated patience that he had planned some particularly special evening or event for us both to share. Without exception, after I had met Lewis, I always cancelled my plans.

'I lived in a spartan, rented flat in Islington and, one March day, was putting the finishing touches to a painting of daffodils – you could almost smell their wild, heady scent – when my phone rang and I saw Lewis' name flash on to the screen.

'"I've sold the last of your paintings, Laura. Let's move in together to celebrate!"

'I didn't have much to pack and so, less than a week later, I moved into Lewis's penthouse flat.' Laura placed her mug of tea carefully down on a side table and suddenly stood up, folding her arms tightly across her chest and bowing her head. She started to pace to and fro, her features pinched with real anguish. 'Cathy, it was terrible! I soon became a virtual prisoner. If I picked up my phone, Lewis would demand to know who I was ringing or texting. He learnt my passcode and I caught him on more than one occasion reading through my messages. Many facets of his character that I had only suspected started to show themselves in earnest. I remember one night I came in later than expected, and before I could sit down, Lewis snatched my phone and entered the passcode.

"I knew it!" he hissed. "You're having an affair!"

"What are you talking about?" I protested.

"This *Nicola* that you have just thanked for a great afternoon is really *Nick!* Don't try to deny it!" And he hit me across my mouth with the back of his hand.

'Lewis's paranoia poisoned every aspect of our life together. If he did allow me to leave the flat, I had to promise to be back by a certain time, otherwise physical violence or mental abuse would follow. Our lovemaking became almost totally an expression of disgust, rather than one of love, and this too was abusive and violent. I could no longer paint, because Lewis would make sure that my time was occupied with things that *he* had planned, things that *he* wanted to do. And – it's almost impossible to believe now – I stayed because I felt that, somehow, without him, I was a failure, and that, somehow, he would change.

'Things came to a head several months ago. It was my father's sixty-fifth birthday and, as she had done since his stroke five years earlier, Mum was planning a party. It was, of course, expected that I should be there and I genuinely wanted to escape the dark existence into which I had been drawn in London. Above all, I longed to spend time with my grandfather in the safe and wholesome little world which he had created on his farm. It's a hill farm Cathy, above the snow-line, high and remote – and to me it has always been a magical place … Anyway, on the Friday morning of my father's birthday weekend, without telling Lewis, I left the flat shortly after he did and caught a train to Harrogate. The weekend was bliss – I had forgotten how sane people behave! During my stay I had just one text from Lewis. It said: *"I'm waiting for your return…"*' Laura's voice had become quieter and quieter and finally just petered out entirely.

Cathy waited for what she felt was an interminable length of time before saying gently, 'Laura, you must be tired. Do you want to leave the story there? You can finish tomorrow if you wish, or just leave it all together – you don't have to carry on if it's too painful.'

'I want to finish it, Cathy – there's not much more. It's been really helpful talking about it all – it's the first time I've had the opportunity! It reminds me that I am a person – with a voice, and opinions … and a story …

'Like a fool, I returned to London and went back to the Canary Wharf flat. Although it was mid-afternoon and I thought Lewis would be out, he wasn't. He was sitting motionless in a chair opposite the door of the lounge. As I came in, he stood up without a word, and crossed the room in two strides. I find it difficult to remember exactly what happened next, but I know that I must have lost consciousness, because I came to outside the door of his flat, surrounded by my ripped and bloodstained clothes and my handbag which had burst open and spilled its contents across the black granite tiles. Fortunately, as the flat was the penthouse, there was no one else on that floor and so, dazed as I was, I managed to pull on most of my clothes and drag myself to the lift. I pressed the button for the ground floor, but I must have fainted before the lift had reached ground level.

'I was told later that the concierge had discovered me and phoned for an ambulance. I had broken ribs and severe head trauma – and I was as sure as I could be that Lewis had raped me. When I had finally recovered enough to tell the hospital my story, they called the police, but by then it was too late for forensic tests to prove the rape.

'I was discharged from hospital several days later and the police escorted me back 'home' to the penthouse flat, still badly bruised and with my clothes still torn as I had nothing to change into. When the door was finally opened by Lewis, and he was challenged by the woman police constable who had accompanied me, he looked directly at me, undisguised disgust on his face.

'"Did I assault this woman? Are you serious? I wouldn't touch her for fear of catching something. Good day."'

Chapter 6

Even though she had listened to Laura's stilted and heart-breaking story until midday, years of shift work meant that Cathy woke automatically around tea time ready to start her night shift from 9pm. She didn't quite know what to expect as she walked quietly towards her sitting room, where she had installed Laura on a sofa bed. Would her unexpected guest be awake; would she perhaps have left? Cathy felt herself hoping fervently that the fragile bond of trust that had started to build between them the previous day would be sufficient to encourage Laura to feel safe in the tiny flat – and to stay.

Opening the door silently she saw Laura still sound asleep, curled like a child in the foetal position. Strands of hair lay damply across her face and Cathy saw with compassion that she had been crying – she must have been crying in her sleep.

The noise of the kettle boiling at last roused Laura, who sat up, eyes wide and startled, looking around her and snatching the duvet to her chest – almost as protection.

Maintaining as calm a voice as she could, Cathy called from the kitchen, 'Tea or coffee, Laura?'

'Tea would be lovely – thank you!' and then, looking around the neat space in which she sat, she asked, 'Am I quite safe here? Can I really stay?'

With her best professional reassuring smile, Cathy popped her head around the sitting room door. 'Yes, on both counts! Now would you like to shower before or after we eat?'

With a huge sigh of happiness, Laura lay back on her pillows and smiled. 'Before, please!'

⇥⊪⇤

'The extensive menu today centres around eggs – boiled, scrambled, poached or fried – and toast.'

Laura turned a flushed and happy face towards Cathy. 'Scrambled please – and lots of toast, if I may?' She had scraped her wet hair back into a bun and was wrapped in a towelling bath robe that Cathy had given her. It had a 'C' emblazoned on the front and Laura had asked, 'C for Cathy?'

'No, C for Champneys!' Cathy had replied. 'I obtained it illegally on a hen weekend!

Laura sat and ate the food placed before her as if she was ravenous – which she almost certainly was. As she bent forward, the bath robe fell forward and open.

'Have you hurt yourself, Laura?' Cathy asked, immediately concerned.

'Hurt myself? What do you mean?'

'Well,' said Cathy, looking more closely, 'that looks like a scar, or a wound or something …'

'This!' exclaimed Laura, lightly touching the large strawberry-shaped birthmark on her left breast. 'It's been the bane of my life! High-necked tops, bikinis that cover, rather than reveal – something I was born with, Cathy. It's not sore, it's just annoying!'

The women chatted as the last vestiges of the late autumn day faded and Cathy drew the curtains. Turning on the lights, she said quietly, 'Laura, I've been thinking.'

'You want me to leave!'

'I do *not* want you to leave,' Cathy reassured her. 'I have just been wondering whether you should contact your family to let them know where you are. Have you been in touch with them recently? Do they know what happened to you, Laura?'

Her companion shook her head.

'But why not?' asked Cathy gently.

'In a nutshell, my parents would have been shocked and would have been all too ready to show their disgust. My brother – he would probably have laughed dismissively. And my grandfather – well, it would have broken his heart.'

Cathy glanced at her watch, standing up and putting on her coat. 'I need to go to work, Laura, but, after our somewhat random mealtimes today, why don't you make yourself some cocoa and try to sleep again. There are books and magazines over there, by the window and I'll try to get something other than eggs for our supper tomorrow!'

'I don't know how, but one day I will try to repay your kindness.'

'For now, following medical instructions – cocoa and bed – are thanks enough! See you tomorrow, Laura.'

Half an hour later, walking across Waterloo Bridge once more, Cathy shivered as she relived the events of the previous night and felt as delayed reaction the full weight of what she had done. She shook her head in the bitter November air as if to dismiss the tide of unanswered questions that were bombarding her. How long would Laura have to stay with her? Would Laura's family want her to move back to live with them? What did Laura's future hold? What did her own future hold? Had she been a fool to trust someone entirely unknown to her?

Only time would answer these questions, but in the meantime, Cathy hoped with all her heart that her instinct to care and protect the vulnerable had not in this latest instance let her down.

Chapter 7

Geoff Jamieson shrugged on his waxed jacket, turning up the collar against the rain that was sweeping almost horizontally up the dale and was streaming down the west-facing windows of his square, stone farmhouse. He jammed on his cap over his thick white hair, whistled to his dog, Fly, and skirted around the range of traditional stone outbuildings to his large, purpose-built sheep barn. In foul weather like today he left the barn open to the field where his newest lambs and their mothers were grazing, so that they were able to take shelter in its warm, dry interior. It was here that Geoff was heading now, to take a head-count of his sheep and their lambs before night came.

His flock of Swaledale ewes numbered around fifty. Sometimes, when old ewes died, it was a couple less; sometimes it increased, when he kept back promising young lambs for future breeding. Most of the year Geoff was comfortable in managing this group of docile, predictable animals but, at lambing time, he had recently become acutely aware that he was, in fact, an elderly man. Setting his alarm for midnight, three a.m., and six a.m. took its toll and he found himself nodding after supper. But he had seldom lost a lamb.

His skill and wisdom as a shepherd were legendary in the dale.

Coming into the sweet-smelling barn, Geoff shook himself, almost with the same vigour as his young sheepdog, before starting to count the lambs and their mothers, marked so that each could be matched to the other. He had lambed a full hundred this year – the sort of return that made hill-farming worthwhile. The ewes were all present, but he reached a count of only ninety-eight lambs, and sighed. As the flock were settled for the night, lambs tucked in close to their mothers' warm fleeces, he didn't think that any had moved – but he would have to re-count. Ninety-eight again. Geoff groaned inwardly. There was nothing for it but to grit his teeth, push his hands deep into his pockets and go out again into that filthy weather. Almost May, and he could swear there was sleet in the wind. Yorkshire was 'God's own country' indeed – but all Geoff could think was that God must be tough!

Settling his cap more firmly on his head, the old farmer steadied himself against the weather outside the tranquillity of the barn. 'Away, Fly!' he commanded the slight, black and white Border Collie who had followed him like a shadow. The dog raced off to the right and was soon lost in the darkness of the night: Geoff mused that he had been right to call her Fly – she flew indeed.

The young dog returned, but clearly her searching run had not found the two missing lambs.

'Come Bye!' ordered Geoff, and now Fly shot away to the left, delicate paws skimming the sodden turf. Geoff waited, but she didn't come back. She must have found something. He lifted his whistle and blew a series of short staccato blasts, but still the dog did not return. Then he heard a regular bark, from quite a distance, over towards the gulley where the spring water supply to his farm poured from the clean limestone of the Dales. Geoff sighed – ah well, good lass, she had done her work.

Flicking on a powerful torch, which he had brought with him from the barn, Geoff walked slowly and carefully across the wet, slippery grass, past the chicken sheds, the entrance to the south-facing fields and on up the gentle rise in the farm drive and the entrance to the spring gulley. He shook his head with exasperation – this was just about the worst situation for any lamb to get lost. Geoff had spent the best part of half a century levelling and improving the fields of *Fell Farm*. But the spring field remained rugged, dotted with sharp boulders and hollows and peppered with gorse.

Fly renewed her barking. She was standing, her nose pointed directly towards the well-chamber, which – Geoff's intake of breath was sharp and his expletive violent – had been opened. The faintest baa-ing sound came from within the chamber. Unthinkingly, he stumbled forward, anger making him careless and, his leg twisting underneath him, he tripped and fell headlong towards the stone slab of the well-chamber, which had been pushed to one side. His torch arced into the sky and landed on its square base, the beam pointing upward to the overcast heavens. Geoff knew no more.

⊰⊱

Jem was beyond freezing. He had been at *The Edge of the World* for a fortnight and was uncertain as to whether he was physically able to stay much longer. His haunted dreams had remained but had become a

26

little easier to manage, because the images in his nightmares were distorted echoes of the reality of his surroundings and it was easier for him to differentiate dream from actuality. When he opened his eyes, panting and sweating, he saw the bare stone, oak shelves and familiar small fireplace of his old bedroom.

Often, in the Friary, he had had dreams which seemed to be relevant to one or more of the other brothers and he had shared them. Sometimes the dream had solved a problem which one of the other men had been pondering; sometimes it would pose a question which brought about change. Howsoever one wished to explain the phenomenon – as a curse or a gift – it was uncanny. But here, in this gloomy, joyless house, there was no need for interpretation. Jem understood only too well the origin of his own, torturing dreams: they were to do with him and him alone, and they could bring about no alteration of the events which had torn his world apart over a decade earlier.

He shivered on his hard bed, wrapping the grey blanket he had brought from the Friary more closely around him inside his sleeping bag. He had been awake for hours because of the sub-zero temperature and finally abandoned his attempts to get warm inside the tangle of inadequate bedding. Slowly he extricated himself from his sleeping bag and stood up, still wrapped in the blanket, arching his back to ease the stiffness in his spine. In a desperate attempt to get some warmth into his limbs, he started to pace to and fro between the bed and the window of his bedroom.

Before joining the Franciscans, Jem had slept here for as long as he could remember – with the exception of a few short, painful months. In daylight, the outlook was breath-taking: down over the dip of fields to the farm boundary and the sheer drop in the dale side to what was now the reservoir. But Jem remembered the days before the flooding of the dale, when his eyes had scanned over farm fields to the deeper reaches of the valley, which held the tiny hamlet of Laikinthorpe. There the chapel that he had attended with his parents stood austerely next to an inn, appropriately named *The Good Shepherd*, and ancient stone cottages were scattered along the narrow tracks which intersected at the centre of the settlement. The whole dale had been horrified when it had been announced that the upper reaches of their beloved Lokisdale were to be dammed to form a reservoir, to serve the ever-increasing population of Harrogate and Leeds. And they were outraged that the unspoilt and historic settlement of Laikinthorpe would be flooded in the process.

The surface of the reservoir was implacable, unchanging, and Jem shivered as he thought of the myriad secrets its waters must conceal. Ripples of light from the moon and stars occasionally enlivened its surface – but not tonight. Tonight all was black, all was bleak.

Jem leaned his forehead against the cold stone of the window embrasure, shivering uncontrollably. Why wouldn't his haunting thoughts go away? He had prayed for ten years for forgiveness and yet nothing changed. As usual his thoughts circled, torturing him. He had to get out of this dank bedroom – simply had to get some movement into his limbs, maybe have a hot drink, even though his destination was the hardly more hospitable kitchen. Jem walked slowly, by the light of a candle, towards the staircase, intending to light the filthy, rusted range which he had managed to resurrect.

But by the round window at the top of the staircase he paused, his attention caught by a light he didn't recognise, shining steadily upwards towards the leaden sky.

Jem had not lived in the Dales for most of his life without developing a keen awareness of the unexpected. In this harsh, demanding environment, humankind had to look after its own. He opened the heavy front door, surmounted by the eroded date stone proclaiming that the farmhouse had been built in 1653, and stood outside, listening attentively. Years of working on the farm, and then in the orchards and gardens of the Friary, had heightened Jem's hearing and he was attuned to the slightest sounds of the natural world. First, he heard the wind in the grass and the gorse surrounding the ancient house; then an owl, flying overhead on silent wings, betrayed only by its call. Finally, more distant, he heard an insistent, distressed barking and realised that the light he had seen from the top of the staircase and the barking were coming from the same direction.

In an instant, his mind was made up. The range would take ages to fire up sufficiently to boil the water. He would warm up just as quickly by walking briskly in the direction of the light and the barking dog.

During his years in the Friary, Jem had stayed almost the same size, although he had broadened and become stronger. The clothes he now wore were those in which, nearly eleven years earlier, he had arrived at the community of Franciscans over towards Skipton, but tonight, in the unseasonal rain and sleet, he realised how threadbare they had become. He slung his cloak – which the Guardian had insisted he take with him – around his shoulders and draped an old sack over his head. It would have to do.

He strode swiftly over the heather and low-growing bilberry bushes, and out through the entrance of his family farm, glancing automatically at the outcrop of rock lying like a sleeping beast to the side of the building. He followed the narrow moorland road and then, guided by the light and sounds which marked his destination, turned down a bridle-way for a couple of hundred yards before reaching the gate of *Fell Farm*.

Almost immediately he could see the origin of both the barking and the unwavering beam of light. To his left, the land fell sharply away and he could hear the rushing sound of a spring surging from the bank beneath him. In the faint yellow light of the torch, he saw a young dog, on her feet and standing guard over the body of a man which lay at an awkward angle against the spring chamber.

Jem leapt over the wire fence and in a couple of strides reached both dog and man. 'Good lass,' he murmured, praising the young sheepdog and caressing her head and ears before turning all his attention to the soaking-wet man, lying with his leg twisted awkwardly underneath him. Jem carefully folded back the collar of the waxed jacket which the old farmer had turned up against the weather. 'Mr Jamieson?'

Geoff Jamieson blinked hard, bringing himself back into consciousness. 'Oh it's you, is it, Jeremiah Walker? I heard you were back in these parts.' The old farmer impatiently wiped away a trickle of blood which was seeping from a deep cut in his temple. 'Those bloody lambs have nearly been the death of me! They're in there,' he gestured to the partly-open stone chamber into which the spring gushed. But, in moving, he winced with pain.

'You must keep still, Mr Jamieson,' urged Jem.

'Since when do I have to do what the likes of folk like *you* tell me to do?' the injured man retorted with surprising energy.

'Because you are hurt, possibly badly hurt; you are soaked through; and you may have concussion. Do you have a phone in the farm?'

'Humph!' exclaimed Geoff Jamieson. 'I've got a portable phone – a mobile my son calls it. He got it for me and nagged me until I started to use it. He said it was either that, or they would force me to sell the farm and move into a retirement bungalow in the town! I tell you, it would have been death by degrees! I was just about to call the doctor when you came up and poked your nose into my business.'

Jem suspected that the old man had been unconscious for some time and that no phone call had been attempted – it had been at least half-an-hour since he had first seen the tell-tale torch light. 'Fine, go ahead. I will just sit here and keep you company, Mr Jamieson.'

'Don't want – or need – the likes of you on my land.'

'I will try to get to those lambs then, whilst you phone. And Mr Jamieson, please make that a 999 call – not just to your doctor.' Reluctantly Jem left the side of the old farmer and approached the spring chamber. He managed to reach his arm down to a stone shelf where, against all expectation, he found the tiny twin lambs, relatively warm and dry, since they were shielded from the freezing rain outside and much of the spray from the spring in their hiding place. He tucked them both inside his cloak.

All the while, Jem was listening for signs of a conversation between Geoff Jamieson and the emergency services. He heard nothing and, looking at the old man, saw that, once again, he had slipped into unconsciousness. Holding the lambs with his left arm, Jem retrieved the mobile phone from the old farmer's limp hand. He punched in the emergency number and summoned an ambulance then, moving himself, lambs and dog against Geoff's inert body he tried to create as much warmth as he could for the injured man.

Mercifully, the paramedics arrived within thirty minutes and Geoff was stretchered away to the ambulance, wrapped in a thermal blanket, before it headed off at speed towards Harrogate General Hospital. Jem watched the flashing blue lights as they reached the main road and disappeared into the night, the sound of the siren still audible for some minutes as the vehicle followed the twists and bends of the valley road. Dripping wet, still clutching the lambs in his left arm under his cloak, Jem secured the entrance gate to *Fell Farm* behind the ambulance and thoughtfully stroked the young sheepdog. With a hundred and fifty ewes and lambs on the farm without a shepherd, and a shivering sheepdog by his side, what, exactly, should he do now?

Chapter 8

The weeks and months slid by, and Cathy and Laura settled into a low-key, but comfortable routine. Cathy followed her punishing schedule at the hospital and Laura fitted in with the cooking, shopping and cleaning which form the mundane framework of domestic life.

One bright spring day Cathy was on lates and sat, yawning, catching up with her newsfeeds: so much unrelieved gloom! On top of the relentless flow of hurt and injured human beings that crossed her path, the pictures of destruction in Syria and of violence in streets not very far from where she sat made Cathy feel that she needed some lighter relief before she stood against the tide of need that would meet her later that evening.

She glanced at the pile of magazines and scattered papers on the low table in front of the window and wandered slowly in that direction. Moving a copy of *The Big Issue* to one side, she saw several sheets of neat – almost decorative – handwriting, and read:

Lucy Luccini lived in Chelsea. She was a white cat, with sleek fur so perfectly-groomed and spotlessly-clean that it didn't look real. She lived in a white house, with a front garden protected by ornate railings, which was full of white flowers.

Lucy worked in advertising. Hers was the poised face that haughtily surveyed an immaculate kitchen; hers the green eyes that scrutinised expensive food laid before her by the human beings with whom she lived; hers were the perfect, pink-padded paws that glided over the black and white marble-tiled halls of the great and the good ...

'That was soooo good!' Laura burst through the front door of the flat, brandishing a bunch of slightly dishevelled daffodils.

'I assume you mean your run? Good! But where did you get those from?' grinned her friend.

'Just picked them! There are loads in the parks and along the roadside even!'

'Laura, you can't just pick flowers like that! They're municipally owned!'

'Oh for goodness sake, Cathy! Go to Farndale!'

'Is this some sort of new insult, Laura?' Cathy smiled.

'Don't be daft! Farndale is in the Yorkshire Moors. There are tens of thousands of daffodils there and you can pick *armfuls*. No one will tell you off – there, beauty is for everyone to share. But anyway, these are for you,' she smiled handing over the flowers.

'That's really kind of you, Laura! I'll try and revive them with CPR – or possibly a vase of fresh water!'

'What have you been up to, then? Do you mind if I have an apple?'

'Of course not! Just coming round really and trying to prepare my mind for the daily dose of human need.'

'How can you keep on working as you do, Cathy, day after day, night after night, dispensing advice, care and healing?' asked Laura, munching her way steadily through the apple.

'Because I believe it's what I am best fitted for – how I can best contribute to society … but I could ask you the same question! How can you produce lovely things like these?' Cathy fanned out the exquisitely written and illustrated sheets of paper which she had unearthed on the table in front of her. 'I thought you were an artist, not an author: your illustrations are wonderful, but your words make me want to read more!'

Laura swiftly crossed the tiny kitchen and gave Cathy a hug. 'When you rescued me, I felt that I would never be happy again. I will never be able to thank you properly. You have given me safety, space and understanding – so much so that a couple of weeks after I started to live here, I tried to start painting again.'

'I suspected it, but never saw any real signs.'

'But Cathy, I hated it! It seemed so pointless, just depicting flowers or leaves, without any real context and so, almost without making a conscious decision, I started to write the sort of stories I used to write when I was much younger – before I went to Art College – and to illustrate them. I watched the pigeons strutting about on your neighbours' roofs; and the comprehensive personal hygiene of that white cat that comes to sit on your garden shed. Once again, I started to imagine animals with human characteristics.'

'So the white cat is the origin of the spoiled model-cat in *Lucy Perfect Paws*?' asked Cathy.

'Yes – and the pigeons are the paparazzi who constantly photograph her as she sashays along the streets.'

Cathy frowned slightly, seeking to understand. 'What sort of stories are you writing, Laura? Presumably they're for children …'

'Mmm – not necessarily,' mused Laura. 'I suppose you could say that I am trying to create modern fairy tales – and I love a good fairy story now, just as much as I did when I was ten! Readers will accept themes – moral stories, if you like – that they would never otherwise accept, when animals, rather than human beings, are the protagonists. Can I be serious with you for a minute, Cathy?'

'Of course.' Cathy's patience was infinite; and she listened to the unburdening of her friend's heart – however frequent – with patience, or eagerness, depending upon the amount of energy her demanding job had allowed her.

'When I met Lewis, I was shocked at the evil, twisted way of living into which he drew me. I had come across it before I met him and had skirted around it, never encountering it directly. I don't think much of how life is led down here in London, Cathy. People lie and cheat to get their own way. They believe that money can buy them anything – and the sad fact is that, usually, it can. Perhaps if I can produce books that are of high enough quality, I can make people realise how empty this sort of life actually is. Apart from you, I have met no-one that I think is half-decent since I came down here to Art College. That's a terrible indictment of society and a waste of nine years of my life!'

'Nothing's ever a waste, Laura, whatever you feel now. But you can't draw the cat and those pigeons forever! You will need more subjects, or models, or whatever you call them.'

'I know, Cathy, and I'm not sure how to begin to say this. We have become such good friends and I owe you so much – I owe you my life.'

'But you are leaving.' It was a statement, not a question, and Cathy's heart felt physically heavy in her chest as she spoke.

'I've got to. I need to get back to the countryside I grew up in. There seem to be more animals than people per square mile in Yorkshire! And I love it – I've tried to explain to you how much I do! There is space, kindness and honesty and people seem to have time – for living.'

'Listening to you talking about Yorkshire, I have come to understand a little of what it means to you – however sad I will be to lose your companionship.' Cathy stared down at her hands, short-nailed and neat, folded in her lap, always consciously controlled.

Laura continued, articulate and passionate, 'I'm going to see if I can stay with Grandad for a while – until I can see where things are financially. He is well into his eighties, maybe even more, but has no help feeding and caring for his small flock of sheep and a fluctuating population of chickens! Perhaps he will let me live with him in exchange for help with the animals, or anything else that needs doing. You must see. You do understand, Cathy?'

'I do. But I will miss you – so much,' Cathy sighed, adding almost inaudibly: 'You will never know how much.'

Chapter 9

As the last faint sounds of the ambulance disappeared into the night, Jem was left alone in the bitter, driving rain, on another man's farm, with no company except his neighbour's sheep and the slight young dog standing at his side.

'Come on then, my lass, we need to find shelter.' Jem spoke softly to the Border Collie, bending to stroke her sodden fur. She was shivering now – whether with reaction, cold, or exhaustion, Jem wasn't sure.

He followed the tarmac drive of *Fell Farm* as it swept in a curve back towards the farmhouse, outbuildings and sheep barn. Whatever else he did, he would have to warm up the lambs that were still tucked inside his cloak as soon as he found the means to do so. They were young and he had seen life too often snuffed out prematurely because of cold and wet. Fly trotted obediently at his heels.

As he entered the sheep barn, Jem smiled despite himself: what a set-up! It was clean, dry, spacious and airy – exactly the conditions that sheep needed in order to thrive. He remembered how, when he was a boy, a neighbouring farmer had nodded sagely when several of his breeding ewes had taken it into their heads to scale the perimeter drystone walls of their farm and then wander off into a nearby quarry.

'Aye, born to die – that's sheep for you!'

Shepherding was an art, not a science, mused Jem. You had to be several steps ahead of the helpless, strangely all-absorbing creatures, when you were a shepherd. It was a way of life, never just a job. As he surveyed the barn, Jem wondered if his father, involved with a range of complex spiritual issues that Jem only half-understood, had ever realised just how devoted he had been to those wilful, illogical animals in his father's flock. He doubted it. But he knew, looking at the content, munching ewes and suckling lambs, that he had missed this shepherding way of life more than he had realised. Anything that Jem had done with and for his father's flock had been the butt of criticism but, patiently, he had continued to do his best, when his father had been absent for hours, or sometimes days, involved in activities to do with the Chapel he attended so fanatically.

Leading off the barn to the south of *Fell Farm* were several stables, in one of which was a heat lamp which presented Jem with the solution to the most pressing problem on his mind – the potentially hypothermic lambs. Taking with him Fly and the young animals, which were already showing worrying signs of disinterest and torpor, Jem threw a bale of fresh straw into the stable and turned on the heat lamp. In the warm, red glow, he slit the binder twine that kept the bale together, shook out the sweet-smelling golden hay and spread it thickly over the floor of the stable. He then grabbed a couple of rough sacks heaped in a corner, stripped off, laying his sodden clothes on the straw where the warmth of the heat lamp would gradually reach them and, wrapping himself as best he could in the sacking, curled up with lambs and dog in the unbelievably sensuous heat of the lamp. Life as a friar had made Jem even tougher than had his Dales upbringing, but tonight he was cold and exhausted and, curling the young dog into him, for companionship as well as warmth, Jem slept until the remarkably loud bleating of the lambs assured him that they were now ready to be returned to their mother for feeding.

⊰⫯⊱

'Father, what were you thinking of?' Geoff Jamieson's son, Michael, bit tentatively into one of the most edible hospital biscuits he had managed to find.

'Doing my job, lad – running my farm.'

'But you broke your thigh, you were concussed, and you nearly died!

'Don't be daft. It were an accident – that's all! Even you, Michael, with your careful bank manager ways, couldn't have foreseen what happened. Accidents are accidents – unexpected – that's that.'

'How about if that neighbour of yours hadn't found you, father?'

'Humph!' Geoff grunted. 'He's no neighbour of mine.'

'Father, don't be so ... so intransigent! Jem Walker is geographically your neighbour and, in Biblical terms, your neighbour indeed!'

'Oh for God's sake, Michael, don't start being sanctimonious with me! Whether you know it or not, I object to that young man's very existence! Go and write your sermon for Chapel next weekend!'

Michael Jamieson sighed deeply. His father seemed totally indestructible. It was true that Geoff had very nearly died – the consultant who had received his father into A & E a week earlier had been brutally honest with him.

'When your father was admitted, I would not have given him a ten percent chance of survival. Whoever phoned the emergency services undoubtedly saved his life.'

Michael had never been too sure of the background to his father's hatred of the Walker family. He knew that before his father had married Lily, his mother, he had been engaged to another woman, and wondered whether his father's animosity stemmed somehow from this relationship.

Michael Jamieson was worried. He sat, hands folded carefully in his lap, watching his father. Geoff had closed his eyes, but Michael was unsure as to whether he was actually asleep, or simply excluding him through feigning sleep. Even in a hospital gown, his father looked indomitable: mouth closed in a firm line, the network of lines on his face denoting a life of hard work and tough decisions. The hospital had made it plain that Geoff was not, under any circumstances, to return to his isolated hill farm alone. His age and the nature of his injury – his left thigh bone was badly broken – made this impossible.

'Could your father come to stay with you until he has recovered?' the consultant surgeon had asked.

'The problem is his farm,' Michael had replied, running his hand through his thinning hair. 'He has a flock of around one hundred and fifty sheep at the moment.'

'Couldn't you or your wife manage to feed them or whatever needs doing?'

'Impossible, I'm afraid,' Michael stated categorically, shaking his head firmly. 'After my stroke, I just cannot undertake work that is too strenuous, and my wife is simply too busy.'

The consultant stood up abruptly. 'Ah well, I am not an agricultural adviser, nor a social worker – just a repairer of damaged human beings. Make whatever arrangements you can, but one thing is absolutely certain: your father cannot be discharged from hospital without our being assured of appropriate support and after-care. Good afternoon.'

The only solutions that Michael had come up with were either to sell the farm – and he knew that his father would never agree to this – or to somehow ask an experienced shepherd to act as caretaker until his father was recovered enough to return. And the only person he could think of who would fit the latter description was, ironically, Jem Walker! Michael decided to try again.

'Why do you dislike the Walkers so much, Father?'

The old man's eyes shot open. Michael's suspicions had been right – he had not been sleeping.

'Amongst other things, because there is bad blood in their veins. It showed itself in the past and it has shown itself again in young Walker's life,' grunted the old farmer.

'Please help me understand,' said Michael, in his best Bank Manager tones. 'If I understand, things will be much easier.'

Geoff Jamieson paused, sighed, and, in a controlled and measured voice, began his story.

'Jeremiah Walker's grandfather, Ezra, and I were good friends when we were lads. We were on Lokisdale cricket team and we did everything together – walking, shearing, even stick-making, although we were pretty rubbish at it. We sat next to each other in junior school and ended up in the same class when we went to the high school. People used to call us David and Jonathan. You with your Bible ways will understand that better than most: we were inseparable and I thought we were true friends. Anyway, the War came along and there was excitement in the dale. We were young and we thought we were immortal. Ezra and I started to ask girls out for walks or for a beer in the local – usually girls we met at dances. We went through quite a few I can tell you! But no one serious until I met Jennifer.'

'Was it love at first sight, Father?' Michael asked, smiling a little patronisingly.

Geoff looked at his son with distaste, his clear blue eyes boring into Michael's. It was an eternal mystery to him how he had managed to father such a weak namby-pamby lass of a son! 'Don't know about that … but, yes, I loved her with a young man's extreme feelings, not the deep abiding love that lasts a lifetime – aye and becomes stronger through that lifetime – which I felt for your mother. We became engaged just months before I was called up and joined the Green Howards Regiment. The army sounded just down my street: adventurous, risky, active, seeing the world, but Jenny was beside herself.'

The old farmer had become pale and thoughtful – evidently reliving his past. 'Jenny was bonny, with soft red lips and shining, dark hair, and that night we sat by the range until the early hours with me just stroking and threading my fingers through her beautiful long curls. It was 1943 and I was nearly nineteen. I tried to reassure her, explaining that I couldn't bear to think of the land which had bred me and her being taken over by Hitler and I was prepared to fight for our future – hers and mine. I said that I would be back before she knew it, maybe even by Christmas, and that we would arrange a Christmas wedding. She smiled and cried at the same time and I was puzzled by the look – almost of fear – on her face. Eventually, just before dawn, she nodded and said that she must leave before my parents were awake.'

'But this is a happy story so far, Father! What happened to make things go so wrong, because clearly they did. You married mother, not Jennifer – why not?'

'Because Ezra bloody Walker married her!' shouted Geoff.

The door flew open and a nurse stepped briskly into the room.

'Now then, Mr Jamieson, you know you mustn't get yourself all excited like this. I would have thought that some would have known better.' She looked accusingly at Michael, before saying to him in tight, clipped tones, 'If you cannot keep your father calm, then I think you should go, Mr Jamieson.'

'It won't happen again, nurse,' Michael mumbled, biting his lip.

'All right, but I am just outside!' warned Nurse Raymond.

'Please continue, father,' Michael implored. 'I never knew any of this.'

Once again, Geoff Jamieson's steady, steely gaze settled on his son. 'I had been away in Sicily for two months and Jenny had written at least every week to me. Her letters gave details of the weather, the state of lambing, prices of lamb and wool – all things important to me – to us both. But then, one day her latest letter came and, as usual, impatient, I tore it open. It said:

"Geoff, I have news. I am expecting your baby. I suspected it before you went away, but now I am sure.

44

When did you say you were coming home? It is a long time until Christmas."

'A long time indeed! My regiment was under pressure and it was impossible to be granted leave. I can't remember how I replied to her, I was so upset and worried for her, but I assured her of my love and tried to explain the impossibility of returning quickly in these circumstances.

'I heard nothing from Jennifer for two months then she wrote me just a couple of terse lines:

"Ezra and I were married last Saturday. I still do not show that much and we can pass off the baby as Ezra's if we are lucky. Yours, Jennifer Walker." '

Father and son sat, silently, whilst the side-ward clock ticked off the seconds.

'What happened when you came back, Father?' asked Michael.

'Well, it was way past Christmas! Sarah had been born. She had lovely auburn hair just like our Laura – same colour as mine used to be. Everyone had accepted what Jennifer and Ezra had said – that she was their child, born early, and Jenny was already pregnant with another baby. How anyone could have acted like that. How any friend could have betrayed another like that … David and Jonathan indeed!'

Geoff Jamieson was agitated. His gnarled hands gripped and twisted the crisp hospital sheets, as he fought to regain some measure of calm.

True to her word, Nurse Raymond was certainly 'just outside', and entered the small side ward like an avenging angel. 'Goodnight, Mr Jamieson,' she admonished Michael, firmly holding open the door for him to leave.

Chapter 10

'Hello dear.' Michael's wife, Orla, greeted her husband absent-mindedly, pushing up heavy-rimmed spectacles on to her high, white forehead. 'Had a surprise today. Laura wants to come home. Well, to be more specific, she wants to stay with your father.'

Michael sat down at the kitchen table and looked at his wife, thinking how attractive she was still. She had dark hair – without a hint of grey – finely-formed features inherited by Laura, and open, clear eyes, which she insisted on disguising with those hideous spectacles. It had been a mystery in Lokisdale when the lovely, outgoing Orla Carr had agreed to marry the stolid Michael Jamieson. As always in the closely-knit market town of Lokisbridge, there was surmise and gossip, ranging through suggestions that she was "getting too old for the marriage market" to her "being in the family way". But the final consensus had been that she had married for respectability and "prospects", a favourite word amongst the careful Yorkshire folk.

Michael sighed and complained querulously: 'I would have thought that by our time of life, our affairs would have become easier, not more difficult! That was the whole point of moving nearer to Matt – and my father – for support and for convenience. But no one seems to do anything ordinary in our family! Why doesn't Matt find a nice Dales' girl and settle down? He is getting close to forty.' Belatedly taking in what his wife had just told him, he paused, digesting the information, before saying, 'But I suppose Laura's visit could be a blessing in disguise. She could take care of Father and relieve us of one worry at least.'

'Filial love!' muttered Orla under her breath, before adding audibly, 'Are you OK, Mike? You look quite pale. Do you want me to call the doctor?'

'Oh, I have just had a dose of family history of the most passionate kind,' Michael said wearily. 'It's exhausting listening to Father when he rants on like that.' And he gave his wife an outline of what Geoff Jamieson had told him earlier.

'I wouldn't fret over-much if I were you, Mike. That sort of thing must have happened many times during the war years. I am sure that the Dales used to be a hotbed of incest and intrigue!' she added, tongue in cheek. Even after over forty years of marriage, Orla's husband was often totally unaware of his wife's rather sardonic sense of humour and took what she had said at face value.

'Yes, I suppose so,' he mused. 'But there is something else that he didn't have time to tell me. I'm sure of it! A fury of a nurse interrupted our conversation. It's another part of the story that centres on the Walker boy.'

'The Walkers are an interesting family … and wasn't there was some sort of scandal? Maybe your father was going to talk about that. It must have happened just before we moved here, because I remember at the time I noticed a lot of lip-tightening and tutting on the part of people who came from the old Dales' families, whenever the Walker family name cropped up.'

Orla stood up and walked quickly to the window. She looked out over the regimented rows of bedding plants in their over-manicured back garden, pressing her forehead against the cool glass of the kitchen door and closing her eyes. Over the long years of her marriage, Orla had consistently supressed her natural instincts for excitement and change, and had learned to channel these into her academic work. But occasionally, she found herself longing for something unexpected to happen in her life, which would surprise and delight her. Today was one of those occasions and looking at her introverted, anxious husband she found this longing almost unbearable. She couldn't wait to get back to her third-year students' essays on the Iliad, where a beautiful woman was the cause of war and men fought and died for their principles. Jerked back to the present, Orla bit her lip when her husband sighed peevishly. 'I can't recall, Orla. I was trying to come to terms with so many changes in my life at the time. I missed my job, York, and our beautiful house there so much. I still do!'

Orla sighed resignedly. 'Are you ready for lunch?'

⬗∥⬖

'He … what?' Laura shook back her mane of thick, unruly hair. 'Why didn't you let me know?'

Laura had arrived later that same afternoon and had scarcely entered her parents' house before she asked about her grandfather. Now she stood facing her mother with an expression which combined disbelief and disgust in equal measures.

'We were going to, dear, but …'

'I'm going to visit him – right now. You say he is in Harrogate General? I will need to take your car, Mum.'

Only half-hearing her mother's response – 'Of course, darling' – Laura snatched the keys from the carefully-organised row of hooks and abruptly left her parents standing in the kitchen: Orla concerned and Michael non-plussed. Watching her daughter striding towards her small car, shoulders set and head held high, not for the first time, Orla sighed, regretting all that she had sacrificed for security and status.

⊰∦⊱

Nurse Raymond, who had summarily dismissed Michael Jamieson the previous day, nodded approvingly and smiled as the slender, auburn-haired girl raced across the ward into the side room where Geoff Jamieson was propped up on his bed, reading a copy of the *Farmer's Guardian*.

'Grandad, are you alright?' Laura carefully enfolded the old man in her arms and kissed his forehead.

'Course I am, lass! What have they been telling you?'

'Not enough!' Laura declared passionately. 'I had no idea you had had this accident until an hour ago. I came as soon as I could'.

Glancing out of the corner of her eye at the conversation between the old farmer and his granddaughter, Nurse Raymond was delighted at the transformation she was witnessing in her patient. Geoff Jamieson's face had lit up and his features had softened when he smiled at his young visitor – he even imperceptibly straightened his shoulders.

Half-an-hour later, Laura stood up. 'It's decided then. I will move in with you and then you can return home. Whatever needs doing on the farm, I will do it. You needn't worry about anything apart from getting better!'

Chapter 11

Laura drove her mother's car through the gate to *Fell Farm* and followed the curving track to the farmhouse and stone outbuildings. Her father had told her that it had been five days since Geoff had been taken into hospital and Laura was beside herself when Michael had reluctantly admitted that neither he, nor Orla, had been to the farm to check on the livestock since Geoff's accident.

'Oh, for God's sake!' she had exclaimed impatiently. 'There are lambs there at the moment. It's cold and wet – they could die! They could all be dead by now – five days in a state of hypothermia leaves only one outcome. Don't you care, Dad?'

Michael had started to mutter something, embarrassed and shamefaced, but Laura cut across him. 'It really doesn't matter what *you* thought and felt, Dad – not in these extreme circumstances. I'll drive up to *Fell Farm* this afternoon and see what is happening. I just hope Grandad has some lambs to sell this year!'

She jumped out of the car, anxiously scanning the fields and farmyard, ready for the worst. But, to her surprise, everything seemed remarkably orderly. It was a cool, bright day and the sheep and their lambs were grazing contentedly in the meadow next to the big purpose-built sheep barn. The water troughs had been filled and fresh hay had been placed next to the lamb feeders, in which there were still traces of supplementary food.

Laura frowned, puzzled at the signs of very recent shepherding. From the other side of the barn, she heard a long, piercing whistle and within seconds saw Fly, her grandfather's black and white Collie, racing down to the southern boundary of the farm. The dog circled slowly behind a ewe and her two lambs, who had been showing too much interest in a section of the boundary wall from which some of the stones had fallen away. You could almost read their minds, Laura thought: any minute now they would scale the weakened wall and jump out of *Fell Farm* land. But the Collie had intercepted their break for freedom and, stalking behind them carefully, head level, steps measured, she drove them back to whoever was whistling.

Laura ran lightly to the end of the stone outbuildings and around the sheep barn. A tall, broad-shouldered man was bending to gently caress the ears of the dog that had just so effectively done her job.

'And who the hell are you?' she asked.

Jem looked up sharply and caught his breath. At that moment Laura reminded him vividly of a pre-Raphaelite painting which the Guardian of the Friary had in his room: it was of the Archangel Michael, about to attack Satan who had appeared in the form of a serpent. St Michael's intense blue eyes blazed, his hair formed a vivid cloud around his ivory-pale face and the look on his chiselled features was one of undiluted anger. If Laura had possessed a sword, Jem was convinced that it would now be pointed at his heart.

'This is my grandfather's farm. I say again, what are you doing here?'

Jem straightened his back and returned her direct gaze, holding her blue eyes with his dark brown ones.

'My name is Jem Walker. I found your grandfather after his accident and I've been keeping an eye on the place since then.' He bent once again to stroke Fly.

Laura was wrong-footed – but only for a second. She was used to the direct, insolent stare of the men she met in London, whose eyes rested only for an instant upon her face before slipping insidiously down her slender body, dwelling lasciviously on those parts of her anatomy which interested them most. A man who held her gaze strongly and steadily, acknowledging her as a fellow human being rather than a sex object, was refreshing indeed.

Laura lifted her chin slightly, realising that her challenge had been out of order, but defiantly maintained her position. 'Well, in that case I must thank you,' she acknowledged.

Since her experience with Lewis, she had wanted no contact with men and spoke to them only when she absolutely had to. Every natural inclination in her urged her to approach this stranger and shake his hand, but she simply could not bring herself to do this and so, maintaining her distance, she introduced herself. 'I'm Laura Jamieson, Geoff's granddaughter. I am going to live with him and so he will be all right now. I can look after the farm. But thank you for your care and attention.'

Jem smiled slowly and his reflective, thoughtful face was transformed.

'That's just great, then. Good to meet you.' He turned on his heel and instantly Fly was on her feet, ready to follow him. Smiling gently, he paused and bent to stroke her silky head and ears, before commanding her to 'Stay, Fly'. Then, without a backward glance, he strode away along the farm drive and out into the bridleway.'

Fly whimpered quietly, sitting by Laura but gazing after the man whom she had started to regard as her new master. Unconsciously mirroring Jem's gesture, Laura bent to stroke the young dog. She hadn't the first clue as to how to handle a sheep dog, or to look after sheep, or anything related to the farm really but, with her grandfather back home, he could tell her and she could follow his instructions. She would learn! They would be fine.

⋙⋘

Jem's long stride carried him swiftly across the springy heather. How he had enjoyed those few precious days at Geoff Jamieson's Farm. He had immediately taken on the care of the sheep, working from first light, when he washed in the stone chamber of the icy farm spring, to his bedtime, when he curled up in the hay barn next to Fly. Some of the almost negligible rental money he received in respect of grazing rights to the land at *The Edge of the World* he had spent on bread, cheese and apples in Lokisbridge. But above all, beyond all these rudimentary comforts, *Fell Farm* held none of the dark memories which seemed to seep from the very stones of his family home. In the warm stable of Geoff Jamieson's well-tended, well-organised small farm, Jem's agonised dreams had not visited him and he had been so exhausted at the end of each long day's work that he had slept, dreamless.

The age-old lines of drystone walling; the fields full of sheep; the moor sweeping away until it met the sky in a bold, carefully-drawn line – Jem registered none of these things, because his mind was fully occupied with the woman he had just met. During his years as a monk, he had focussed as intently as he could upon devotion, work and prayer, constantly praying for forgiveness. But, insidiously, in the middle of the long dark nights, thoughts of the few women he had known would disturb the calm immensity of his sleep and he would long for a loving touch, a warm smile, the sort of partnership that could transform his life without the thronging shadows of the only meaningful relationship he had ever known …

⇥║╞

Laura unlocked the farm door and went into her grandfather's rather dark, old-fashioned kitchen. The solid-fuel Aga – where Geoff cooked himself meals, boiled his battered kettle and warmed up lambs that had been born in rain or snow – was out, and the old stone house smelt musty and felt dank. Laura shivered involuntarily. She glanced around, mentally listing priorities, then took a deep breath, went out to the car and unearthed another thick jumper. She had seen her grandfather clean out and light the Aga countless times, and so proceeded to remove the ash and load up the fire box from the scuttle which she knew was kept in the utility room. Within half an hour the ancient range had started to emit its usual comforting heat. Geoff Jamieson scorned central-heating and so Laura had to use her ingenuity to air the house: she lit the living room fire and the wood-burning stove in the snug, opening all the doors so that the heat would gradually circulate and warm the house through.

Her mobile rang. 'Laura, it's Mother here. Will you be coming home for lunch?'

Laura was still seething about her parents' attitude towards her grandfather's accident. Her mother had always been an academic, but these days seemed to be even more deeply-immersed than ever before in a seemingly endless series of obscure classical texts. As for her father, the word hypocrisy sprang to mind. How could he preach to others about doing good, when he had never provided the slightest support for his own ageing father! She took a deep breath, trying to get her anger under control before replying, somewhat tersely, 'No, I won't, Mum – but thank you for checking. There is so much to be done here, if Grandad is to return home. I'll warm up some soup or something. See you later.'

Laura went into the north-facing, stone-shelved larder. There was a block of Wensleydale cheese, some mouldy bread, potatoes and a couple of tins of tomato soup. Looking at her grandfather's meagre provisions, Laura blinked back tears. How *could* her parents bear to live the very comfortable life they did, only a few minutes by car away from an elderly relative who clearly did not have either the inclination, or possibly the means, to feed himself adequately. She angrily emptied the can of soup into a saucepan and opened a lid of the Aga, basking in its warmth whilst stirring her lunch with a wooden spoon. Laura never bothered overmuch about eating – there always seemed much more important things to do. As she impatiently ate her lunch, munching automatically on a slice of the heavily-trimmed cheese, she started to think.

She knew that she had been harsh with Jem Walker. If it hadn't been for him, her grandfather, she knew, would be dead. She rubbed her eyes wearily, remembering Jem's soft brown hair and the way in which his smile had been generous and completely open, with a lack of guile shown only, in Laura's previous experience, by the very young. She also recalled how her natural reaction was to shake Jem's hand, and winced at how she had been physically unable to do so. Would Lewis Devrille's toxic legacy never end?

Staring out of the mullioned window across the small front garden, where her grandfather still found time to cultivate Grandmother Lily's favourite plants – Sweet William, Primroses and Wallflowers – Laura was shaken out of her reverie by the sound of her mobile phone.

'Cathy! How wonderful to hear your voice! How are you?'

'Oh OK, Laura. More importantly, how are you? I need to talk to you.'

'And I to you! How much I have to tell you!'

And so the emotional, bitter narrative poured out of Laura: her parents' neglect of Geoff Jamieson; his accident; and her frustration at how she had handled her meeting with Jem.

'I felt so rude, Cathy! This man had saved my grandfather's life and I just could not act like a decent human being! I kept seeing Lewis's distorted features sort-of overlaying this man's – his name is Jem. Will I ever leave that nightmare behind? It's been almost a year …' She spoke through gritted teeth and her voice betrayed her frustration.

'Laura, of course you will. It's still early days. Sometimes people never get over an experience such as yours. I think you have done brilliantly! How is your grandfather now?'

'He's OK. Thank God I am in a position to move in here and support him, Cathy! I honestly don't think my parents would notice if he dropped dead at their feet! But I'm sorry – I have just wittered on about myself – how are you?'

'Well … I have been in better situations,' Cathy replied hesitantly. 'I was laid off yesterday. More NHS cuts …'

'Oh, Cathy,' Laura exclaimed penitently. 'I've just been going on about myself and you are in this awful situation. Maybe I've inherited my parents' self-centred genes! I'm so sorry.'

'No need to apologise,' Cathy reassured her friend. 'The big worry is my mortgage. It's hefty, as you know, and I just can't sustain it without any income, so I'm going to have to put my lovely little flat on the market.'

'But you can't! Everything in it represents a milestone as far as your life is concerned. I remember how you told me the stories behind your things, as you were nurturing me back to normal life: the rug from your holiday in Istanbul; the lovely bed-linen your mum bought you as a birthday present; the quirky line drawing you found in Borough Market … your flat's the place where I found myself again. There must be something we can do – how about temping, Cathy?'

'Not really,' replied her friend, somewhat evasively. 'Anyway, the purpose of my call – apart from asking how things are at your end – was to enquire whether you felt like some company? I can instruct agents tomorrow and give them the keys. I can't really do anything useful here and it's quite difficult just staring at the same four walls – however much I love them!

Originally I had thought that I could find a cheap B & B somewhere and just keep you company but, after what you have just told me, perhaps I can be of more use than that: perhaps I can help you with your grandfather. I have worked with a lot of elderly people and you can't care for him *and* run the farm.'

'Oh Cathy, I would love that!' exclaimed Laura. 'When can you get here?'

'The day after tomorrow?'

'Done!'

Chapter 12

As she had promised, Cathy arrived two days after her telephone call. She looked tired and, Laura thought, the best word to describe her appearance was 'beaten' – almost as if, from left-hand field, life had dealt too harsh a blow for her to parry effectively.

She met her friend at Harrogate train station in her mother's car and, after giving her a hard hug, bundled her case and bag into the boot. Cathy thought ironically how the tables had turned: she was now in the weaker position, and Laura was the one who looked fit and glowing with health.

'So is your grandfather home yet, Laura?' Cathy enquired.

'Nearly,' Laura responded, putting a positive spin on the situation. 'I have explained to the hospital that we need just a couple more days to get the house ready for his return. They were most impressed when I explained that a London nursing sister was coming to share his care with me!'

Cathy said nothing, and Laura glanced sideways to see her friend's head bowed and tears in her eyes.

'Nursing was always what I wanted to do – even from being a small girl,' Cathy gulped. 'I put sticking plasters all over my dolls and teddy bears and drove my mother mad when I tried to bandage up our cats' legs – they were forever getting the bandages caught on plants in the garden. It's all I'm any good at ...'

Laura rested her left hand lightly on Cathy's thigh and said very seriously, 'It's not, you know. You are good at connecting with people who are lost and feel that they are worthless and have nothing left to live for. You are good at listening, not talking *at* someone. You are good at making a home the *best* place to be. And above all, Cathy Munro, you are utterly brilliant at being a friend!'

Over the next couple of days, the women worked together to ensure that the snug was converted into a comfortable and convenient bedroom for Geoff. An added bonus was the small ground-floor bathroom which lay directly off the snug. Cathy advised on the layout of the room, making sure that an upright chair was placed by the window in front of a small round table, and that there was ample light for reading.

'If your grandfather wants to watch television, he can join us in the living room,' she explained to Laura. 'We don't want him becoming too solitary or withdrawn.' Placing a vase of late daffodils on the table, Cathy put her hands on her hips and smiled at Laura. 'Right, I think we're ready.'

⊰╫⊱

Geoff and Cathy got on well from the start. They were both capable, direct people, who said what was on their minds. Neither could stand any nonsense or insincerity – the innate cause of Geoff's impatience with his own son.

'So, you're my lass's friend from London?' Geoff's bushy, white eyebrows drew together slightly as he surveyed the neat, compact figure of Cathy, who had accompanied Laura to collect her grandfather, adding, 'You don't look strong enough to handle the size and weight of someone like me.'

Cathy smiled. 'Appearances can be deceptive, Mr Jamieson. *You* don't look strong enough to handle a hundred and fifty sheep, build drystone walls, or milk a cow!'

The old farmer burst out laughing. 'I can see why our Laura gets on with you. Come on. Let's get me home.'

Laura observed that the Dales' air had the same effect on her grandfather as it always had on her. After he had been helped out of the car by the two friends in front of his old stone farmhouse, he breathed in deeply and almost immediately some colour returned to his cheeks. She noticed the visible relaxation of his shoulders, the slight straightening of his back. Cathy assembled the wheelchair borrowed from the hospital and expertly manoeuvred Geoff into it, pushing him slowly through the small garden so that he could see the awakening signs of spring. Then she wheeled him in through the front door and to the right, where the snug lay, clean and bright and warm, ready for the old farmer's return.

'Here we are, Mr Jamieson,' Cathy said. 'We've put all your sheep trialling awards on the shelves there, to remind you of past victories, together with some bedtime reading. There's a bottle of water, and some squash if you fancy something stronger. We are having a casserole for dinner tonight and I would like you to eat in your room, as I don't want you to become overtired.'

'Yes, Matron!' Geoff inclined his head in a mock bow.

'And if you continue to be as obedient as this, I may allow you up tomorrow to watch television,' she grinned.

Happily, the relationship between Cathy and Laura's grandfather continued in this vein. But although Geoff was apparently still his bluff, ironic self, Laura detected a tiredness in him that she knew he was not acknowledging to anyone.

Chapter 13

Cathy was never still. Laura had noticed that as far as her friend was concerned there was always something to be cooked, or cleaned, or tidied. One evening, long after Geoff had gone to his room, Cathy was dusting. 'This is your grandfather, Laura, isn't it?' she asked, running the duster around the frame of a small black and white photograph which showed a tall, broad man gazing down at the small blond woman at his side. His gaze was adoring and the strength with which he drew the woman to him was still evident after all the years which had clearly elapsed since the photo was taken. His adoring gaze was returned, steadfastly.

'Yes, and that's my lovely grandma, Lily. They always looked at each other like that: as if they centred their lives on each other – which they did, I suppose.' Laura sighed. 'It's so odd seeing him like he is now, Cathy. He's so tired and vulnerable; I used to feel that as long as grandfather was here, the world was a safe place to be in. My happiest times were spent here at *Fell Farm*.'

'Fancy finishing up the wine?' her friend asked. 'There must be a good couple of glasses left.'

Laura swirled the deep red liquid around her glass, smiling, remembering. 'You know the old, beamed building in the High Street that houses the Craft Shop? Well, it used to be the most perfect library. On cold winter days the librarian, Mrs Pocock, fired-up the black, cast-iron range in one of the front rooms and I was always enticed in, to sit with the friends that I had made during my frequent stays at *Fell Farm*. We used to curl up in the worn leather armchairs and read the books that were set around on low tables. It was more like a private library than a public one and, from time to time, Mrs Pocock would organise exhibitions, featuring the work of a particular author.

'Over the years it had become a family tradition that we should stay with my grandparents at Christmas time because there was nothing that Grandma Lily loved more than cooking and caring for her family. One holiday, a few days before Christmas Day, Grandfather had been out for some time, checking the sheep. When he came into the kitchen, he breathed on his fingers to thaw them out and leant against the Aga over there to warm his back. After a few minutes he buttered himself a piece of toast and poured tea from the pot on the kitchen table, announcing that he was "Going to take a break from the farm for an hour or two, and introduce our Laura to one of my favourite people." My father had a pile of Bank reconciliations to work through and had taken over the snug which, as you know, the wood-burner always makes warm and welcoming. My mother was dominating the kitchen, having spread out on the kitchen table a pile of essays on Virgil's Aeneid which she had to mark, and she simply smiled vaguely at Grandad's comment. As you can imagine, I was very excited and jumped up and down whilst my grandfather tried to put on my favourite little red coat, hat and gloves.

'Who is this friend of yours, Grandad?' I asked, curiously.

"Ah, she always makes me laugh. Always puts me in a good mood and gives me something to think about," he replied with a smile, ruffling my hair.

'Grandad kissed my grandmother goodbye and, hand in hand, we walked down the hill to the main street of Lokisbridge, past the holly wreaths on front doors and shops decorated with tinsel and baubles for Christmas, until we reached the library. My grandfather stopped there and together we gazed at the library window. It had been transformed into a magical land where animals lived and interacted together just as our neighbours and friends did. Against a backdrop of posters of fells and meadows full of flowers; of snug kitchens and gloomy woodland – the landscapes in which the author sets her stories – Mrs Pocock had recreated the world of Beatrix Potter, using china figures, soft toys, and small, child-hand-size books. It was entrancing, Cathy!'

Cathy was quiet for a while, then asked, 'Beatrix Potter – didn't she have something to do with conservation and the Lake District?'

'Yes. She had a restricted and rather sad early life, which was typical of a young girl living in Victorian times, but she ended up buying *Hill Top* farm in Sawrey in the Lake District and marrying a local solicitor. The income from her books funded the purchase of further farmland which she gifted to the National Trust on her death. In perfect miniature, she captures the lakes and mountains of the district; and her hedgehogs, rabbits, foxes and mice live in farmhouses which depict in detail aspects of the interior of *Hill Top*. When my grandfather took me to visit her farm a few years after the exhibition in the Library, I saw for myself the ranges, dressers, stone fireplaces and ornaments with which she furnishes the homes of the animals in her stories. Her tales are a perfect blend of fantasy and reality; and always, there is a moral, threaded through the beauty of the illustrations and the directness of the language. They still have impact – even after a century.'

'And your grandfather introduced this influence into your life?'

'He did, and so many other things as well …'

'Devoted husband and grandfather, skilled shepherd, with a sense of humour and deep-rooted kindness – he sounds like the perfect man!'

'He is, Cathy. The only one I have ever known.'

Chapter 14

It was a Tuesday, a couple of weeks after Cathy had arrived. Geoff was doing well, but still spent a considerable time in his room. Laura had tried to follow his instructions to the letter so far as running the farm was concerned, but she had no real knowledge or understanding of farming, having perceived it only from the outside. For anyone observing a well-run farm, backed by skills acquired over decades, everything appears to be easy, undramatic and predictable.

One morning, Geoff was sitting at the table that Cathy had placed in front of the window in his bedroom. He was toying with a rather tattered notebook, which he placed face-down as Laura walked in with his morning cup of tea.

'You're up early, Grandad!' Laura exclaimed.

'Aye – well it's beautiful sheep weather today,' smiled Geoff, kissing his granddaughter on the cheek.

'Didn't sleep well then, Grandad?' Laura asked, concerned.

'OK – but I kept thinking of your grandmother – she were so like you! It's uncanny. Full of life, and fun, and love … I still miss her you know, our Laura …'

Laura sat down opposite her grandfather.

'She was very lovely. I remember, even when I was a little girl, I loved the scent of her – lavender and another sort of scent ...'

'Jasmine,' responded Geoff promptly. 'She loved that Jasmine perfume you could buy in Boots – clean and fresh and natural, she always used to say.'

Laura blinked back tears. She remembered the Hermès and Chanel with which Lewis had entrapped her. How much hard-won profit from her grandfather's farm did one bottle represent?

Geoff took up a black and white photograph of Lily that he had placed on the table in front of him. 'When we were married, we came back here together on our wedding night – no honeymoon for us farmers. I carried her over the threshold, she was such a bit of a thing, and as I set her down she smiled at me and said, "Right you are then, Geoff, it's time to do our rounds with the sheep." She took off her lovely lace wedding-dress and put on her work dungarees and wellingtons and out we went together. And do you know, Laura, that's how it was for the rest of our time together – shoulder to shoulder in life and on the farm, supporting each other. She hadn't had an easy life before we met, but she was a brave and beautiful lass – just like you, my girl! All the work we did here together was for the future of our children – but we just had your father ...'

Laura saw that her grandfather's head had drooped to his chest and she wasn't sure whether he had actually fallen asleep, or whether he was overcome with regret or sad memories. So, laying her hand on his arm, she said clearly and very distinctly, 'It's just as well your granddaughter inherited your passion for farming then – and Grandmother's! I will always carry on your beliefs and traditions, Grandad – always.'

Geoff squared his shoulders and raised his tired eyes to hers. 'You're a good lass – my best lass!' he said, gripping her hand in his.

⊰⧚⊱

Following the routine set out by her grandfather, Laura walked the fields three times a day: at seven in the morning, at midday, and in the evening, just as dusk was falling. After kissing her grandfather goodbye, Laura grasped his shepherding crook and started her first tour of the fields. Her fingers ran over the smooth, carved sheep's horn, following the lines of a miniature sheepdog, alert and ready for work, underneath which were proudly set the words: *Geoff Jamieson*. His shepherd's stick had accompanied him to national and international sheep dog trials and Laura remembered how her grandmother had glowed with pride watching her husband's skill as he penned a tricky cohort of sheep at the renowned Longridge course. She recalled her grandfather's stalwart figure, legs apart, arms wide, brandishing his stick almost as a weapon; and the admiring laughter as a farmer turned to Lily Jamieson and said, 'Reckon them yows are more afeared of Geoff than of his dog!'

Laura inhaled deeply and gripped the stick tighter, feeling the smoothness of the horn where her grandfather's rough fingers had gripped it for decades. She would be worthy of him – she *would*. Whatever it took, she would never let the Jamieson legacy die.

The land was peaceful after the frenzy of the dawn chorus some three hours earlier. Laura checked the chickens, opening the door to the poultry house and hearing the usual range of clucks and ruffling as the birds emerged, stretching wings and legs in the May sunshine. She went on to the field near to the lambing barn, where she had left the sheep the night before and scanned the field from left to right.

To her astonishment, neither in the field, nor in the barn could she see any animals. She was certain that she had secured the gate between that field and the next but, quickening her pace, she almost ran to double-check. Empty. Panic began to tighten like a knot in her stomach. She shaded her eyes from the low, rising sun and scanned the land as it rose to a small enclosure where the farm ram – an enormous pedigree Suffolk tup – was kept. He was on his hind legs, gazing over the drystone wall, seeming to be as keen as she was to find the flock that he headed. Laura was extremely wary of this animal, called for some reason 'Old Charlie' by her grandfather. Whereas the sheep and lambs seemed docile and gentle, in Laura's opinion the tup didn't even *resemble* a sheep. Where the ewes' faces were smooth and neat, the ram's was almost fissured, his nostrils wide and flaring, his skull heavy and huge. She remembered her grandfather, several years previously, telling her that two Suffolk tups had butted a man to death in Masham and, looking at the powerful animal, its massive head still and watchful, she shivered and ran on.

Away to the left – the west – Laura could just catch the outline of the next farm. During her childhood visits Geoff Jamieson had never spoken of his neighbours, and their walks had always led away from the brooding dark buildings of the neighbouring farm. A few days earlier curiosity had prompted Laura and Cathy to walk along the bridle track which was, effectively, the entrance drive to this unknown neighbour. Eventually, almost obscured by gorse, matted reed and sedge, they had come across a dilapidated gate on which was crudely burnt probably the most surprising name they had ever seen: *The Edge of the World.*

'Why on earth do you think it's called that?' Laura mused.

Cathy paused for a moment. 'Could it be something as simple as its situation? It looks over the land and the reservoir that lies in the valley, as if it is actually on the edge of the world.'

'Mm – best explanation I can think of! But the place is so dark and forbidding that it could almost be called *The End of the World.* No wonder Grandfather always avoided coming here.' Both women had laughed uncomfortably, and moved swiftly on.

Laura completed her frantic tour of the fields. The sheep were nowhere to be seen and panic gripped her. She didn't want to disturb her grandfather with the news that, with the exception of the tup, his entire flock had disappeared overnight. She was almost certain that, if she did this, Geoff would insist on getting out of the house and helping her to search for them, so she ran back to the barn, breathing quickly. Calling Fly out of the stables where she slept overnight, Laura snatched up a plastic feeding bucket into which she threw a handful of sheep nuts, the food supplement that ensured that the lambs flourished and came early to market. She remembered how, when a very little girl, she had seen her grandmother shaking the bucket and enticing sheep and lambs to follow her. Because she hadn't a clue about how to handle a sheepdog, Laura thought that she could follow her grandmother's example and use the sheep nuts to recall the straying animals.

Panic was causing Laura to act in sheer desperation so, as well as arming herself with the sheep nuts, she tried to recall everything she could from her observations of her grandfather handling his sheepdogs and decided to use one of his commands at random: 'Away!'

From the high round window in *The Edge of the World* farmhouse, Jem watched, concerned. From this viewpoint, he could see the northern fields of Fell Farm, including the small enclosed tup field, but not the barn, nor the emptiness of the southern fields. He had stayed away from Geoff Jamieson's farm since his meeting with Laura. There could be no mistaking the ice-cold reception that she had given him and there was no point, Jem reflected philosophically, in seeking a repetition of this by another visit. He watched Fly circling away to the right, following the anti-clockwise fetch signal. Bless her, you could almost see how puzzled she was at being sent to fetch sheep that were not to be found in that direction. The young dog ran in a wide arc before returning, to stand, attentive head to one side, paw raised, looking to Laura for direction.

Jem watched Laura, who was standing utterly still, hands clenched by her sides. He was too far away to see that she was practically in tears by now, but frustration was visible in her every aspect, stemming from having to face something beyond her experience or capabilities. She took up the bucket and started to rattle the sheep nuts in it, calling all the while as she walked swiftly down to the sheep barn. Jem knew the reputation of the Suffolk ram on the neighbouring farm and had been told that Geoff only kept him because of its pedigree and ability to father outstanding lambs. As Laura and Fly moved further away, almost out of his field of vision, Jem caught his breath sharply as he saw the sudden collapse of part of the drystone wall surrounding the tup field. The ram, overwhelmingly attracted by the rattling of the bucket and the smell of sheep nuts, had managed to haul his enormous weight up and over the wall, sending stones rattling and sliding in all directions. Jem hesitated no longer as he watched the tup starting to move at a surprisingly quick pace, with a rolling, weighty gait, towards the unsuspecting Laura. Praying that he would be in time, Jem hurtled out of his farmhouse, racing across his own land before vaulting nimbly over the boundary wall into the fields that belonged to Fell Farm. He pulled his sheepdog whistle from his pocket and blew a series of loud, urgent blasts on it. Fly was a skilled, well-trained dog and, desperately trying to recall the exact topography of the field which contained Laura and Fly and the now rapidly approaching tup, Jem aimed to attract the dog's attention so that she would turn and intercept the animal. He was running as fast as he could towards the field in which he knew not what drama was unfolding. Scrambling over the wall, he saw that what he had prayed would happen, had actually done so. Fly, head down, was holding the huge ram with her 'eye' – the atavistic threatening stare of the sheepdog. The tup had his head down and Jem knew he was considering charging the unbelievably vulnerable-looking black and white dog which confronted him. A knot of fear and respect rose in Jem's throat. This huge animal must weigh at least eight times as much as the young dog now facing it. If it *did* charge and butt the dog, Jem couldn't be sure what the outcome would be.

Laura remained motionless, one hand on the field gate, poised to see whether there was anything in her power that she could do to help the little dog. This was absolutely beyond her experience and she was frustrated and angry with herself because she didn't know what to do for the best – and she blamed herself for putting the sheepdog at risk through her own ignorance.

And then, the decision was made: bowing its shoulders and dipping its huge head, the tup ran at Fly. Jem could hardly bear to watch the outcome, and was already striding towards the charging animal with some hope that he could come to the rescue of the young dog. But he had underestimated her bravery and Geoff's training. At the very last second, Fly leapt at the ram and sunk her teeth into his muzzle. The ram was literally stopped in his tracks and shook his head, trying to fling off his determined opponent.

Jem watched the confrontation, hand hovering on his dog whistle. Should he command Fly to leave hold of the animal she was fighting to control? The ram continued to toss his great head about, but still the courageous Collie clung on. Agonised, Jem decided not to interfere but to leave her to her own instincts. Eventually, after what was probably no more than thirty seconds, but which seemed interminable to both Jem and Laura, Fly let go, landing lightly a metre or so away from the tup and, unbelievably, started to approach it again, head lowered, teeth bared, fixing the great animal with her unwavering stare. She was panting and must be feeling the effects of the vigorous shaking she had just experienced but, steadfastly, she stalked closer.

Then the unbelievable happened. Old Charlie turned and lumbered cumbersomely back towards his small enclosure. Jem whistled to Fly, commanding her to drive the animal back towards the small field from which he had escaped a few minutes earlier. Jem kept pace with the dog and opened the gate to the field, into which the tup entered. As Fly guided him in, Jem examined the damage done by the dog. It was superficial – painful enough at the time, but easily dealt with later by an application of iodine. Jem closed the gate, picked up a sheep hurdle, left at an angle against the wall from earlier shearing, hoof trimming or other sheep husbandry, and put it securely in place over the damaged wall to act as a temporary repair.

Fly was standing waiting for her next instruction, and Jem whistled softly to her, calling her to him: 'That'll do, Fly,' he murmured, squatting and holding his arms wide to praise and welcome her to him. Realising she was now off-duty, Fly flattened her ears and came, tail wagging like a silky fan, to the man she had grown so fond of when they had shared the warm stable together in late spring. 'Good lass, that's my lass,' he murmured, rubbing her ears and shoulders.

Chapter 15

Laura watched the man and the animal. What a strange contrast they were: the dog eagerly displaying her affection, rolling over on her back, then jumping up to play around Jem's heels; the man quiet, controlled, every movement spare and restrained. Laura was shaking with reaction – she realised that even her teeth were chattering slightly – as she watched Jem come towards her with the long, easy stride of the born Dalesman, Fly playing at his heels.

'I don't know how to thank you,' she stammered.

Jem shook his head slightly and asked, rather abruptly, 'What were you doing?'

In the drama of the last few minutes Laura had, unbelievably, forgotten the cause of her unfortunate attempt at shepherding, but now she exclaimed, with renewed anguish, 'My grandfather's sheep – they've gone!'

'When did you last see them?' asked Jem.

'At nine o'clock yesterday evening. I've tried to follow my grandfather's routine and walk around the farm morning, afternoon and last thing at night to make sure that everything's all right.'

Jem nodded his head in approbation before recalling the weakened part of the southern drystone wall he had noticed earlier in the spring, and asked again, 'Have you noticed a break in any of the boundary walls?'

Laura shook her head.

'Stay here,' Jem said, whistling up Fly, who was on her hind legs, lapping water from a sheep trough.

'No,' replied Laura vehemently. 'They're my grandfather's sheep. I may be the most useless apology for a shepherd this side of the Watford Gap, but I'm coming with you.'

Jem grinned at her, and once again she glimpsed the transformation brought about by his smile, when the careful control and veiled emotions momentarily evaporated.

They walked together down the long field to the south of the sheep barn.

'I suspected so!' commented Jem, as they approached the boundary wall. A tell-tale tumble of stones, surrounded by hoof prints in the bruised grass, showed how the flock from *Fell Farm* had made their foolish break for freedom.

Jem scrambled over the wall, commanding Fly to follow him into the surrounding scrub. Laura stood back from the pile of stones over which the sheep had escaped, watching closely, trying her hardest to learn. The Collie disappeared from view as she circled wide, following her handler's instructions. Seconds passed, minutes, and then Laura became aware of a pattering, then a quiet thudding noise. Ewes and lambs were being driven quietly but steadily by Fly back towards the gap in the wall. Keeping her distance, zig-zagging to keep any stragglers close to the flock, her control was superb. The lead ewe saw the broken wall and scrambled over it, back into Fell Farm land, and swiftly the others followed. Jem counted the sheep as they passed him.

'How many does your grandfather have in his flock, exactly?' he asked Laura.

'One hundred and fifty,' she replied.

'Full house then,' confirmed Jem, grinning broadly.

Jem stayed by the broken wall and insisted that he should repair it immediately. To risk again the escape of the entire flock would be foolish indeed, so Jem explained that once sheep knew that there was a breach in a field wall, they would, without question, return to it. Laura walked thoughtfully back to the farmhouse, glancing back just before she entered to see Jem busy rebuilding the broken wall. Shaking her head, she realised sadly that there was so much she had taken for granted, so much knowledge of sheep and walls and dogs – an entire world that she had participated in, but only as an outsider, an observer. Laura's mind was made up. Whatever obstacles, whatever objections her grandfather put forward, she would explain what had just happened and would suggest that Jem Walker should become their shepherd.

But the conversation that she was rehearsing in her mind was abruptly cut short, as she entered her grandfather's bedroom with his mid-morning cup of tea. She had expected to see Geoff either dozing or reading one of his many past copies of *The Dalesman*. Instead, the farmer was still sitting in the chair by the window, one hand resting on the old, brown-paper-covered notebook open in front of him and the other cupped protectively around the photograph of Laura's grandmother. But Geoff Jamieson's hands were still and his eyes sightless. At last his indomitable spirit had left his ageing body and the farm to which he had devoted his life.

Laura glanced down at what her grandfather had been reading. It was a diary, and she looked at the last words that Geoff Jamieson had read:

August 2ⁿᵈ 1951

Lily Jamieson ... Lily Jamieson ... I can't believe that this will be my name until the day I die. I have married my wonderful, indestructible, loving Geoff, who stands between me and the difficulties and hurts of the world.

Today he promised that he would love and comfort me, whatever life throws at us, "'til death us do part". He is so utterly a man of his word and this made me feel the safest I have ever felt.

And I will do my best to make him the happiest I can, through all the days of our life together.

At the end of the page Lily, clearly an accomplished artist, had drawn a tiny, exquisite scene: a flock of Swaledale ewes, grazing quietly in front of *Fell Farm* in summer fields full of flowers.

Chapter 16

It was July, and gradually Laura had started to anticipate and manage the acute sense of loss which faced her on waking each morning. She still felt the pain like a kick in her stomach, but fought off the feeling of desolation by reminding herself that, through her grandfather's bequest, she now had the care of *Fell Farm* and would, to her last breath, defend the land, the animals and the way of life that had meant so much to Geoff Jamieson.

She pushed back the white lace bedcover, reflecting that summer time in Lokisdale must be the best time and place on earth to be. When she had moved into the farm in the spring, she had decided to use the largest upstairs bedroom where there were windows facing both south and north and, today, they were both open wide to the fragrant, flower-scented air. The south-facing windows led the gaze down across the dale to the wooded slopes opposite. Then, away to the left, the view opened out as the land flattened and dipped towards the Humber estuary where, on the horizon, a tiny spiral of steam from a power station curled into the hot still air. The windows facing north overlooked the lush green grass of *Fell Farm* land, where newly-shorn ewes and their now well-grown lambs grazed contentedly. Laura walked across the sun-warmed pine floorboards to these windows and breathed deeply. Ever since she was a small child, she had felt tension or anxiety slip away from her as she inhaled the Dales' air. It seemed like a heady distillation of flowers, crystal-pure water filtered through the limestone crags, and the sweet natural scent of well cared-for animals: it was indescribable! Gazing at her lambs and ewes, endless blue sky and fragile harebells moving gently in the warm breeze, Laura wondered how she could ever have left Yorkshire and, at that moment, vowed to herself that she never would again.

⮜╫⮞

She thought back to that late-spring day when she had discovered that her grandfather had peacefully passed away. She had raced upstairs, calling for Cathy, who had slept through the drama of the previous few hours. It was ten o'clock and Cathy was still in bed. As she came to know her friend more intimately, Laura was astonished that Cathy was naturally a late riser. This increased her respect even further, as she realised that the countless very early mornings and interminable night shifts were counter-intuitive to Cathy.

'Laura, what's wrong?' she asked instantly.

'Cathy – it's grandfather. I think he's dead …'

Cathy jumped out of bed and grabbed her dressing gown. She ran downstairs just behind Laura and they went into Geoff's bedroom together. After a brief examination of the old farmer, Cathy gently closed Geoff Jamieson's eyes for the last time.

Laura had been too shocked to cry. The previous few hours had brought her closer to real tragedy – to danger and loss and death – than she had ever been before. The memory of her attempt at suicide flashed briefly across her mind. How tawdry and meaningless that desperate gesture had been. Here, every day, ordinary men and women faced danger and death in the course of simply living their lives. She thought of the simple, touching words that the grandmother she had hardly known had written and, for the first time since that attempt on Waterloo Bridge, she felt thoroughly ashamed of her actions.

When Laura had telephoned her father to tell him the news, there had been an imperceptible pause. She could have sworn that she heard a slight sigh of relief and then the predictable words, 'Ah, but he has gone to a better place, dear. He was very elderly you know, and …'

She had simply hung up, disgusted, and with Cathy had seen to the arrangements.

One of the most straightforward things to decide was where the wake should be held. Really, there was no question – it had to be *Fell Farm*. Geoff would have wished the final celebration of his life to be nowhere else. Laura knew that the number of people likely to attend the funeral would run to many dozens and, helped by considerable quantities of tea, and – as the evening wore on – several glasses of wine, she and Cathy had made what they hoped would be sufficient sandwiches and cake to do justice to the kind and generous man so beloved in Lokisdale.

The vicar, Simon Tempest, had hardly known the tough old farmer who only stepped down into the neat market town when absolutely necessary, to buy food or take an animal to the vet – or to share with his beloved granddaughter the simple things that meant a lot to him.

But Laura's father had provided him with a carefully-written eulogy, running to several pages, which was more to do with the ancient origins and respectability of the Jamiesons than with the tough individuality and deep kindness of the man who had passed away. Laura had gritted her teeth during the service as the real achievements – and certainly the real essence – of the grandfather she had adored were diluted until the eulogy could well have applied to any aged farmer who had spent decades caring for his family and his flock.

Later, at *Fell Farm*, Laura was still deeply upset as she watched her father and the vicar munching their way through an unbelievable number of ham, cheese and tomato, and beef sandwiches. Wiping his mouth fastidiously before turning his attention to the cake, Michael shook his head and sighed, 'Ironic that it was the Walker boy who should find my father after his accident …'

'Why so?' asked the vicar.

Michael raised his eyes to the heavens and sighed again, 'Oh some complex and ancient feud between my family and "those damned Walkers from *The Edge of the World*" – sorry Simon.'

Guests ate and drank their fill and drifted away leaving the farm at peace once again, held in the embrace of the moors and bathed with the sweet, clean air of the Dales. The awkward church service and the greed of her father at the wake were, Laura thought, as nothing compared with the fine life that her grandfather had lived. Everyone who had attended the service had known Geoff for the man he had been, not the caricature that had been presented during the service.

Geoff now lay next to Lily, his wife, in the small churchyard at the heart of the dale. The situation was beautiful, utterly tranquil and entirely appropriate. Geoff Jamieson's final resting place was in the land that had bred him, and the rough headstone marking his grave would be buffeted by snow and wind, by rain and sleet and scorched by the sun, as he himself had been during his life. But, Laura thought, on her frequent visits to place flowers on her grandparents' grave, most fitting of all was the bleating of the sheep which dotted the fell-side around the little church.

Chapter 17

Two weeks after Geoff's death, Laura felt that the time was right to visit Jem Walker and ask him to be her shepherd. She had completed her early morning tour of her farm and had seen the expert job that he had made of the broken wall through which the entire Fell Farm flock had escaped. It was only a fortnight ago, although it seemed like a year, thought Laura, as she walked slowly up the bridle track, savouring the early morning birdsong and the fragrance which always hung heavy in the air at this growing time of year. Mist lay across the fields and the deep valley which held the reservoir as she walked, trying to muster her thoughts.

She really did not know this man at all. He was unusually quiet and reserved, and only twice had she seen him smile – but this had been a truly unforgettable experience as the radiant smile had transformed his appearance. Laura skirted the boundary wall of her farm, hearing the bubbling song of a curlew as it rose through the mist and disappeared into the blue sky that she knew would appear later that morning. Further on a lark soared, with the intention of landing far from its nest to lure away any predator from its eggs or its young. Her eyes watched the bird gather height, becoming almost indistinguishable from the mist, and then disappearing entirely to exist only as melody. Her eyes dropped again to the earth. She was rapidly approaching the granite gateposts and broken gate of Jem's farm: *The Edge of the World.* The appropriateness of the name struck Laura once again. She had never seen anything quite like the way that the farmhouse and barn had been built on a limestone ledge which, like an eagle's eyrie, overlooked the reservoir which lay below it.

Laura walked silently past the decayed, leaning gate, her eyes facing the bank of mist which hid the reservoir from sight. She had never set foot before on land which belonged to the Walkers and every step took her on a voyage of discovery. The house lay to her right, rambling and ancient, and shadowy in the pale early morning light. There was no garden, just scrubby grass, and to her left lay a rocky outcrop which reminded Laura of her trips to Brimham Rocks with her grandfather years earlier. She smiled as she remembered him struggling to explain to her eight-year-old self how wind and rain had eroded the Millstone grit rocks and created a world of fantastic pinnacles and pillars. She had no interest in the origin of the Rocks, but remembered the feeling of warmth and complete security as she had trotted along, her small hand enclosed gently by his large, calloused one.

Lost in memory, she gazed at the strange formation. In this mist it almost looked like a sleeping dragon – or dinosaur – and, as her imagination kicked in, peopling this eerie landscape with huge prehistoric or mythical creatures, she saw a slight movement.

Sitting motionless on the rock was a small child – a boy – whose ginger curls blew gently in the slight breeze. He was gazing with utter concentration at the mist-covered landscape in front of him and holding a toy – a painted wooden lorry. Involuntarily, Laura stopped and watched. Usually small children moved or fidgeted, or played, throwing stones or sticks, but this child did not stir. Had it not been for the wind lifting his hair, Laura would never have noticed him. It was very early for a child of only three or four to be out by himself, and it could not be good that he was sitting motionless on a misty, damp morning such as this. Without thinking, Laura stepped forward.

'Hello,' she started to say gently, but, looking at the child rather than the boulder-strewn land in front of her, she stumbled and had to stretch out her hand to catch hold of a rowan tree to keep her balance. When she looked up again, the child had gone.

⊰))⊱

Jem was leaning against his battered range, waiting for the kettle to boil. His breakfast invariably consisted of a slice of bread and a cup of tea with no milk. His years at the Friary had accustomed him to periods of fasting and he ate only just enough to live. If he could not buy food, he drank water and ate any wild fruit or nuts that he could find. Jem was reliving the day, two weeks earlier, when he had last seen Laura. He couldn't get her out of his mind. Her composure in the face of danger – and later tragedy and loss – was striking and he remembered how, in the face of so much drama, her behaviour had been controlled and self-contained. Her beauty was unforgettable and he began to wonder whether she could be one of those rare human beings whose loveliness matched their goodness. Firmly dismissing these as idle thoughts, he brought his attention back to the pragmatic business of surviving. Finally, the dented kettle was emitting steam and he poured the boiling water on to the last of his tea bags, stirring it thoughtfully.

Just how long could he remain here, he pondered. Since his return, he had worked steadily to patch the ruin of a farmhouse so that he was relatively dry. But quite how he was going to tackle the wilderness that surrounded it had, so far, escaped even Jem's ingenuity. The dreams had started to haunt his nights again, bringing back the desperate feelings of betrayal and loss that he could just not seem to escape. Although he didn't need much, he did need *some* money and the scant rent he received for allowing a neighbour to graze his sheep on *The Edge of the World* land just about allowed him to buy the basics for survival. The need to renew some of his clothes, which were now literally falling apart, was becoming pressing and he grimaced as he felt the cold of the stone-flagged kitchen strike through the worn soles of his shoes. Jem's natural reserve and his disinclination to mix with people who, a decade earlier, had been so ready to condemn him meant that seeking work locally was just not an option. But quite what else he could do without transport he couldn't begin to imagine.

The stagnant air reverberated with the sound of the cracked bell that hung by the front door. Jem never jumped, but he was startled and left the shadowy depths of the kitchen, crossed the hall and opened the heavy oak door.

'Mr. Walker – Jem – can I come in?' asked Laura.

'Of course,' he replied, thinking that the woman standing on his doorstep, with hair curling in damp tendrils around her flushed face, was the last person that he had expected to see on this misty, damp morning.

'Would you like some tea?' he asked.

Laura shook her head. 'No – thank you – but I would like to talk to you.'

'That's just as well, since I have just used my last teabag!' Jem laughed.

He gestured to the kitchen, the only place that offered a modicum of warmth and comfort. He had placed an old armchair next to the range and had spread his friar's cloak over the seat to provide padding against the springs which fought to escape the scratchy horsehair. Laura, however, did not sit down, but stood with her back to the range, looking at him with her usual direct, open gaze.

'Jem, I need a shepherd. Would you consider helping me?'

Jem shut his eyes briefly, almost as if he were sending a swift prayer of thanks to the God who had sustained him, despite everything.

For the third time since meeting her enigmatic neighbour, Laura saw his face irradiated and transformed by a wide, generous smile.

'I would be delighted, Laura,' he replied.

Chapter 18

The weeks that followed were quiet and altogether golden. Laura would always remember that summer because of the intensity of the events that happened during the long, sun-filled days and the way in which it seemed to stand alone – unrelated to what had passed and to what was to come.

She came to see that, in asking Jem to become her shepherd, she had put the farm into the best of hands. Gradually, and with great thoroughness, he worked his way around *Fell Farm*, attending to the maintenance jobs that a shepherd only has time to do in the summer – that brief respite between lambing and tupping time. He checked all the boundary walls and had to make a fair number of repairs: watching him choose and shape the stones, coaxing them skilfully into place, Laura realised that the farm had started to become too much for her grandfather. Jem sharpened and cleaned the tools he needed for his shepherding duties – sheep shears and hoof clippers – as well as general gardening and maintenance tools. Subtly, under his sure, experienced touch, the farm changed. The gate was newly-painted, the grass cut, walls were solid and steady and no longer patched up with sheep hurdles where they had grown weak. Once more, it became alive, orderly and well-run as it had been when Geoff and Lily had been young.

Laura found Jem's presence deeply comforting. He seemed to be a part of the gently-changing seasons and the slow rhythms of farming life. There was a rightness about his actions – firm, sure and gentle – as he steered the farm and its animals through the complexities of the farming year.

Sometimes, Laura reviewed her relationships with significant other people in her life and was shocked by the outcome of her reflections. She had never related particularly closely to her parents, because their life philosophies were alien to her. They seemed totally enrapt with things that, to Laura, just did not matter: her mother was taken up with texts written many centuries earlier by people who were long-dead, and about a society that was no longer relevant; while her father was almost entirely self-absorbed. Matt she was fond of, but couldn't say that she knew him any longer – at more than ten years her senior they had little in common. Cathy she loved like a sister, but felt that there were whole tracts of her personality that she had not revealed. She had never really known her grandmother, Lily, who had died when Laura was only a girl, but having read part of her diary and seen her beautiful little sketch, Laura started to suspect that they would have had much in common. Her grandfather she had loved as a soul-mate: someone who cared about what she cared about and who found humour and joy where she herself did. Lewis – Laura shuddered as she remembered him – his cold intensity and the narrowing of his eyes and mouth as he said, or did, something that she found abusive or disgusting.

But – her mind returning full-circle to her shepherd – Jem was quietly self-contained, serious and caring, but showed from time-to-time tantalising glimpses of a warmer and much more complex personality.

⊰◁║▷⊱

Cathy was a natural carer. She watched quietly as her friend and her shepherd worked, talked and laughed together. Seeing their mutual absorption and the obvious pleasure that each had in being with the other, she occupied herself with what she was happiest doing – looking after them. She cooked for them, fed them, and called them into the kitchen when she thought they needed rest and refreshment.

One hot day, when Cathy decided that four hours of physical work – even in the shady interior of the barn – were quite enough for anyone, she gave her usual call that lunch was ready from the depths of the spotless farmhouse, whose door stood open to the summer air. Since her arrival, Cathy had transformed the interior of the house, scrubbing paintwork and floors, painting with light, bright colours, and making curtains and cushions. It seemed to Laura that she never stopped working, but what she didn't fully realise was that her friend was immersing herself in cleaning and redecorating as an antidote to brooding on the vocation that she had lost.

Responding to her call, Laura and Jem left the hay barn where they were working together and walked up the stone steps to the house, chatting animatedly.

'And so you see, I am writing and illustrating modern fairy stories!' explained Laura, somewhat defensively, due to every single aspect of her work having been trashed by Lewis during their relationship.

'A mix of Beatrix Potter and folk tales – I suppose you think that's stupid …'

'On the contrary, fairy stories are some of the most complex works of literature. They combine folk memory, superstition and the supernatural, *and* usually deliver a powerful moral.'

'Did they teach you that sort of thing at shepherding school, Jem?' Laura quipped. She asked the question without thinking, embarrassed and feeling vulnerable because their conversation had moved on to something that meant so much to her. Only after she had spoken did she realise how patronising she sounded – and Jem's thoughtful and serious answer made her feel even worse.

'No, but I love reading,' Jem said quietly. 'And I didn't go to college to learn about shepherding – I learnt through practical experience. My father thought I was a bit of a let-down loving poetry and novels … and never let me forget it. The only books I was allowed were borrowed from Mrs Pocock's library.' Seeing Laura's flushed face and downcast gaze, Jem tried to lighten the tone of the conversation by adding, 'Father and I hardly communicated for years – except in dog whistles!'

Grateful for Jem's sensitivity, Laura readily moved on to this shared memory. 'So Mrs Pocock changed your life too, Jem? Did you ever see that exhibition about Beatrix Potter?'

'I did, although I pretended to be a bit aloof, I remember … I was after all nearly thirteen!'

Laura smiled. 'So you have not been a shepherd all your life?'

'No. I was a monk – a Franciscan friar – for ten years.'

'Really?' The incredulous question escaped Laura involuntarily, and immediately she could have bitten her tongue out. But this time she apologised directly. 'Oh Jem, I'm sorry. That sounded so rude. I have just never met a monk before.' This got worse and worse. Would she ever be able to hold an easy, spontaneous conversation again?

'Why did you decide to become a monk?' she gabbled. 'I suppose you had to pray all day and attend church services and things like that?'

'Do you normally answer questions that you ask other people before you give them time to respond?' Jem asked laughingly, running his hands through his thick brown hair. He folded his hands quietly on the table in front of him and paused, collecting his thoughts. He wanted to speak honestly and seriously about his faith and a way of life which had meant so much to him for so long; but equally was determined not to damage Laura's evident lack of self-confidence. 'We did pray, yes, and sing hymns and follow services, which we called the daily offices; and we willingly completed our allotted work to ensure that our community had food to eat and a clean friary to eat it in. But the wonderful thing about the Franciscan order is that it is based upon love – love for all Creation, love for animals and the natural world and for the seasons, as well as love for God. It was an inspirational and fulfilling way of life and I will never forget the joy and peace I felt within the walls of the Friary. But I could not continue in the Franciscan order because too many distracting thoughts interfered with what I should have been concentrating on. I decided that I had to leave the Friary to face the things – the really hard and difficult things – that had happened to me here in Lokisdale and to make peace with myself. If I can't make peace with myself, I can never make peace with others and certainly not with God.'

Jem hesitated, gazing into his tea then, when he finally lifted his dark eyes to hers, she saw that they were full of anguish.

'Sometimes in life, something happens that is so awful that the only way of dealing with it at the time is to escape, effectively to stop the world and to retreat for healing and renewal. Ten years ago, something utterly insupportable happened to me. I left my home here and sought sanctuary with the Franciscans. Although I gradually became able to live with myself again, I could not completely banish the thoughts and vivid dreams that reminded me of … of what had happened. Because of this insistent interruption, I found I could not be true to my calling. I couldn't dedicate myself wholly to prayer and devotion and banish the concerns of this world, and so I left and came back here to the farm where I was brought up.'

Further conversation seemed impossible. Laura realised that she had opened a door to a world of pain that her gentle shepherd tried to keep firmly closed when with other human beings; but opened, she suspected only too frequently, when alone. She felt guilty and embarrassed that she had been the key to opening that door and sat once again with lowered gaze, twisting her napkin in her hands.

'More apple crumble?' asked Cathy gently, aware of the distress that both her companions were feeling.

'I'm fine thanks, Cathy,' Laura murmured.

'Yes please!' responded Jem, keen as always to be the peacemaker in a situation that had become awkward.

Cathy grinned widely and heaped his pudding bowl with a further helping of dessert.

'And what is on the agenda this afternoon, Jem,' she asked.

'Erm… probably sleeping,' he laughed.

Chapter 19

Because she had found someone to whom she could entrust her grandfather's sheep, Laura was free to work again, finding inspiration, as she always had, in the animals and the natural world which surrounded her. She realised that, increasingly, the austere beauty of the landscape was impacting upon her creative imagination and that she was starting to combine the legends that had been woven around and through the Dales with the attractive anthropomorphism of her childhood muse, Beatrix Potter. Her tales became entirely her own – quirky, powered by animals involved in their own intense and complex world, but focussing on the eternal beauty of the moors, mountains and wide, surging rivers of the Dales. She was no longer a quiet disciple of her grandfather's 'best friend', Beatrix Potter, but an innovative and individual voice who had started to reflect in her work the many dimensions of the land she loved.

On a perfectly still August day, she lay on her front in one of the dry, fragrant fields surrounding *Fell Farm*, drawing the robin hopping along the top of the wall outside the kitchen, looking quickly to his left and his right, before he fluttered to the ground to pick up crumbs and seeds. He just *had* to become a postman – active, chatty, into everyone's business, gathering news and gossip wherever he went. And the origins of the society through which he moved was held in the stones of the wall along which he made his way, the panoply of history which started with the fossils entombed forever in the hard limestone.

Laura was so involved in capturing the exact angle of the small, feathered head and the bright, black eyes of the bird that she hadn't noticed Jem walk quietly up behind her. He chuckled and she spun around, jumping lightly to her feet. The barriers with which Laura had surrounded herself and her work had been lowered – if not entirely demolished – by the excruciating conversation over lunch several days earlier. She had been drawn into trusting Jem much more as she noted that he strove to protect, rather than ridicule, her sensibilities. And so now she faced Jem with a smile, rather than embarrassment.

'He's such a busybody, isn't he?' Jem grinned. 'The village nosey-parker!'

'That's exactly what I was thinking! He's here, there and everywhere, poking his beak in where he's not wanted and gossiping behind peoples' backs. And all the time the backdrop is the eternal beauty of the Dales, which he and his fellows never perceive, but which has determined why their community was founded and why it continues to exist.'

'Do you see human characteristics in all animals, Laura?'

'Most of them,' she nodded. 'And usually the more unattractive traits, to be honest – traits that are easy to parody: greediness, ignorance, aggression, rather than calmness, goodness and beauty.'

Jem stood and looked at her without speaking for several seconds, then closed his eyes briefly, ran his fingers through his damp, dark hair and asked, 'Laura, are you busy for the rest of the day? The sheep are settled and the lambs are just growing as you watch them. They don't need any intervention from us at the moment.'

Taken completely off guard, Laura blushed. 'Not really.'

'If you want to see animals that are gracious, beautiful and calm, I can take you to see them this afternoon,' he added.

⊰◉⊱

If anything, the afternoon seemed to get hotter as they walked along together in easy companionship, sometimes chatting inconsequentially about the majestic landscape which swept before and around them, sometimes saying nothing at all. One of the things which Jem appreciated most about Laura was that she did not talk for the sake of talking, as did many women. He noticed that when she was silent, it was then that her other senses appeared to be working at their utmost intensity. She would glance to left and right, inhale deeply and sometimes just stop, obviously listening to birdsong or to the sound of water. Occasionally she would stoop to touch a flower, or reach out to follow the circling pattern of lichen on a drystone wall. Never had he met someone so completely in harmony with their surroundings.

They passed Jem's farm and struck off on a path that descended to the valley bottom, just beyond the church where Geoff Jamieson and generations of Lokisdale families lay peacefully in their dreamless sleep.

The track led alongside the River Loki and started to rise gradually to the moor which lay at the head of the dale.

'See that wood?' Jem gestured ahead where a dense area of mixed beech and oak woodland clothed the side of the dale. 'That's where we are heading.'

'Great – I'm very hot!' exclaimed Laura. 'It'll be good to get into the shade. Are we going to see some sort of deer?'

Jem shook his head.

'Well, it can't be a badger or fox at this time in the afternoon!'

'It's not.'

'You're infuriating!'

'I know …'

The track entered the wood and climbed steadily as the river fell away to the right into a steep-sided gorge. Determined not to be drawn into further guess-work, Laura just walked quietly along, noting old metal lamp brackets driven into the limestone to their left and the smoothness of the paved path which they followed.

'What's this place called?' she asked.

'*The Crying Wood*' replied Jem.

'Bet there is some sort of ancient legend surrounding *that* name.' Laura's eyes flickered from right to left, committing to memory the twisted shapes of the oaks, the jagged boulders, the white, turbulent waters of the river as it surged over the stones strewing its bed.

'Bound to be, but I am not sure what. I believe that the wood was a favourite haunt of Victorian ladies and gentlemen who wanted to immerse themselves in the picturesque: hence the smooth pathway and the carefully-lit track. I've come here since I was a boy, to collect firewood and – well, you will see …'

They walked for some minutes, deeper into the woodland, climbing all the time. Eventually the pathway started to level out and Laura glimpsed sunlight ahead. She guessed that they were coming to the end of the trees and were about to emerge on to the moor beyond. Before they did, however, Jem gestured to a large flat stone. 'Sit down here, Laura. Wait, and watch. This is one of the places I have come to swim for as long as I can remember.'

Laura realised that they had been following the course of the river. At this point, having risen from a moorland spring somewhere beyond where they were sitting, the river swelled and had formed a deep pool, cupped and held by the boulders which surrounded it. The water lay, surface unbroken, mirroring the trees and, far above, the hot blue sky. It was nearly five o'clock and beyond the wood the air shimmered with heat. They sat, for some minutes, in total silence and Laura felt herself relaxing, almost slipping into sleep.

Virtually on the borderline of consciousness, Laura heard a slight rustling above her. Shaking herself into alertness, she looked up to see heavy, white birds gliding down from a cliff to their right, to land, almost without a sound, in the deep, clear water of the pool. Geese: huge, pure white geese. Elegantly, they dipped their heads in the cool water, not frenetically, like smaller water fowl, but regally, consciously allowing the glistening drops to cascade down their necks and merge once again with the water's surface. They were silent, magnificent and, within this context, utterly surreal.

Words were superfluous. Laura was wholly absorbed in the birds' attitude of aloofness and their sublime beauty, vivid against the primeval background of tumbled rocks and ferns. After what probably amounted to twenty minutes, the geese came out of the pool and stood, fanning their open wings gently in the still, warm air of the summer's afternoon. They looked like some mythical bird – a phoenix perhaps – as they waited for their wings to dry. Then, almost as if responding to a silent signal, they took off, aiming for the gap in the woodland ahead, their two-metre wingspan lifting them effortlessly into the sultry air and enabling them to soar above the earth until they disappeared into the brilliant slanting beams of the summer sun.

'That was one of the most beautiful things I have ever seen,' whispered Laura.

Jem just sat and looked at her. Still, composed, her eyes blazing with the vision of beauty that she had just experienced, he thought that he had never seen a woman so entirely lovely.

'I must go back now,' Laura murmured.

They said nothing as they returned. Laura was still entirely enrapt with the otherworldly loveliness that she had just seen, whilst Jem was enrapt with the woman who walked quietly by his side.

Chapter 20

That night both Jem and Laura lay sleepless.

If anything, it seemed to have become hotter and, even with opposing sets of windows in her bedroom wide open, Laura found the air sultry and oppressive. She had tried to sketch the geese, to recapture their ethereal, exquisite grace, but everything she produced seemed a poor reflection of the beauty she had seen earlier that day. She was restless and frustrated at her artistic shortcomings, but there were a host of other, less well-articulated, feelings that surged in her mind, making sleep impossible.

Less than half a mile distant, Jem lay on his back staring into the darkness of the bleak room in which he tried to sleep. His preoccupation was simpler: he was beginning to realise that the overwhelming love that to this point he had felt only for his God was growing in his heart for his neighbour. But mixed with this new feeling of joy there was bitterness and pain, because to Jem she was pure and lovely and untainted by the creeping evil that he felt had defiled him.

At two o'clock, he gave up on sleep and lit a candle. Walking slowly to a cupboard next to the cast-iron fireplace, Jem opened the black oak door and took out a battered biscuit tin. He took a deep breath, paused and then removed the lid, carefully lifting out a faded photograph and a tiny curl of hair. He gazed intently at the photo and stroked the hair lightly with his forefinger, before replacing the items in the box and returning it to its resting place.

Since sleep was impossible, Jem went down to the kitchen and lit the camping stove that his wages from *Fell Farm* had enabled him to buy. He filled his new aluminium kettle and placed it ready to boil. What luxuries! Sipping his tea, Jem sat in the broken-springed chair and closed his eyes, his mind in turmoil. Was it possible to put such pain and wrongdoing behind him? He knew himself very well and was satisfied that he had repented and asked for forgiveness for the terrible things that had happened ten years earlier. Could he now entertain the hope that he may be able to move on, that the unthinkable could happen and that he could actually feel a deep, well-grounded, mature love for a woman? Maybe, but the inescapable, devastating thought arose: even if he could move on, would Laura – would anyone – be able to accept him after what he had done?

⊰〉Ⅱ〈⊱

Laura could stand it no longer. At first light – around four-thirty – she got up. She was so restless she just had to move, she had to walk somewhere – anywhere. It was a perfect morning. The sky was clear and held that opalescent colour only seen before the sun actually rises above the horizon on a warm, still day.

Laura tiptoed along the landing, past Cathy's room, and helped herself to a glass of water from the kitchen. She decided not to take Fly – the morning seemed too untouched and silent for even the most steadfast of companions – and, moving almost as quietly as the rabbits and sheep that had already started to crop and nibble the grass, Laura followed the farm track, then the small moorland road which led down into Lokisbridge. She found it fascinating to pass houses and farms where people still slept and were oblivious of her passing. It seemed to her that at this time of the morning there was a blanket of stillness thrown across the tumult of human life and for a few precious moments there was peace. She felt a tingle of excitement as she passed Jem's farm, wondering whether he too was awake, and she smiled in anticipation of the conversations that they would share later that day.

Apart from sheep and birds, it seemed to Laura as if she was the only living thing that stirred on the moor that morning. As she descended the steep slope into Lokisbridge, she glanced at the small church and the churchyard where her grandfather was buried. She had not visited his grave for a few days and decided that now would be a perfect time to go in and sit on one of the oak benches placed in the churchyard here and there, quietly remembering the happy times they had had together.

Geoff Jamieson and his wife lay under an oak tree, behind the church and to the left, against the wall which separated the consecrated ground from the moor. Laura moved silently around the low stone building, but then saw something that stopped her in her tracks. Kneeling in the dewy grass, a little beyond her grandparents' grave, was Jem. He was placing wild flowers awkwardly in a jam-jar placed under a rough wooden cross, which leaned slightly. His fingers were lightly touching the ground and she just heard him whisper, 'I'm sorry. I'm so sorry.' He then placed the palm of his hand flat on the ground for a few minutes before starting to get to his feet.

Laura fled – back along the footpath between the gravestones and out into the still-silent street of the town. She flew along the pavement and turned into the first narrow passageway on her left. She had to find somewhere to hide and, breathing hard, she swiftly made her way into the centre of a labyrinth of narrow, cobbled alleyways. Leaning against the wall of an old-fashioned hardware shop, she finally stopped, her imagination whirling: just when she felt as if she were getting to know this complex man, she had witnessed something which perplexed her utterly.

She waited for perhaps half an hour, until she could be fairly sure that Jem was no longer in the churchyard. Her mind was racing uncontrollably. It was unthinkable to return home to the comfortable routine of breakfast and early morning television news with Cathy, so she ran past the now empty churchyard, up the track to *The Crying Wood*, following the route that she and Jem had taken the previous day. With every step, Laura struggled to analyse what she had felt when she had witnessed the simple, elemental gesture that Jem had made in the churchyard. It was as if he was laying his hand on the heart of a beloved person. And how did that make her feel? Confused? Puzzled? Eventually, inexorably, the answer came: she had felt jealous.

Surrounded by the full force of early morning birdsong, Laura raced up the pathway through the woodland thinking that, somehow, if she could regain the position of peace and tranquillity that she had achieved yesterday, her mind would once again become calm. Breathing deeply because of the speed at which she had run, Laura stopped just a few metres from the rock where she had witnessed the unforgettable spectacle of the white birds bathing, then spreading their wings, then flying above the expanse of the moor. But then, once again, she caught her breath. There, beneath her, swimming effortlessly in the pure, cold water was Jem. He was naked and as unselfconscious and graceful as the geese had been, revelling in the cool purity of the water. She could see the tanned expanse of back, shoulders, arms and legs and the vulnerable pale areas that were never exposed to the heat of the sun.

With tears in her eyes, Laura turned away. Those exquisite white birds had been beautiful, but Jem was the most beautiful thing she had ever seen. He was such a part of the elemental grandeur of Lokisdale and seemed utterly removed from the corruption and evil that she had encountered in London. With the things she had experienced and done there, how could she even dream that she could draw close to such a man? She moved silently through the dappled shade, back towards the path through the woods and, as she glanced back, just once, towards the pool which had surprised her with such visions of beauty, she saw a slight movement in the bracken. It was the child she had seen sitting on the rocky outcrop at *The Edge of the World*. This time he was lying on his front, clutching the same battered wooden toy and smiling down at the unsuspecting figure of Jem.

Chapter 21

Whilst Cathy was washing up after lunch, Laura was sitting at the kitchen table, distractedly adding detail to a drawing of their large white cockerel. It was impossible to give the work her full attention as she couldn't get out of her mind the picture of Jem, swimming effortlessly in the cool woodland pool, nor the small child lying still and almost obscured by the bracken and flowers which dotted the floor of the wood. The presence of the child – always alone and often in far from safe situations – disturbed her immensely. She had returned home, quiet and pale, and had refused anything to eat at breakfast time. Cathy had tried to engage her in conversation, but everything she said was received either with silence, or with a non-committal murmur.

Laura had taken a mug of coffee outside and had spent a large part of the morning sitting on the wide stone gatepost next to the chicken hut, sketching their arrogant white cockerel as he strutted up and down in front of his chickens. Eventually, she became lost in her observations, reflecting how astonishing it was that a relatively small creature could produce such a volume of noise, and frowning at the inevitable posturing of male animals. The male bird stalked with a long-legged stride in front of the hens, every so often thrusting his head forward and emitting an ear-splitting sound. It was clear that he was propositioning one, or all, of the females, and eventually a small and quiet brown hen succumbed to his attentions. Laura watched, horrified, as the enormous cockerel leapt on to the female, pecking her neck savagely as he mounted her. Suddenly it was as if she was witnessing, as a third-party, Lewis's perverted and violent treatment of her. Cursing under her breath at the agonising contrast between this reminder of her relationship with Lewis and the pure wonder of her developing feelings for Jem, Laura had snapped her sketchbook shut and walked quickly back to the house.

Cathy was attuned to Laura's every mood and immediately noticed that something had disturbed her friend deeply. During lunch, she chatted inconsequentially about her visits to Lokisbridge and to Ripon, but apart from the occasional nod or murmur, Laura said nothing. Finally, Cathy reached across the table and laid her hand gently on her friend's arm. 'What's upset you, Laura?'

'Oh, just a flashback ... about Lewis ... how that man haunts me! How can the exploits of an oversized arrogant chicken upset me so much!'

'The exploits of a chicken!' echoed Cathy, bemused.

The absurdity of the situation struck both women at once and the tension was broken as they burst into peals of laughter, ending in Laura giving her friend a hard hug.

'Come on!' Cathy whipped off her apron and firmly hung it up on one of the hooks next to the Aga. 'Let's try out the fruit of my ill-gotten gains and go to find somewhere cool to sit!' Cathy's flat had sold quickly, realising a small profit after the mortgage had been settled, making it possible for her to buy a second-hand car, which she and Laura shared.

⊰⊱∦⊰⊱

The abbey cloisters were quiet and cool – exactly what both women were looking for. They sat for some time in the comfortable, companionable silence that good friends share, but finally Laura turned to Cathy and said, 'Earlier, when you asked me whether there was something wrong, there was – there is. Well, actually, there are two separate things that are bothering me.'

Cathy nodded and smiled encouragingly. She was on the brink of adding a throw-away comment to the effect that it was pretty obvious that Jem was on her friend's mind. But, because she knew how sensitive Laura's emotions could be, she just continued to sit on the cool stone bench which ran around the cloisters, hands quietly folded in her lap in a controlled, self-contained gesture that was habitual to her, waiting for her companion to speak.

'Well,' Laura started hesitatingly, 'I can't seem to get Jem out of my mind.'

'To be honest, my lovely friend, that is not a surprise. You light up when you look at him. And … can I be honest?'

'Please.'

'He is similarly transformed when he looks at you.'

Cathy wasn't sure what Laura's reaction would be – possibly, she thought, embarrassment, laughter or denial. But what she had not expected was for Laura to cover her face and to start to cry silently. Cathy hugged her friend to her and quietly stroked her hair away from her face. But Laura shook off her friend's embrace, impatiently jumping up and wiping her eyes on her arm.

'I *hate* myself like this! Why on earth am I bloody *crying!*'

'Don't be so harsh on yourself,' Cathy began.

But Laura cut across her gentle words, driven by her own frustration, 'If he knew what I am – what I have done – he would never look at me again, Cathy! I know he wouldn't. I'm tainted, spoiled, second-hand goods – all those things and more. I didn't even love Lewis! I was just obsessed by him.'

'You can't read peoples' minds, Laura. Jem isn't superficial. I can't explain precisely why, but I am sure that he would never condemn you. I am certain that he would understand.'

'Well,' Laura took a deep breath, 'I am never likely to find out what his reaction would be because I couldn't ever tell him. And if I can't admit these things, how can a … friendship … or anything else develop between us? It's an impossible situation.'

'Laura, there are things that sometimes one just has to talk about, but there has to be a right time. You don't know everything about me. But you will, one day, when the time is right.'

'Well, you are hardly a woman of secrets, Cathy!'

Cathy didn't respond, and her expression was unfathomable. 'And the second thing on your mind?'

'Well, this is really weird. I have seen a little boy – probably about three or four, no more – twice now. The first time he was sitting on a rock on Jem's land, when I went to ask him whether he would become my shepherd; and the second time was earlier this morning, when he was lying on his stomach, just watching Jem and smiling. I should have mentioned seeing the child when I went to Jem's farm, but I was so anxious to find the right words – not to patronise him or anything – that it slipped my mind.'

'And no one was with the child?'

Laura shook her head: 'No. That's what is so strange. He's so small, so vulnerable. Anything could happen to him.'

'Jem needs to know, Laura. It's strange that the child was sitting on Jem's land, but it's downright peculiar that he was watching Jem without his knowledge. You need to tell him.'

Chapter 22

Laura genuinely wanted to learn some of the skills she saw being expertly practised by Jem. Apart from the safe, warm feeling of just being with him, she was that rare thing, a life-long learner, and was fascinated to see the range of tasks that a shepherd had to routinely undertake in order to keep a small flock of sheep healthy. Jem was a good, patient and careful teacher, assessing his student's readiness for each task. And, in that most searching and complex bond of learning and teaching, Jem and Laura grew ever closer as each cloudless blue days of that unforgettable summer came and went.

At first Laura just watched, but was gradually encouraged to join in with the more straightforward jobs. Frequently the sheep's fleece had to be trimmed with dagging shears when it had been fouled, to avoid the dreaded fly-strike and ensuing mastitis. On a monthly basis the flock had to be wormed, so Jem held the sheep's heads whilst Laura administered worming drenches, smiling as she saw, or possibly imagined, the pleased expression on the animals' faces as the cool milky-coloured liquid seemed to quench their thirst. Laughing and working side by side in the neat yard in front of the sheep barn, the wind lifted and mingled Laura's cloud of auburn hair and Jem's darker brown. Cathy, keeping them supplied with tea or cold drinks as necessary, had seen this phenomenon on more than one occasion and had felt a lump rise in her throat at the way in which Nature, at least, had joined her friends together without qualm or hesitation. She recalled Lily's simple words, which she had caught sight of when she had closed Geoff Jamieson's eyes for the last time: *And I will do my best to make him the happiest I can, through all the days of our life together*. This land was so elemental and flock husbandry literally a matter of life or death. Seeing her friends living, working and laughing together, nothing seemed more natural to Cathy than that they should do exactly what Lily had declared she would do – make each other the happiest they could through all the days of their life together.

The more complex task of inoculating the flock against the range of standard sheep diseases was undertaken by Jem alone, but he explained exactly what he was doing to Laura, suggesting that she should wait until her confidence grew a little before attempting this more intrusive procedure.

One hot day Laura and Jem had been working together during most of the morning. It was time for the monthly routine of checking the feet of each ewe for signs of infection, and paring back any parts of the hoof that had become overgrown. The rhythm of Jem and Fly's work together was perfect. At Jem's low, short whistle, the sheepdog would send a sheep from the barn through the sheep crush, down to the area just outside the sheep barn where Jem was working in the shade. He would expertly catch the ewe off-balance, using her own weight to twist her over so that he could examine the hoofs, paring or applying iodine as necessary.

'My brother Matt is coming over this afternoon, Jem,' Laura remarked.

'Right,' Jem replied non-committedly, concentrating on holding still a particularly large and active sheep, whilst cutting away part of her front hoof. 'Where does he live, then?'

'Ripon. He's a vet.'

'Well, that's useful!' grinned Jem. 'He could have done this job for you!'

Laura smiled back. During the summer her hair had lightened and the dusting of freckles on her nose and cheeks had darkened. She looked exactly what she was – happy, healthy, relaxed and fulfilled.

'How many more sheep are there in the barn, Laura?' Jem asked.

'Fifteen.'

'I should be finished in another forty-five minutes then – at most. I think I'll stop then and go for a swim if that's all right with you. The home comforts at *The Edge of the World* are not too spectacular.'

'Jem, don't you ever want to spend time doing all this' – she gestured expansively at the picture of orderliness which surrounded them – 'on your own farm?'

The shadow that always crossed Jem's face when his family farm was mentioned did so once again.

'No.' He replied curtly. 'It would be pointless. Going back there is like leaving a wholesome, bright place where there is laughter and wellbeing, for the darkest pit that ever existed.'

Laura hesitated.

'So why do you continue to live there, Jem?'

Jem put down his tools and paused before he replied.

'Would you understand if I said it is a sort of penance? And besides, I have nowhere else to go, Laura. Some of the most bitter times in my life have been spent there and I somehow need to become stronger in order to face the memories that godforsaken place constantly throws at me.'

'I would be lying if I said I did understand, Jem. But I respect your decision. At least you get visitors there sometimes, though,' she added, trying to move away from what was clearly difficult ground for him. 'No-one apart from the postman and delivery people and the odd family member ever seems to darken our door!'

'I don't, Laura,' Jem replied.

'But shortly after grandad died, when I asked you whether you would consider being our shepherd, there was a little boy in your garden – well, land.'

Jem blanched. 'What? What did he look like?' He stood up suddenly, releasing the sheep he was holding.

'He was about three or four years old, small and slight with curly, ginger hair. He was sitting quite still, just looking out across the reservoir and holding a wooden toy quietly in his hands. And I saw him again Jem, in the wood.'

Jem made a sound that was almost indescribable. It was part sob, part howl.

'No! And where did you see him?'

'The first time, on the rocky outcrop … and then lying in the bracken near the pool where we watched the geese …'

'I must go,' Jem cried and, dropping his hoof knife, strode away, along the winding drive.

Chapter 23

Shaking with shock, Laura watched her brother's dark blue Land Rover stop briefly on the farm drive, as Matt attempted to engage Jem in conversation. But, hands in pockets, head down, Jem didn't even break his stride in his haste to leave *Fell Farm* behind.

'Hi, Lau. Is that your new shepherd?' Matt Jamieson asked curiously, jumping lightly down from his vehicle. 'He doesn't seem a very talkative type!'

'Er, he isn't,' stammered Laura, desperately trying to pull herself together to welcome her brother, whom she hadn't seen since her grandfather's funeral. 'Come in, Matt. Cathy has been slaving over a hot Aga making every sort of cake she could find ingredients for!'

Slipping his arm over his sister's shoulders, Matt walked with her to the house. He shared the same vibrant looks as his younger sister: tall, slim and suntanned through spending the majority of his working life outside. He was one of the large animal specialists in his practice and, although only thirty-eight, held a respected place in the Lokisdale farming community. He ducked his head slightly to avoid the low lintel of the kitchen door, extending his hand as he went into the kitchen.

'Hi, Cathy. Good to see you again! How's life in Yorkshire then, compared with the great metropolis?'

'Hi, Matt. Great, thank you. I love it here.'

Matt sat down at the heavily-laden kitchen table and rubbed his hands together.

'Where shall I start? This looks amazing! I haven't stopped since breakfast. Serial calving going on in Lokisdale today and I'm starving.'

As the afternoon slipped by, Laura knew she was being over-quiet. But however hard she tried, she just could not forget Jem's harrowing reaction to her description of the little boy she had seen. Several times, she shut her eyes briefly, trying to push away the cry of utter despair and the bleak, agonised look that Jem had given her.

'Are you OK, Laura?' asked her brother, eventually.

'I think I must have had too much sun,' Laura replied. Perhaps I'll go and work in the snug. It's cooler in there. The *Fable of the Foxes* is calling for my attention'

Laura went through the sitting room to the snug. She and Cathy had carefully converted it back to its original purpose after Geoff Jamieson's death and it was warm, bright, and freshly painted in a clear daffodil yellow. Laura had bought a desk and this now faced the window, so that maximum daylight could fall on her workspace.

Since Jem's care of her sheep had allowed her to start working again, Laura's creative imagination had been at full stretch, observing the range of animals which surrounded her at *Fell Farm*. And always her sketches and stories reflected the elemental splendour and savagery of North Yorkshire. The bullying white cockerel; Fly, the devoted sheepdog; the busy-body

Robin; and the ethereal white geese, all came to life and acted out their stories under her skilful pencil strokes. But over recent weeks, there had been one storyline that had come to demand all her attention and it was to that that she now returned. She opened her sketch pad of thick, A3 sheets of paper and, frowning, looked at the preliminary sketches for the *Fable of the Foxes*, one of her modern 'fairy stories'. Carefully, she selected a pencil and examined its point.

Laura's mind was most definitely not on her work today but, almost of its own volition, her hand continued to move across the creamy sheets of paper, creating a little world within her world. Laura shook herself with impatience as her thoughts constantly returned to Jem. What was that indefinable something that she found so fascinating? And then she had it: wholesomeness. He was wholesome in the same way as a beautiful animal was wholesome and good to look at. The self-seeking arrogance that she had encountered in most twenty-first century men was absent in Jem. He was clearly very intelligent, but was perfectly satisfied shearing a sheep, or paring its hoofs. He was satisfied with what life dealt him.

Almost unconsciously, her mind occupied with the enigma of Jem's character, Laura sketched one of her brightest and most vivid childhood memories: a fox cub curled and sleeping in the terrifying vulnerability of infancy. She added fine details: tiny pricked ears, pink inside and edged with soft fur; the brush, not yet bushy as it would become in adulthood, curved protectively around the fragile body.

And then, almost as if the pencil had a life of its own, she drew a wolf standing just to the cub's left, mouth open and fangs bared, yellow eyes narrowed in its grey pelt, drops of saliva falling and darkening the cub's soft golden fur. To the right, she sketched a fully-grown male fox, magnificent and in his prime. Steady gaze, brush held stiffly, teeth and claws ready to engage with the evil presence opposite: protecting, loving, cherishing the cub lying at his feet. The two adult animals stood almost heraldically, one guarding, one threatening, the unsuspecting fox cub lying in its baby sleep between them.

As the sketches gained definition, Laura gradually tuned in to the conversation in the kitchen. She heard her brother's low laugh and a comment that was inaudible. Then she heard Cathy say, 'No, no I haven't yet. There is a right time for everything, as I was saying to Laura only yesterday.'

'Well better sooner than later, is my advice,' declared Matt Jamieson firmly. 'By the way, if you want to explore further in that direction, why don't you come with me to York? There are some first-class bars and clubs there. I am thinking of paying a call over the weekend, as I'm not on duty. I have a spare seat in the Land Rover ...'

Laura couldn't catch her friend's response, although she did hear her laugh, low and melodious.

Chapter 24

The *Fable of the Foxes* continued to take shape over the next few days. Laura's tales were usually fairly straightforward and were satisfying in their simplicity, featuring archetypal values such as honesty, integrity, bravery and patience – and the opposites which threatened them – but Laura felt that this one was different. A dark vein, heavy with violence, had crept into this modern fairy story.

'But what do *you* think, Cathy?' Laura asked her friend thoughtfully. 'Usually my stories are full of sunshine and parody. This one is full of darkness and a sort-of unnamed threat.'

Cathy leant against her friend's desk, thoughtfully turning the pages of her sketch book. 'It *is* different, Laura. But consider some of the traditional fairy stories! They're certainly not all sweetness and light. *Hansel and Gretel, Little Red Riding Hood, The Snow Queen* – they are all tragic, and all contain violence. I wouldn't worry. Just see where this story takes you.'

'I hear what you say, but it is almost as if this is being dictated to me. Where did that wolf come from?'

'Well, pretty obviously your imagination …'

'Yes, I know Cathy, but as I was drawing him, and the cub and the fox, each animal was imbued with the character of a specific human being. The wolf is an evil presence, ready to spoil and destroy; the male fox, a force for supreme good; and the poor mite in the middle – the cub – is the victim.'

Cathy was listening carefully but this figurative language was beyond her: she excelled in the practical and the tangible and so all she felt she could do was to repeat her previous advice. 'See where it takes you, as I've said. If you don't like it, you can always tear it up.'

Laura acquiesced, but still felt deeply disturbed about the way in which she seemed to be acting as the channel for a story whose development and outcome she did not yet know, or understand.

⇥∥⇤

Over the next couple of weeks Laura was drawn back, again and again, to the same sketch. She accentuated different aspects: the vulnerability of the cub, the self-contained beauty of the male fox and the malevolence of the wolf. One cool, bright September day she sat and realised that the picture was finished, apart from the setting, the background. Her mind immediately went to the hollow in the flowery field by the river in which she had come across the cub on that summer walk so long ago, and was surprised to find that it was still etched unforgettably on her mind. But somehow this gentle setting was inappropriate for the two males who, she was certain, were in some sort of battle over the juvenile, so she discarded this idea. Then, in a flash of inspiration, the black, stark rocky outcrop on *The Edge of the World* land came into her head. Perfect! She remembered the jagged points and pinnacles of the rocks and recreated them on the page in front of her – and the images of the animals sat perfectly within this setting.

Jem had returned to *Fell Farm* the day after his sudden exit and continued to work with a quiet intensity. He didn't avoid Laura, but she felt that he had stopped seeking her company and their easy companionship seemed to have disappeared.

Laura's head was bent over her drawing, as she was carefully shading the rocks to catch the planes and sharp spines of their shape. She raised her head, to ease the slight stiffness in her neck and saw, to her amazement, Jem gazing at her work through the window. He looked utterly stricken, then, when his eyes met hers, she saw a quiet determination blaze in them as he turned on his heel.

Moments later she heard his voice speaking to Cathy and, seconds after that, there was a knock on the snug door.

'I must speak to you,' Jem said. 'Please can you come with me … as soon as you can, Laura. I just can't stand this any longer.'

It would be impossible to refuse him, as Laura could see that he was barely keeping control over his emotions.

'Where are we going?' she asked. If she was to leave the house with Jem in this state of mind, at least she would tell Cathy her destination.

'*The Edge of the World*,' he replied grimly.

⊰⊪⊱

Jem strode ahead of her, head down, seemingly oblivious to everything around him, until they reached the grim, disintegrating pile.

'Come in, Laura.' It was an order, not an invitation. Jem led the way up a narrow stone staircase, which wound around the chimney of the kitchen inglenook to the rooms on the first floor.

What a dismal place it was! Gloomy and harsh, no colour brightened the bare, stone walls, no carpets softened the black oak floorboards. Jem walked quickly along the landing to a small bedroom which faced directly out over the reservoir. The rocky outcrop where she had seen the child lay just within sight to the left.

Jem pulled open a wooden cupboard, to the left of the small cast-iron fireplace. He took out a dented biscuit tin and, for a few moments, held it still in his hands. Then he took a deep breath and opened the lid. 'This is the boy you saw, out there on the rocks, isn't it.' Jem was making a statement of fact, not asking Laura a question. Jem held out a rather faded photograph which showed a small boy, wearing a green knitted jumper, long grey socks and scuffed shoes, sitting on a swing, smiling with all his heart at the person who had taken the photograph. He was unmistakable. His pale, heart-shaped face was surrounded by a mop of thick auburn curls and, as when Laura had seen him herself, he was clutching to his chest a wooden lorry as if he would never let it go.

'Yes, Jem, it is. Who is he?'

'My son, Joshua.'

Chapter 25

'You think I have led a blameless life, a pure life, as a monk … but it was a life of penance for the terrible thing that I did. If the Franciscans wore a hair shirt, I would have worn one. I would still wear one – but their way is gentler.'

Jem's face was wet with tears.

'When I saw that drawing, I knew I just had to speak to you. How did you capture one of the dreams which haunts me?'

Laura was speechless. Her mouth was so dry it was impossible to respond to Jem's impassioned outburst – even if she had an answer to his question. Jem turned his back to her and gazed out over the reservoir, which was sparkling in the autumn sunshine, making a vivid contrast to the dark, sparse interior of the farmhouse.

'I told the Guardian of the Friary my story, and now I must tell you. I feel that you and Cathy have created a false picture of me as some sort of saint, whereas I am some sort of demon! Thirteen years ago, when I was seventeen, I met a woman. She moved into a rented cottage in the village of Laikinthorpe, which is now hidden by that.' Jem gestured to the surface of the reservoir. 'She was older than me, probably ten years older, but I became fascinated by her, with the obsession of the young experiencing for the first time what they believe is love. She had a gentle attractiveness, with the sort of hair you have – exactly the same colour and wildness. Through the whole of that long, idyllic summer we were never apart: we met on the moors, in the woods, here when my father was away, but mainly in her little stone cottage. I had no idea where she had come from, or what her background was. I was such a boy! All I knew was that I had been bewitched by her. I had never slept with a woman before but I couldn't resist her. We became lovers, secretly, because my father would never have approved. He was an evangelistic zealot with a dominant, iron-hard personality in which there seemed to be no room for compassion or gentleness. Our family had always been ruled autocratically, without laughter or love because, before her death when I was fifteen, my mother had been oppressed by and completely subservient to my father.'

Laura watched Jem, gazing sightless out of the cracked, filthy window, over *The Edge of the World* land, down to the reservoir. She was experiencing such mixed emotions that it was impossible for her to articulate them, even to herself.

'At the end of the summer, she told me she was expecting a baby. I held her in my arms and assured her that I would protect her and our child. I told her that I would speak to my father and explain what had happened, and that we would be married. I had finished my 'A' levels and could find some sort of job which would support us all. I would ditch the idea of university. She was overjoyed.'

Eventually, Laura managed to speak. 'What was her name?' she whispered hoarsely.

'Ruth.'

'What happened, Jem?'

'I spoke to my father. Our family had always followed the tradition of using biblical names for children and Ezra, my grandfather, had unbelievably called my father Nehemiah, the prophet who succeeded Ezra in the Bible. It was a bitter and difficult conversation because, although my father condemned university as a waste of taxpayer's money, he believed that with a well-paid job I may be able to bring capital back into the farm, to repair and to restock. Grudgingly, he agreed to meet Ruth. It was to be for Sunday tea.'

Clearly, Jem was going through agony, retelling his story. He ran his hands again and again through his hair and eventually leaned his forehead against the broken glass of the window. He shut his eyes.

'Ruth walked in. She had put on her best summer dress, which still fitted her – just. My father, in a typical, dominant gesture of his, was facing away from the parlour door as she entered, looking through some religious commentaries that he had on the book shelves.

"Father, can I introduce Ruth?" I stammered nervously. Slowly, Nehemiah Walker, my father, turned to face us. Then a look of anguish, such as I have never seen before, crossed his features and he clasped his hand to his chest.

"You promiscuous fool!" he exclaimed. "This is your sister! You have impregnated your sister! You abhorrent, perverted apology for a human being."

'I was completely aghast. I remember feeling that the whole world was spinning out of control around me. Hardly coherent, I managed to ask my father what he meant and how could that be. His response was brutal and to the point.

'"That fool, Geoff Jamieson, fathered a baby on your grandmother Jennifer, before she married your grandfather, Ezra Walker. They called the baby – my half-sister – Sarah. She lived here for a while, first at *The Edge of the World*, then down in Lokisbridge. She walked me down to school for a couple of years, but when I was ten, she went to 'seek her fortune' in Leeds. She found a job in a factory and eventually married well: the manager of the clothing company she worked for. She had inherited the red hair and white skin of the Walkers, which can always ensnare unsuspecting folk,' my father said scathingly, looking poor Ruth up and down.

"Well, your grandparents died, and the farm came to me. My half-sister wrote to me – mainly at Christmas – to tell me that she and her fancy husband were happy enough, but one thing blighted their lives: they couldn't have children." Once again my father looked at my poor Ruth, who seemed to be fading away before his onslaught. "And one thing was blighting *my* life, and that was lack of money. Anyway, to cut a long story short, your mother became pregnant with our first child."

'He jabbed his forefinger at Ruth in a violent, uncouth gesture: "Her!"

"It seemed an easy solution. We would give this lass to Sarah in exchange for a certain sum of money which would save the farm. With the devil's irony, she even had the same colouring as my half-sister, which would help when nosey folk asked too many questions."

'Coming back abruptly to the present, Nehemiah glared at Ruth. "God knows why you should decide to return to this place – maybe to get money out of me? Your mother was always soft – took after her natural father most likely. She kept in touch with me over the years, sending photographs and so on, imagining that I would be interested in what was happening to you – so you had this address, didn't you?" He approached Ruth, towering over her, so that she backed away from him, towards me. My father was a bully and, seeing her fear, he turned back to me and exclaimed scornfully, "So you see, by not following God's laws, you have committed one of the greatest sins possible. God help the child that will be born of this unholy union. And another thing …"

'But, Laura, he said nothing more because I hit him with as much force as I could, put my arm around Ruth and left this house, thinking never to return.'

Laura's mind was spinning, but of the many emotions she felt, the chief one was of compassion. This poor man! Made a scapegoat through no fault of his own, how could he have borne such news? She couldn't stand aside any longer. Just for once she had to make a spontaneous, warm gesture, irrespective of what he thought of her, or she of him, or what her past had been. And she did. She walked up to Jem and encircled him with her arms. She had not held a man since Lewis, when all she had experienced was a creeping feeling of revulsion. Now, holding Jem, she felt only the steady thudding of his heart and a slight shuddering that told of the intensity of emotion that he was going through; whilst in her own body she was flooded with a warmth and longing that she had never expected to feel. Jem relaxed slightly back into her embrace and continued.

'The next seven months were terrible. I moved into Ruth's cottage and tried to sooth, as best I could, her horror at the situation she found herself in. She wasn't a bad person, Laura, quite naïve I think. She told me how Sarah, her 'mother' had described Lokisdale as the best place on earth to live, and that this had prompted her to visit, to discover the dale for herself. She reassured me that she had never had any intention to ask my father for money – but she needn't have bothered explaining, she was too straightforward a person for a scheme like that.

'I told her again and again that no blame attached to her – for anything. There was only one person I blamed and have continued to blame, and that is me. Of course we didn't marry – we couldn't! Clearly, Nehemiah Walker had done his worst and had spread our tragic little story far and wide amongst the people of Lokisdale. People stared at us when we had to go out to buy food or to go to the doctor for ante-natal check-ups. Even the nurse looked askance as we walked in to the examination room together.

'Joshua was born – eventually. Ruth's labour was difficult and lasted nineteen hours – to be honest I think she had given up on life. She was an uncomplicated person, as I say, and my father's revelations had shocked her immensely. Joshua lived, but Ruth did not – probably it was better so. She is buried in the churchyard – ironically, close to your grandfather. No wonder he hated my family. No wonder he hated me!'

Chapter 26

Rain started to spatter against the cracked glass of Jem's bedroom. Grey clouds had gathered from the north and the chill in the unheated, dilapidated house seemed to intensify.

'I loved my little boy. He was so beautiful. He inherited his mother's hair …' Jem turned and threaded the tips of his fingers lightly through Laura's chaotic auburn curls. 'There was no one who could care for Joshua, and I felt that I had no choice but to return to *The Edge of the World*. I bought an old pram and parked it wherever I was working around the farm, and Joshua was as good a baby as I had ever come across. He slept a lot, and when he woke, he smiled – just as if he was delighted to be in the world. As he grew older, I bought a baby sling and we went everywhere together. I used to lay him on the large, flat stone near the pool where I swam, or tuck him into the hollow on the rocky outcrop near the entrance of the farm. He would stretch out his little hands to me and, when I picked him up, he would cuddle his head into my chest. He never cried. He didn't make a sound. He would just smile, a wide smile that lit up the whole world for me. The terrible mistake I had made and the consequent loss of his mother – an innocent woman – was in some measure compensated for by his sheer joy of life.'

Jem had gently pulled away from Laura's arms and stood, stroking the photo of his baby son, lost in memories.

'Didn't you get any help from your family, Jem?' Laura asked.

Jem raised his eyes and looked directly at her. He shook his head vehemently. 'Help? As I say, my mother had died a few years earlier and we didn't have a clue where my father's half-sister Sarah lived. Although she had sent photos and school reports, she never sent an address where she could be contacted. Nehemiah Walker wanted me to have Josh adopted and ranted again and again about the shame that I had brought to the Walker family and the way in which my son was a living reminder of this.'

'Couldn't your father see anything of himself in the child?' Laura asked hesitatingly.

'No. He had coarse grey hair and the most unsettling eyes I have ever seen in a man – they were amber – animal eyes.' Jem shuddered. 'Like that wolf you have drawn so vividly – like the wolf that haunts my dreams.'

'Jem, where is Joshua now?' prompted Laura gently. 'Was he adopted in the end? You were hardly more than a boy yourself …'

'No, Laura, he wasn't adopted. I will try to finish the story – well, as far as I am able to "finish" it.'

Jem paused, as if gathering every ounce of strength he could. He gently brushed the ginger curl with his lips before replacing it with the photo in the battered box, and turned to face Laura, his back to the window which was now streaming with rain. 'As Josh became older – nearing two – I admitted to myself something

I had been aware of almost from the moment he had been born. He never spoke, or laughed, or made any sort of sound at all. My son was mute. You can imagine what Nehemiah Walker had to say about that! "The sins of the fathers will be visited unto the children" was one of the most frequently-heard things in this house of pain and anguish.'

All Laura could say was, 'Oh, Jem …' The sky had become even darker, and what little light there was in the room was behind Jem, making it impossible to see his expression. But from his voice, Laura knew he was struggling to continue.

'I took him to the doctor and various specialists. Physiologically, he was fine, and so they said that the barrier to speech must be psychological. I wracked my brains over the whole of his short life, from his conception to that present moment and, apart from the bitter exchange between myself and my father, could identify nothing that could have damaged his mind. I refused all suggestions that he should be sent to a Child Mental Health clinic for investigation. Even if he never said a word, I loved my son and, somehow, I would create a life for us both that did not rely upon language, but upon experience and emotion and most of all upon love.'

Laura just had to provide some sort of comfort for this man and so, once again, she reached out to him, holding his icy hands in her warm ones. His hands closed automatically over hers, enveloping their softness with the muscle and strength of hands that had worked all their life bringing order and care and health to animals – and had gently held, fed and cared for his small son.

'It was the year that they decided to flood the dale. They were offering silly money to anyone who could gather the sheep, or help with the excavation, or become involved in the thousand and one complex tasks that creating a reservoir entailed. Joshua was growing fast and needed new clothes and boots. He had started to run about bare-footed because, presumably, his little red boots hurt him. I earned a pittance: nothing from this place and very little from the odd shepherding jobs that I was able to pick up. I resisted applying for any of the reservoir posts, because I knew I couldn't take Josh with me. Health and Safety notices were thick on the ground and they would never allow a small boy anywhere near the site but, eventually, I gave in. Josh had just turned three. This biscuit box contained a birthday cake that I had bought for him in town ... I told my father that I would be applying and asked whether he would keep an eye on Josh if I did. Tersely, he agreed.

'Well, it was a disaster. It was very close to the time when the dale was to be flooded. The river Loki had been diverted and dammed, people from the cottages housed elsewhere, and the chapel deconsecrated. I returned home after that first day's work to find Josh sitting on the rocks by the entrance to the farm – where you say you first saw him. I have never had much money, but I had made him a wooden lorry, which he loved. He took it everywhere with him – even to bed – and he was holding it on his knees, as he gazed out over the dale where I had been working, which is now the reservoir. As soon as he saw me, he ran towards me, holding out his arms. I could see that his face was grubby and that he had been crying, but worst of all he had a bad graze on his forehead, so I whisked him up in my arms and cuddled him, took him inside and made his tea, telling him about my day and how much I had missed him. Of course, Josh couldn't tell me anything, but before he went to bed that evening, he clung to my legs and tried to hide from Nehemiah – I find it so difficult to call him my father!' Jem was telling his story through gritted teeth and his clasp on Laura's hands had tightened so much that it was painful.

'I bathed Josh carefully and put some antiseptic on his forehead. When he was tucked up in bed, I told him one of the stories from my primary school days, about a family of little pigs who lived in a cottage in the woods with their guardian. In this house of imagination, everything was warm, happy and gentle, so different from the bleak, hard home we had to live in here.

When he was safely asleep, happy and smiling once more, I tackled my father about the state in which I had found him. I was furious and was barely able to keep my temper.

'"He's a right namby-pamby!" Nehemiah retorted. "Just like his father! Talk about soft. Just had a bit of a tumble, that's all."

'I rang the contractors to say that I just couldn't come again because of child-care issues and, for a couple of weeks that was that. Anyway, the day came when the reservoir was to be filled: there was a sense of expectation, but also of fear, across Lokisdale. The landscape that folk had known since birth was going to be changed forever and everyone felt unsettled. It was ten o'clock in the morning and Josh and I were out mending one of the walls at the back of the farm. I had shown him how to build a drystone wall and he was intent on making a miniature one of his own and he tapped my arm every so often to show me his progress.

'My father came out of the house, shouting that someone wanted me on the telephone urgently and, scooping Josh up into my arms, I ran in. It was the reservoir contractors. One of the local landowners had let sheep stray into the area which, in a few hours, would be covered metres deep in water. His shepherd was sick and they wondered whether I could gather the sheep and return them to their own land. Because good publicity was vital in such an enterprise, and the voice of a local influential farmer was loud in these parts, the contractors promised me £1000 for a morning's work. Very, very reluctantly, I agreed.

'Replacing the telephone receiver slowly I turned to my father.

'"I said I would go – just one more time. If anything – anything at all – happens to Josh whilst I am gone, you will wish that you had never been born."

'He narrowed his inhuman, amber eyes and pushed his head forward, a little closer to me. "I wish I had never been born in any event," he hissed. "What a cursed family I have begotten!"

'I actually thought at that moment that he had lost his mind, so intense was the look of hatred on his face. But I would be gone for only a couple of hours. Surely nothing could happen to my boy in that short space of time. I grabbed my dog whistle and called up Sweep, our black Border Collie. Josh was standing on the rocks, trying to smile as he waved me goodbye. My father was standing close to his side, looking down at him with an unfathomable expression on his face.'

Laura couldn't help herself: 'Oh, God, what happened?' she cried.

Jem replied bleakly, 'That's the problem – I don't know. The sheep took under two hours to gather. Sweep was working like a magician, doing everything perfectly. I almost ran home, so concerned was I for my little boy. As I raced along the road from the contractors' huts, I became aware of a rushing sound – already the dammed water of the river Loki was pouring down the hillside into the valley bottom. By the time I got home an almost unbelievable amount had already gathered and where there used to be fields and walls was now standing water.

'I immediately ran to the rocky outcrop which was one of Josh's favourite spots. As I turned the corner, I expected to see his rosy cheeks and tousled curls, arms outstretched as always, as he ran to greet me in his own special, silent way. But there was no sign of life there. I went swiftly into the house, shouting my son's name, but there was no sound – nothing at all. Starting to panic, I shouted my father's name – nothing. I searched every room, every corner of our outbuildings and land, but still nothing.'

Jem sat down suddenly on the bed, holding his head in his hands.

'There was an investigation, of course. A comprehensive search was organised by the members of my father's chapel, now hidden deep under those dark waters, but nothing was ever found. We didn't have a car and no one had seen Nehemiah and Josh walking down to Lokisbridge or catching a bus. They just disappeared off the face of the earth and I have been left ever since with a space in my heart that nothing can fill and a two-fold feeling of guilt: for becoming involved with poor Ruth in the first place and for losing my precious boy in the second. Some of the local people actually accused me of getting rid of my father so that I could inherit the farm, and getting rid of my son because I was ashamed of him! Now do you understand about my penance, now do you see why I took refuge in a Friary for ten years?'

Laura was crying silently now. Never had she heard such a bitterly tragic story. There were many things she felt like saying, and doing, but all she did was whisper, 'Yes, Jem, I understand. And the small child I saw, how could that be Josh? He must be all of eleven now ...'

Jem wiped his hand across his eyes. 'Yes,' he affirmed. 'He would be eleven next March. You saw his ghost.'

Chapter 27

Cathy sat listening to Laura's account of Jem's shocking and deeply moving story. Laura was pale and agitated as she poured out the facts, mirroring the angst and sorrow that Jem himself had shown in his dark, comfortless bedroom. Cathy didn't say a word, didn't interrupt once, but when it was clear that Laura had finished, she stood up silently and walked to the window. Coincidentally, at that moment Jem appeared, walking from the barn out into one of the southern fields with Fly, as always, at his heels.

'I don't think I have ever heard anything so utterably sad,' Cathy murmured. 'How that poor man has been able to carry on is quite remarkable. He must have enormous inner strength. Despite opening his heart to you, he has continued to face the responsibilities that he agreed with you when you asked him to be your shepherd: he's been coming earlier and earlier, and leaving later each evening, Laura, because he wants your flock to be ready for tupping time. He told me that the Dales folk have a saying: "Put the ewes to the tup on Bonfire Night and you will have lambs on April Fools' Day." Pretty typical of the sardonic sense of humour the people round here seem to have.'

'He may be his usual diligent self as far as the animals are concerned, Cathy, but he has hardly spoken to me for the last forty-eight hours.'

'Come on, Laura! Are you surprised? Having shared his story with you frankly and without reservation, he now feels completely vulnerable when he sees you. How would you feel if you had told *him* about Lewis – all the grisly, graphic details? Would you just walk up to him as if nothing had happened, a huge grin on your face? Of course not!'

Laura nodded. How she appreciated Cathy's forthrightness and common sense! It was two days since she had heard Jem's heart-wrenching story, and initially she had had to manage the ensuing maelstrom of emotions without the comforting presence of her friend, who had spent the night in York.

Over the past few weeks, Laura had started to realise that Cathy was developing a life for herself away from the farm. She volunteered on a regular basis at St Mark's, the primary school that Jem had attended, and had accompanied Matt to York on a couple of occasions.

'Shall we go for a walk, Cathy?' Laura asked. 'I could show you *The Crying Wood*.'

Cathy hesitated for a few moments. 'Laura, I don't quite know how to say this, but you really should come down into town more. You are almost becoming a recluse. Everything is very intense up here. The landscape is harsh, life as a hill-farmer is tough, and you are so deeply involved with your stories. There *are* other things to do – you don't have to work all the time. Let's go to the museum and discover some of the history of Lokisdale.'

'I didn't know there *was* a museum in town.'

'Mm! As I said, you need to widen your perspective a bit.'

⊰∦⊱

The museum was small. Originally it had been a three-storey terraced house in one of the side streets of Lokisbridge, but about ten years previously, just after the creation of the reservoir, a local history enthusiast had bought the property and devoted several years to collecting artefacts, photographs and stories relating to Lokisdale and the surrounding district.

Used to the slick London museums, full of digital imagery and interactive displays, Laura and Cathy didn't quite know what to expect when they entered the distinctly *non*-technological, traditional Dales townhouse. On the ground floor, a series of rooms authentically re-created the interior of the house as it would have been when it was built – in the late Georgian or early Victorian age. The living room had an inglenook fireplace containing a black, cast-iron range, with an open fire and kettle set upon the hob. From the bressumer beam hung an iron griddle, and Windsor chairs with patchwork cushions flanked the range, in front of which was a chaotically-coloured rag rug. Sepia photographs and samplers crowded the walls, and delicate china was set on a round table, as if ready for tea time. It was enchanting! They passed through to the scullery, similarly fitted out with range and a wooden clothes' drier, suspended on a pulley from the beams of the ceiling. In the far corner, adjacent to the rear yard, there was a circular galvanised washing tub. Centrally positioned on a pine table, surrounded by neatly-tied bunches of lavender, was a framed notice, announcing that '*This museum of rural life has received the Local Museum of the Year Award*' for three consecutive years.

'Well, I can't say I'm surprised,' Laura commented. 'I think it is beautifully done. It takes me back to the Library I told you about that I visited with my grandfather when I was a little girl: it's like walking into a chapter of a history book! Such a shame that the Library has become just another craft shop. I'd love to show it to you.'

'That is a pity, yes,' Cathy agreed. 'I love this sort of thing. You feel as if you are visiting someone else's home in the distant past and you kind-of learn by osmosis!'

They went up the steep wooden stairs to the first floor, where exhibits were arranged as a museum collection rather than in an historical setting.

The first display cases showed the geology and prehistory of Lokisdale. They explained how the millstone grit was laid down millions of years earlier and how weather had eroded the top levels of the rock surface to create oddly-shaped outcrops of stone, Brimham Rocks being the most well-known example. The display was contextualised by local photographs, and Laura exclaimed as she bent closer to see one more clearly.

'Cathy, look, these are the rocks at *The Edge of the World*! It was here that I first saw the little boy.'

Without a word, Cathy gently touched her friend's arm and encouraged her to move on, to the rest of the display cases.

The next room was devoted to the creation of the reservoir and contained various pieces of furniture salvaged from houses and buildings in the valley before it was flooded. One striking item was a huge wooden box-pew from the chapel.

'I've never heard of a box pew before,' commented Cathy, standing on tiptoe to peer over the top of the structure. She saw names, incised in a careful, even script and a game of noughts and crosses scratched in the dark surface.

'No … it's enormous!' agreed Laura. 'I don't know how you could have seen out of it – it's almost like a little room.'

'I suppose the minister used to stand above the congregation, and at a higher level, so people would have to look up to him physically, as well as morally,' Cathy added.

'Well, one would hope so, but if you were a child, it would be awful!' Laura said indignantly. 'Like being imprisoned! No wonder children scratched their unstimulating surfaces to play games. You wouldn't be able to see a thing – just these four wooden walls and all you could hear would be a boring voice, droning on. You would be in your own restricted world, unable to escape. Look, the catch is at the very top of the door, on the outside! No child would be able to open it, or reach it. I think it's cruel!' She felt cold and angry looking at the barbaric device invented by a generation who were determined, against all odds, to indoctrinate their young – even to the extent of effectively imprisoning them and literally making them a captive audience.

The entire story of the making of the reservoir was there, neatly set out and documented with photographs and newspapers of the time. It was only slightly more than a decade earlier, but the display captured how a whole village had become history in a space of a few short months. Some photos showed men and women standing outside their homes, looking lost and sad, forced to evacuate houses that had, in some instances, been in their family for generations. There was an interior shot of the chapel which caused Laura to explode.

'For goodness' sake! It looks just like a prison! Those unspeakable pews are everywhere. It's horrible and I'm glad it's disappeared under water! And look at that gigantic stone cross, dominating everything – it looks like a weapon rather than a religious symbol.'

'Laura, don't get so upset! There are plenty of examples of disgusting human practices far worse than this example of religious fervour! How about the man-traps over there that they dug up when building the dam? They could maim or even kill people, not merely indoctrinate them! Come on. Just time to go to the top floor before tea.' Cathy linked her arm firmly into her friend's and they climbed the next staircase to the top floor.

The third floor of the museum was devoted to 'Myths and Legends of Lokisdale' and contained the usual array of Victorian photographs of 'ghosts' and 'fairies' – mere shadows on the celluloid which could have been anything, or nothing. Letters written in sloping copperplate handwriting told of alleged encounters between inhabitants of Lokisdale – themselves long-dead – and various unexplained phenomena. Framed maps of the area showed where legends had grown up and were linked by map pins and tightly-stretched string to photographs of the sites where these phenomena had manifested themselves: natural features, farmhouses, wells and woodland.

Laura's eyes ran quickly over the array in front of her: a girl drowned in a well that belonged to a monastic farm; a dragon that had slept for centuries on a rocky outcrop by the *Edge of the World*; and *Souls' Farm,* built at the highest point of the moor, the most haunted farm in Lokisdale.

'I'm so glad we came, Cathy,' Laura said, pressing her friend's hand. 'There is so much material here for my stories!'

'I won't say Auntie Cathy told you so...'

But, as she entered the final exhibition room, Laura gasped. Directly opposite the door, over the ornate, cast-iron corner fireplace, was a large photograph of the pool in *The Crying Wood* and, rising out of the deep clear water, were beautiful white birds – the geese which she had seen with Jem. Laura flushed as she remembered the last time she had seen the woodland pool, when it had been Jem's beauty that had riveted her attention, rather than the loveliness of the birds. 'Cathy, it's *The Crying Wood*,' she said softly.

'What does it say in the display case underneath?' asked her friend, bending to see the neatly-printed card.

'The legend of The Crying Wood has developed in Lokisdale over at least five centuries. This ancient, broad-leaved woodland used to belong to Loki House, which was flooded when the reservoir was built. In centuries gone by, the trees were managed carefully by the Robinsons, the owners of this, the largest house in the dale; and grottos, paved ways and gas lights were introduced to heighten the sense of the picturesque for the family and their guests. Most of those who know the Crying Wood believe that its most significant feature is the large, natural pool hidden in its depths. It is a well-documented fact that, for generations, great white geese have bred in the woods, swimming in the pool just before evening. And it is a powerful legend in Lokisdale that before a soul passes from the earth, it is

said to journey through the woodland lamenting its sins before inhabiting the body of one of these magnificent creatures – hence the name: The Crying Wood. As the great bird flies out of the woodland towards the open moor beyond, the soul finally gains freedom from earthly sorrows and can reach the eternal light of the heavenly realm.'

'What Biblical rhetoric! Must have been written by one of the old ministers in that chapel,' Cathy joked.

But Laura's expression was deeply reflective as she re-read the legend. 'You should see them, Cathy. There *is* something other-worldly about them. But it's so sad …'

'Well, I find the inflated language quite amusing, actually.'

'No, let me finish. I was thinking about Jem's little boy – Joshua. If he was in *The Crying Wood*, he couldn't have made a sound. Poor little boy …' She reached out and gently followed the outline of one of the birds in the photograph.

'It *is* sad, Laura, but we can do nothing about it! Let's get back to reality and treat ourselves to some cake,' Cathy said, giving her friend a warm hug. 'Cake is the antidote to all sad and uncomfortable things.'

Chapter 28

The tea-rooms were empty. It was now September and, as schools across the country started their autumn term, the annual influx of visitors to North Yorkshire had thinned to a trickle. People had returned to their own urban lives and work routines, having glimpsed for a brief moment the wonder and freedom of the Dales.

A fire was burning in the grate, and paintings of Lokisdale by local artists, who used the tea shop as a showcase to sell their work, crowded the whitewashed walls. Delighted at the arrival of new customers, the small, stocky woman who owned the café smiled warmly at Laura and Cathy, as she moved the vase of chrysanthemums to one side in order to place a staggeringly large afternoon tea on the table.

'I can feel myself putting on weight just looking at that lot,' joked Laura. Usually, Cathy was ready with a laugh and a swift riposte, but she seemed to be concentrating entirely on placing china cups on saucers and stirring the tea in the large brown tea pot.

'Laura, what I said to you back in the farm, about getting to know more people, I think it's really important – for me, for you, for everyone. I don't often mention our first meeting and the weeks that followed, but you had, understandably, retreated deep inside yourself, and it took months before you were ready to face the outside world again. It was wonderful as I watched your character flower when we started to have coffee together in town, to go shopping, to meet some of my colleagues for a drink or a roast on Sundays.'

Laura reached over the heavily-laden tea table and laid her hand lightly on Cathy's. 'I remember it too!' she exclaimed softly. 'It was like coming out of a dark tunnel. I can never thank you enough ...'

'It was a joy and a privilege,' her friend smiled. 'I know I'm not putting this particularly well, but I care for you, Laura, and I need to try to say what's been on my mind for some time.'

Laura nodded and sipped her tea, as Cathy haltingly continued. 'Human beings are made to be social animals and there are hundreds of minute character traits that we need to develop and allow to be developed, through contact with other people. I really miss my parents and my London friends, but I couldn't just stay at *Fell Farm* reflecting upon this feeling of loss. I made a conscious decision to get out, to start to mix with different groups of people and make new friends. I didn't particularly want to volunteer at St Mark's, but the school was in quite desperate need of volunteers to work with small groups of children who need extra support during some of the lessons. There is such a wide spread of ability there, from the children of the doctors and lawyers who commute to Harrogate and Leeds, to the children of local farming families who regard leaving their own remote hill farms as an adventure. Laura, why don't you come down to meet the Headteacher, Miss Wilkins? She has devoted her life to the school here in Lokisdale. She was telling me that she was made Head here when she was only in her mid-twenties and has remained ever since, developing and growing with the school over the last twenty years. She really does care about her children and she is passionate about literature and the arts. Perhaps you could bring some of your work down and maybe use it to stimulate the creative imagination of the children.'

Cathy paused, conscious that her friend had become very quiet. For what seemed like an eternity, Laura was silent and kept her eyes firmly on the sandwiches and cakes in front of them. Cathy slowly stirred a second cup of tea, wondering whether she had overstepped the mark, pointing out what was to her so obvious: no-one could live a solitary, or nearly solitary, life without becoming prey to over-thinking. During the past ten months Laura had transformed Cathy's life. Her compassion had been raised by the blend of innocence and experience that Laura had brought into her world; and her heart sang when she saw her friend laugh, or even smile, at some shared event or encounter. Laura had introduced her to new ways of observing and reacting to the natural world and had stimulated emotions in Cathy that she had not known she was capable of feeling.

Eventually Laura looked up from the fine bone china. 'You are right, my wise friend. Everything has been so intense since we came here. Losing Grandad, being faced with running the farm, becoming involved in creating my stories ...'

'Meeting Jem!' added Cathy, with an affectionate smile.

Laura flushed. 'Yes, Cathy, Jem! He has become the biggest challenge of all! I just don't know how I should act with him anymore. During the summer I really felt that a friendship, a relationship, was growing between us, but it is as if it has just been cut off, or frozen, or something …'

This time it was Cathy who stretched her hand across the table and placed it, warm and comforting, on Laura's cold one. 'Can't you just be yourself, Laura?'

'I wish I could!' Laura exclaimed passionately. 'But I feel as if a chasm has opened between us and we are divided by things that have happened to each of us. Seeing Jem putting flowers on that grave – presumably where Ruth, the mother of his little boy, is buried – I felt as if there was a whole lifetime of experience that Jem has had that I can never touch.'

'And how about Lewis?'

'What do you mean?'

'Jem doesn't even *know* about Lewis, Laura. You have never shared with him how hard you were driven by your experience – to the point where we met.'

Laura ran her fingers through her hair. 'It's yet another thing – a huge obstacle – that stands between us. How *can* I ever tell him, Cathy? Think of the life he has led – he was a monk for years! He has had only one short relationship when he was little more than a boy himself – and I bet there was nothing weird about it! I just don't know what to say to Jem any more. Everything I can think of saying seems so charged with emotion or implications that I can seldom pluck up courage to open my mouth!'

Cathy munched steadily through a thick slice of fruitcake, obviously thinking carefully about what to say next. She took a sip of tea, then smiled warmly at her friend.

'Laura, try to distance yourself from the situation for a while; try to give yourself perspective. Jem's diligence means that he is fully occupied with the sheep at the moment. You, equally, need to be fully occupied with something that is not focussed on Jem! Come to St Mark's with me tomorrow. Meet Miss Wilkins – please!

Sandra Wilkins was an attractive woman in her mid-forties, dressed in a navy-blue, mid-calf-length skirt, white blouse and dark blue cardigan. Laura's first impression was that she reminded her of the Headmistress of the primary school just outside York which she herself had attended nearly seventeen years earlier. Her expressive features and mobile mouth, short dark hair and vivid blue eyes made an unexpected impression on Laura. The executive Headteachers and Heads of academy chains who appeared on breakfast news and in the national papers – hard, suited and booted and focussing totally on how well their schools were performing in the league tables – were light years away from Miss Wilkins. There was a calmness and wholesomeness about the woman that immediately put Laura at ease.

'How do you take your coffee, Miss Jamieson?' the Headteacher asked.

'Black, no sugar, thank you – and please do call me Laura,' she added.

'And my Christian name is Sandra – I've so been looking forward to meeting you and hearing about your work.'

Laura had brought her sketch books which were filled with her small, even handwriting and exquisite drawings of the animals which both crowded her everyday life and inhabited the literary world she had created.

Sandra Wilkins carefully took the sketchbooks over to her desk which was stationed in front of her office window. It was morning break time and she took a moment to scan the playground, raising her hand and smiling to several small children who were vying for her attention. Her face lit up as she watched the skipping, circling, animated throng. Laura tried to start a conversation, but clearly her companion's mind was completely absorbed by her charges and it was only when the whistle blew for the end of break time that she turned, smiled at Laura and sat at her desk, opening the books in front of her.

Completely absorbed, Sandra turned the pages, obviously reading the text as well as appreciating the drawings, and many minutes passed in silence. Eventually, she closed the books, resting her hands lightly upon their covers, turned to Laura and said, 'These are quite remarkable. Cathy has explained to me that you were an artist of considerable standing in London, before you decided to turn your talents to writing and illustrating these sorts of moral tales. We would be honoured if you would consider working with the school. The children's imagination would really take flight seeing these!'

'Would you want me to go into classes and talk to the children? I have never done anything like that, and quite honestly, it terrifies me!'

Sandra laughed. 'It does most people. No, I was thinking it would be more appropriate to make a start during our Creative Arts Festival just before Autumn half term, when we invite artists to be "in residence" for the week, talking to children, parents and grandparents and any other interested parties about their work. The idea is something I introduced years ago, but we can do so much more now we have our wonderful new hall!

School Governors attend and I make sure that my teaching staff supervise the behaviour of the children. All you would have to do, if you are willing, would be to work as you normally do: drawing and writing your stories, whilst explaining the process to the children.'

'I would love to do that, Sandra.'

'Then please put 15th – 21st October in your diary! We would love to have you.'

Chapter 29

Since Jem had opened his heart to Laura, he felt as if he had lost touch with reality. Through reliving every painful detail of his relationship with Ruth, his love for his little boy and his hatred of his father, the past had started to seem more real than the present. He constantly felt that he was on the point of seeing his son again. When he turned suddenly, he would often catch a slight movement, as if Josh had just left the room, or the rocky outcrop, or the sighing, dark woods. He dreamt persistently of his son, of his smile and his touch – even the warm, clean scent of childhood. Less frequently his dreams were of Ruth whom he felt he had destroyed through what was no more than a young man's intense and immature first 'romantic' relationship.

He continued to perform his shepherding duties meticulously, and the *Fell Farm* flock were being thoroughly prepared for the fifth of November when, once again, the age-old annual cycle of tupping, gestation and lambing would start. Jem, too, felt that the easy communication, holding such latent promise, which had started to develop between him and Laura had ceased to exist. But whereas Laura attributed the change solely to the longing that Jem had for the past, Jem knew that he had become withdrawn and silent because he felt that Laura must be utterly disgusted by his past actions. Often he would arrive at *Fell Farm* in the dark before dawn and would leave long after dusk had fallen. Watching his figure leave the farm quietly, bent against the wind and rain, Laura couldn't imagine the sort of existence he must be leading in the semi-derelict, dreary ruin, less than half a mile away from her own warm and comfortable home.

Laura had really taken on board the advice that Cathy had given her after the visit to the museum. Although she had not admitted it, even to herself, the power and honesty of Jem's story had affected her so profoundly that it was as if she herself had suffered some of the tragedy. She now knew that never again would she be in danger of spiralling down into the state of mind that she had been in when suicide had seemed the only answer, but her conversation with Cathy had been a real wake-up call. It had made her realise that instead of wishing to share her 'modern fairy tales' as an ironic commentary on life, she had started to regard their creation as an end in itself. Her involvement with the school's Creative Arts Festival reminded her that there were countless other lives and worlds that demanded her attention outside her own small and relatively constrained one.

'We must look like a travelling circus!' exclaimed Cathy, as she carefully shut the rear door of her vehicle. She and Laura had packed the back of the car with Laura's sketchbooks, pencils and watercolour paints. There was also a large cage, deeply-bedded with clean straw, containing one of their brown hens that clucked softly as the vehicle set off.

'Come in,' Miss Wilkins beamed. 'I have put you over by our tall, east-facing window. I have heard that artists need as much light as possible and this is the brightest part of our hall.'

Two long work tables had been set end-to-end in front of the window which stretched floor to ceiling. A small, circular stained-glass roundel was set into the centre of the window, showing the lion of St Mark and what Laura presumed to be the school motto: '*Fortem esse modestos.*' As she set up her paper, pencils and paints, Laura wrinkled her nose, trying to decode the Latin words. 'Is it something to do with being modest?' she asked Miss Wilkins, who bustled up to ask whether she had everything she needed.

'It looks as if it should be, doesn't it?' the Headteacher replied. 'It actually means: "Strong but gentle". We had a school competition about twenty years ago to decide upon the best way to express the values our school stands for. Linking the lion of St Mark with the saint to whom the school is dedicated was pretty obvious, but it was one of our quietest, gentlest boys who came up with the words.'

'Do you teach Latin, then, Sandra?' asked Laura absent-mindedly arranging pads of paper and pencils for the children to use when they started to sketch.

'Not seriously. It's not really appropriate at primary level. But we do dabble, when we follow the topic of 'The Romans'. I remember though, Jeremiah really became fascinated by the combination of military might and creative genius shown by the Romans. Part of the competition was for the children to give a presentation, explaining the reasons behind the motto that they had devised. Jem explained that it was easy for a strong man to be violent and aggressive but very difficult for such a man to combine his strength with gentleness. His argument was very powerful and almost certainly derived from his relationship with his brute of a father.'

A pot of pencils that Laura was tidying crashed to the ground. 'Sorry – Jeremiah? Do you mean Jem Walker?'

'Yes, I've never known another Dales child called Jeremiah! He was a complete delight to teach: bright, interested in everything, and very, very caring. What happened to him was such a tragedy.'

'He's my shepherd, Sandra. I know the outline of the story.'

'It was so unfair. He could never have guessed who that poor girl really was – none of us did. I have never seen anyone so completely traumatised. He had to stand so much criticism, both covert and direct. In the end he just had to leave Lokisdale – and then it was as if he had disappeared into thin air, just like his father and his little son. No one knew where he had gone, but when he came back this spring it was no surprise that he had become a Franciscan friar. He always loved the beauty of nature and fed birds, hedgehogs, stray cats, foxes – anything that crossed his path.'

Laura did not raise her gaze to meet that of the Headteacher. What she had just heard had complemented her own observations of Jem. Life was so unfair, she thought to herself. There was Lewis – dark, dangerous, sadistic, wealthy, ensnaring any woman he took a fancy to and then discarding them brutally; and then there was Jem – quiet and caring, loving the beauty of the natural world, whose one immature but genuine relationship with another woman had been twisted by fate into becoming something unnatural and bitter.

⊰❘❘❮⊱

The children were very excited as they flocked into the school hall after registration. They had been carefully prepared for working with the range of artists who had now set up their work stations in the hall. As well as Laura, there was a stained-glass artist, who had a small studio in the converted stables of a large Victorian house on the outskirts of town; a weaver, who collected and spun her own wool from her flock of Herdwick sheep further up Lokisdale; and a woodcarver, who had an array of small wooden animals on his table and was busy working on the creation of a dibber, a relatively straightforward article for the children to produce with his help. Laura quietly appreciated the thought and hard work that had gone into setting up the Creative Arts Week at this small school. The chicken, which Laura had decided to bring in case the children's inspiration ran out, clucked quietly and scratched around in her cage whilst Laura took a deep breath and nervously welcomed her first group of children.

They were introduced to her as Paula, Jim and Laisha. Laura had already worked out how to involve the children in the depiction of animals as characters, and the weaving of a story involving their fantasy personalities.

'Who has a pet?' Laura asked her small group. Two hands shot up.

'What sort of pet do you have, Jim?'

'A dog, Miss. He's called Toby.'

'And you Laisha?'

'Two guinea pigs – Ginger and Spice.'

'Is that because of their colour?'

The little girl nodded vigorously.

'Do you know any animals well, Paula?' continued Laura. 'Maybe a pet belonging to an aunt, or friend?'

'We have our farm up the dale,' replied the stocky, rosy-cheeked little girl. 'Me dad has about a thousand yows.'

'Excellent!' Laura smiled. 'Jim, I would like you to jot down five words to describe Toby. Laisha, could you please do the same for Ginger and Spice; and Paula, can you find five words to describe your father's ewes, please.'

'I thought you were going to teach us to become artists, Miss,' Jim remarked slightly truculently, 'not do writing with us!'

Laura laughed despite her nervousness, 'Be patient! I am teaching you how to work as I work.'

Five minutes later, the children had decided that Toby was 'cheeky, greedy, loving, a bit fat and lazy'; that the guinea pigs were 'silky, cuddly, noisy, sleepy and inquisitive'; and that the sheep were 'stupid, boring, played follow-my-leader, woolly and hungry.

'Great!' Laura encouraged them. 'Now choose one of the adjectives – describing words – and draw your animals trying to illustrate that adjective, either through their expression, or what they are doing.'

The children were away. Their imaginations were caught by thinking of how their chosen animal would demonstrate the character trait which they themselves had identified. The results were exactly what Laura would have expected from primary-age children, but they were fresh and funny. Toby's legs bent under his hugely fat body as he wolfed down his dinner; the guinea pigs slept in crudely-drawn rocking chairs; and the sheep clambered cumbersomely, one after another, over a broken-down drystone wall.

'Brilliant!' Laura praised their work warmly. 'And now, let me show you one of the stories I am working on at the moment. It's called *'Robin, the Nosey Postman.'*

Laura opened one of her sketchbooks. She had completed the story during the long summer days when she and Jem had observed the robin together, pecking crumbs outside the kitchen window.

As they turned the pages, the children gave an animated commentary:

'He's just like our postman, Miss!'

'But he is drinking so much tea, going from house to house, where he delivers the letters and sits down and talks to people ...'

'... being really nosey in their houses.'

'He's really naughty, I think! Just look at the way he's poking his nose ...'

'Beak!'

'... poking his beak, into those presents on that lady's table.'

The children were spellbound as the story of the nosey postman-robin unfolded itself. Its moral was the theme of many a traditional fable: a kind lady had bought the postman a birthday present – a mug with a picture of a sheep on it – but because he was a nosey-parker, the postman discovered and dropped the birthday parcel and broke the mug.

'It just shows,' commented Laisha sententiously 'you should mind your own business!'

'Exactly!' The comment came from a tall, good-looking, grey-haired man who had come quietly to observe the group. He extended his hand towards Laura.

'Miles Jefferies. Delighted to meet you. Community governor – I'm editor of *The Dale Echo* – do you get the pun? Not *Daily Echo*, but *Dale Echo*. I was fascinated to see how you worked with those children – you really engaged their imagination.'

'Thank you,' smiled Laura. 'I love this, actually. It really makes me analyse my own creative process – how I observe animals and link the natural characteristics I see in them with human counterparts.'

The children started to fidget, pressing close to the small brown hen that Laura had brought to the school, and who appeared to have laid an egg at some stage during the session.

'Right children, time to move on to our weaver,' Miss Wilkins told them briskly and shepherded them away towards the woman whose mass of coarse grey hair uncannily resembled the piles of Herdwick fleece with which she was surrounded.

Miles Jefferies threw back his head and laughed. 'As long as you don't apply those principles of observation to the human race in your everyday dealings with them,' he said wryly. 'Miss W would be Mother Goose, herding all her goslings along in a neat, fussy and predictable way; Phil Jenkins over there, working away on his wood lathe could well be an old woodpecker, banging away at the same spot with not much impact.'

Laura felt distinctly embarrassed at these comments, which were made loudly and pointedly, so she tried to steer the conversation in a rather more positive direction.

'I think Miss Wilkins is the perfect Headteacher, Mr Jefferies, don't you? She is so kind, vibrant and hard-working – and the children love her.'

'Miles, please. She is also outmoded in her practice. We could do with some youth and real energy here.' He scanned Laura's slim figure quite overtly and her embarrassment turned to anger.

'The children in St Marks's are models of politeness and good behaviour,' Laura retorted. 'Traits that are often sadly lacking in today's society.'

Completely missing the allusion, but sensing potential disagreement, Miles abruptly changed the subject. 'Your work is really very competent. Where did you train?'

Laura told him, adding with some asperity: 'I was invited to exhibit at the Affordable Art Fair in Chelsea when I lived in London. Happily, my *competence* meant that I was successful in selling all twelve of the paintings I entered over the ensuing weeks.'

Laura had forgotten how stultifyingly boring the self-centred, testosterone-fuelled men that she had consistently encountered in London actually were. Miles Jefferies would certainly be more at home in their company than here in this quiet Yorkshire market town. She was desperate to work with the next group of children waiting for her, being kept at a little distance from her workstation by Miss Wilkins. The Headteacher looked slightly flushed – whether with anger or embarrassment, Laura was unsure – and was talking quietly to the group who were in earshot of the loud opinions recently expressed by the school's community governor.

Laura turned and was just about to call across the hall to the Head when Miles touched her elbow, 'Would you like to come out for dinner with me tomorrow night? We could continue this fascinating conversation. *The Pheasant* has had some excellent reviews by my food and wine correspondent. Shall we say seven-thirty?'

Sandra Wilkins was guiding the next group of children in Laura's direction.

'And now, you will be working with Ms Laura Jamieson. Ms Jamieson was a well-known artist in London before she decided to come to live in Lokisbridge. Animals are the subjects of all her stories and I know you will love working with her.'

Seeing the new cohort of children approaching rapidly Laura panicked, her single thought to get rid of this rude, self-opinionated bore. 'Oh, all right,' she muttered, desperate to do anything to make Miles Jefferies go away.

'Where do you live? I will pick you up.'

'No thanks. I'll get a lift and will meet you there. *The Pheasant*, you said – seven-thirty it is.' And finally he went, smiling in a self-satisfied way as he bade her good bye.

Chapter 30

Laura slung her bag in the back of Cathy's Panda, muttering under her breath, 'That bloody man!'

'Er, perhaps you could give me slightly more information as to whom you are referring,' said Cathy gently.

'Miles Bloody Jefferies!'

'Ah! Otherwise known as Miles "The Creep" Jefferies. Don't tell me, he has asked you out to dinner? He tried it on with me, but I told him that he was, er, not exactly to my taste.'

'You told him that?'

'Well yes, I did. Don't forget I am a volunteer and he probably thinks he really needs to keep on the right side of me. Actually, he needn't give it a second thought. I go there not because of the governors but because I enjoy the work and I respect the staff.'

'Oh, I should have told him to get stuffed – I am just too soft!'

'You are what you are, Laura. Your character makes you, you.'

Laura was so glad to see *Fell Farm*: it had become her home like no other house or flat ever had before. It was safe, welcoming and always full of life, with sheep bleating or hens clucking or the light bark of Fly as she went about her work.

It was dark as they followed the curving drive to the farmhouse. Cathy had left the lights on in the house and they shone out into the chilly evening, beckoning them home. The friends half expected to see the tall, dark figure of Jem striding along the drive in the opposite direction, as it was about the time he usually returned to *The Edge of the World* and, as the lights were blazing in the barn too, they assumed that he was still working. However, as they drew level with the barn they saw Jem outside the building, kneeling in the farmyard and bending over something.

'Cathy, please can you stop and drop me off here. I need to see what is going on,' Laura asked her friend.

'Of course. But do you mind if I go and make sure the casserole is still edible? It's been in the oven for a bit longer than I anticipated.'

'Go ahead,' said Laura, jumping lightly out of her friend's car. 'I'm absolutely starving! I can see why Miss Wilkins keeps so slender, working every day with children – you literally never stop! See you in a minute.' Concentrating on making her voice sound friendly and natural, Laura walked swiftly towards the kneeling figure of her shepherd. 'Hi Jem,' she called.

'Laura, Fly was missing for some hours this afternoon. She must have eaten a bone she found somewhere, because it splintered and a part of it stuck in her throat. I managed to get it out, but it damaged her – she has been bleeding pretty badly. Can I bring her indoors? She is OK, but needs warmth and quiet.'

Jem carried the little dog gently up the slope to the kitchen door, which Cathy had left ajar after entering the kitchen. Turning swiftly with hands cloaked in oven gloves Cathy asked practically, 'What can I do?'

'Just put some folded blankets in front of the Aga please, Cathy. Fly is all right, but just shocked and sore, I think.' Jem sat cross-legged on the kitchen floor next to the sheepdog, stroking her and murmuring to her: 'Good dog, that's my lass. Good little dog.'

'If I really can't do anything to help you, Jem, do you mind if I get on with dinner,' Cathy asked.

'No, of course I don't mind – I feel I am intruding!'

'Can *I* do anything to help, Jem?' Laura asked biting her lip.

'Not really, thank you. There's not a lot you, or anyone, can do. I am just going to let her rest and nature will do the healing. You two have to eat. Don't mind me.' And he continued to stroke the little dog and murmur to her, fondling the long silky fur of Fly's ears and the thick black and white coat covering the slight bones.

Laura and Cathy worked easily together in the kitchen. Only the previous day, Cathy had laughed, saying, 'My mother loves cooking and has always said that a kitchen is big enough only for one cook! How come we two can work together?'

'Easy,' Laura had quipped. 'I'm no cook!' And the friends had hugged hard, laughing.

Tonight, Laura set the table whilst Cathy prepared the vegetables. The casserole she had made earlier that afternoon had simmered away in the Aga during their time at school and despite her concern was perfectly cooked.

Cathy deftly chopped broccoli and slipped it into a pan, saying quietly to Laura, 'Let's have some of that red wine we got the other day in Harrogate – and for goodness' sake, invite Jem to stay and eat with us! Say you want to thank him for keeping an eye on Fly or something ...'

Laura set an extra place at the table and put out three wine glasses. She coughed nervously. 'Jem, we cannot thank you enough for looking after Fly. Please stay and share our meal. There is a lot of food here and we hate waste.'

Cathy rolled her eyes at her friend's awkward invitation and added, 'So please wash your hands and sit in the chair nearest to Fly. She won't fade away with her guardian next to her.'

Jem grinned. 'Thank you. I would love to stay. Where would you like me to wash my hands?'

'Oh, here in the kitchen or in the bathroom – just through there,' Cathy replied, gesturing towards the snug and the downstairs bathroom. Jem took off his boots and placed them carefully outside the kitchen door, before leaving the women together.

'That man just pulls at my emotions, Laura!' Cathy whispered when he had left the kitchen. 'Did you see his socks? They were more holes than fabric! But everything about him is so fragrant. Have you noticed? It's like having a dose of Dales air in the house.'

'He must swim every day, Cathy' Laura mused.

'Sorry?'

'Well, his "home" is so very basic. I didn't see a bathroom at all when I went there. He said he swims regularly.'

'Laura.' Cathy took a deep breath. 'Where is your humanity? This man is living on the poverty line – just about surviving. Haven't you seen how painfully thin he has become since we have known him? Without the regular meals all the monks must have received in the Friary, how do you think he would survive without the food we give him? According to what you have told me he has a prototype range; a basic camping stove; one kettle and no hot water apart from what he can heat up in it; very limited food; and one broken chair! Try to think of his well-being rather than your own tangled emotions.' Cathy's tone was, for her, rather sharp and she asked pointedly, 'Can't we offer him more than we are giving him at the moment?'

Laura twirled the wine glass thoughtfully in her hand. 'Yes,' she said simply.

It was one of those evenings when everything seemed to be just right. The food was perfect; the wine was good and, against all expectations, the conversation between Jem, Cathy and, to a lesser extent, Laura, flowed freely. Fly slept deeply, a slight discharge of bloody spittle escaping from her mouth. As soon as he saw this, Jem was up from the table without excuse or apology and knelt next to the little dog, stroking her and saying in the gentlest tones, 'Now, my girl, are you OK?'

Fly's fan-like silky tail flapped a couple of times and she licked her lips before falling back into a deep and exhausted sleep.

'Cathy, that meal was amazing!' Jem placed his knife and fork neatly down across his plate at a precise forty-five degree angle. What did you do in your London life? Were you a cook?'

Cathy smiled at Jem and replied: 'I am so glad you didn't say "chef", Jem, but actually I was a nurse. My mother is a wonderful *cook* and during my childhood I just learnt naturally to care for and look after people. And I love to do it!'

Laura stretched out her hand and clasped Cathy's warmly. 'You certainly do!' she smiled.

Firmly Cathy withdrew her hand from Laura's. 'Jem, I have enough rhubarb crumble to sink a fleet. *And* I have custard. Can I tempt you?'

Jem bowed his head, pushed back his long thick hair, and gave a groan of pleasure. 'Just as well I am not still a monk!' he laughed. 'Your food is enough to tempt the most devout and temperate of men.'

As the meal had progressed, both women had noticed how Jem had visibly relaxed. His face gained colour and the sharp angles of brow and jaw seemed to soften with the warmth, food and wine that they had provided. All evening, Laura had been reflecting on Cathy's words and had felt thoroughly ashamed. She was the first to criticise her parents for being self-absorbed, but she now acknowledged that she herself had been guilty of precisely this where Jem was concerned.

It was nine o'clock. The large casserole was empty, as were the pan of broccoli and the bottle of wine. Fly was sleeping soundly and had even ventured a drink from the water bowl that Jem had put down for her. Both women noticed that Jem's eyes flickered from time to time to the kitchen clock: seven o'clock, seven-thirty, eight-thirty. And now Jem took a deep breath, set his shoulders resolutely, and said, 'I must go.'

Laura, who had been the quietest of the trio during dinner, took a final sip of wine and placed her glass down firmly. 'Jem, please don't go. Please stay here. We have enough room for you here on the farm. Please do stay. I think that Fly needs you, but I also think you need more warmth and comfort than you are getting at the moment. I can't afford to pay you more, but I can offer the hospitality that my grandparents always used to show. Please stay, Jem.'

Cathy cringed inwardly at the fact that her friend had used the word 'please' no less than four times, but folded her hands, bit her lip and said nothing.

Looking across the scrubbed pine kitchen table, Jem realised how very much he wanted to stay – not just as a shepherd, but as a man who wanted to continue to get to know the quiet, beautiful woman who sat opposite to him tonight. Surprisingly, he lifted his head and smiled into Laura's eyes. 'I would love to stay,' he replied simply.

'Thank God!' exclaimed Cathy with feeling.

'… but only outside, sharing Fly's bed in the stable.'

'Well then, at least take some hot chocolate with you, and a blanket,' Cathy insisted.

Jem grinned in response: 'Of course! You never know, I might get hungry in the middle of the night …'

Chapter 31

It was a bitter night. The stars were bright in the clear, frosty air as once again, in the stable he had first used after Geoff's accident, Jem curled his body around the warm, slight form of the little sheep dog.

He had had a wonderful evening. People dining at Michelin-starred restaurants on wine that cost more than the average worker's weekly wage could not have felt more genuinely satisfied than did Jem that night. He bunched up the straw that he had heaped into a makeshift bed and tried to settle his head. But as soon as he shut his eyes, he saw again the pensive, vital face of Laura as she quietly ate her dinner. In his memory, he replayed the conversation which had ebbed and flowed during the evening. She was so complex! One moment all he could see was her talent, her genius, observing an animal, eyes wide and focussed. Next, he saw her laughing like a young girl, sharing a joke with her best friend. And, as a subtext to all these impressions, he found her a lovely, desirable woman. He felt that he could be no more than background to her, so great was the spread of her perception and empathy. He found her intoxicating!

In her bedroom, Laura had drawn back the curtains so that she could see the immense, starry sky. Since she had been a girl, Laura had been fascinated by the legends that surround the constellations: *Orion's belt, the Pleiades, Castor and Pollux,* and usually her mind was full of the mystery and beauty of the universe as she drifted off to sleep. Tonight, however, she couldn't get out of her head her friend's comment concerning Jem as they prepared dinner together: '*Can't we offer him more than we are giving him at the moment?*' Apart from *Fell Farm*, its contents and the animals that it sustained, Geoff Jamieson had not been able to leave his grand-daughter much of a bequest. It barely met the outgoing expenses of the farm and had to be augmented by Laura's savings and limited investments, together with the hill farm subsidy that *Fell Farm* attracted.

Laura couldn't afford to increase Jem's pay, but an idea had been growing in her head and tonight her brain was in overdrive, trying to work out how she could take this forward. She was also replaying some of the conversation at dinner, recalling Jem's gentleness and care for Fly. He was so honest and open and she knew that he deserved equal frankness from her concerning her past life. She gazed, sleepless, out of the un-curtained windows across which the implacable constellations appeared to move as the world slowly turned. To Laura, sleep seemed as far away from her that night as those remote stars. She flicked on her phone and saw that it was three o'clock but, despite the time, she decided that she would just have to go out to the stable where Jem was sleeping and speak to him. If she waited until morning, she feared she would lose her determination to share her past with him.

Slipping on jeans, two thick jumpers and a quilted jacket, Laura tiptoed downstairs so as not to wake Cathy. She quietly unlocked the kitchen door and walked softly by the low, traditional stone outbuildings which stood at right angles to the farmhouse, turning right to the stables and the modern sheep barn. Laura was light and moved gracefully, making no more noise than a cat and she soon reached the stable, outside which she paused to regain her emotional equilibrium. Taking a deep steadying breath, Laura glanced through the window, before she entered the snug little building. In the middle of the heap of straw the starlight showed where Jem lay sound asleep, with body half-curled, his left arm over Fly and his right cushioning his head around which his thick brown hair lay like a tousled halo. Laura stood for several minutes gathering her resolve, then entered the stable, lifting the old, heavy latch.

In an instant Jem was awake and on his feet. 'Laura! Are you all right? Is there something wrong?'

Laura shook her head. She had decided not to procrastinate, but to come straight out with what she had longed, but dreaded, to tell Jem almost from the first time she had met him. 'Jem, I have to tell you something. You have been so frank with me about your past, about your relationship with Josh's mother and all the circumstances which surrounded it ...'

'You want me to leave,' Jem said bleakly.

'*No*! No, please just listen to me, Jem. Have you ever wondered how Cathy and I met?'

'Not really, I supposed you had just come across each other.'

'Well, we did, but it was because I was about to kill myself. I was on the point of jumping into the Thames, because I just couldn't stand the life that I was living any longer.'

Laura had started to shiver. Without a word, Jem gently wrapped the blanket that Cathy had given him earlier around her shoulders.

'I met an art dealer at an exhibition and he told me that he knew people who would buy my paintings. He did and sold several of them, and I had a relationship with him.'

Jem sat quietly, listening.

'It wasn't a normal relationship though, Jem. It was horrible. He was perverted and abusive. He isolated me from all my friends and colleagues and from my family and he hurt me, persistently. After I had come up here, to Lokisdale, for my father's birthday, he hurt me really badly and threw me out of the flat that we shared together. I was in hospital and then on the streets. I have never felt so disgusting, so useless or alone. Then, one freezing November morning, Cathy saw me standing on one of the supports on Waterloo Bridge and offered me the hand of friendship – literally. I owe her so much.'

Still Jem said nothing and Laura quietly covered her face with her hands, closing her eyes and trying to come to terms with the thought that, in the last few minutes, she had almost certainly destroyed any chance that Jem would ever like or respect her. She felt that she never wanted to leave the oblivion of the safe, dark world she had created for herself behind her hands, and would never open her eyes again; but, gently and firmly, she felt her fingers being released, one by one, and then her hands being held in a warm, strong grasp. Then, overcoming her fears, she did open her eyes and gazed directly into Jem's where she saw warmth, acceptance and deep compassion. He said nothing but leant forward and kissed her lightly on the lips, stroking her hair back from her face.

'Thank God you are human,' he said with infinite gentleness.

Chapter 32

Jem bent and lifted the sheepdog into his arms and, silently, without disturbing that moment of complete understanding that they had shared in the stable, they went back together into the kitchen – always warm and welcoming.

'I feel … I feel as if …' Laura started.

'… as if a huge weight had been lifted from your shoulders?' completed Jem. 'So do I, Laura! I felt so utterly unworthy of you, and I believed that it was a mere question of time before you would find an excuse to get rid of me as your shepherd.'

'And I felt that you would be disgusted by what I have just told you,' Laura admitted. 'But you're not, are you?'

'No, of course I'm not,' Jem declared forcefully. 'Let me try to explain. When I was in the Friary, I discovered that the brothers live by several simple rules. The first one is that all human beings are imperfect – every single one. Even the Pope and the Archbishop of Canterbury are imperfect in God's eyes! The important thing is that people should be honest and admit that they are not perfect and, despite that, try to continue to live as good lives as they possibly can.

Honesty is the one and only thing that matters. That and accepting without judgment all other human beings for what they are – flawed, full of complex twists and turns.'

'Even Lewis – the man I told you about – is loved by God, then?'

'Even him, Laura. What sort of little hell do you think he was living in, treating you like that? Most likely, he was abused himself; or maybe he had no self-respect. Certainly, the actions towards you were nothing to do with how you behaved. It was *his* problem – the flaw was in him.'

Jem lent across the table and, hesitating only for a moment, took her hand in his, interleaving his fingers in hers and pressing their palms together. Then, with an infinitely gentle gesture, he kissed the back of her hand and returned it to her.

'Thank God for that!' declared Cathy who, beaming widely and wrapped in a very unbecoming fleecy dressing gown and tartan slippers, appeared at the kitchen door. 'I think that this calls for some tea!'

⇥‖⇤

They had given up on sleep that night. Cathy put the kettle on the Aga and opened a cake tin. Jem pretended to groan.

'I will explode if I continue to eat like this, Cathy,' he declared. 'You are looking at a man whose regime as a monk was to fast two days a week.'

'Well, more fool you!' retorted Cathy. 'As a medical professional I can tell you that the human body is not programmed to fast like that. Maybe not *quite* so much cake, but I am sure that it's good for the soul.'

The minutes ticked around and their conversation ranged from past experiences to matters of sheep husbandry, until Laura said, 'I have an idea I would like to discuss with you both.'

'Yes?' came the almost simultaneous reply.

'That stable, Jem – the one you were in tonight – I think we could convert it to a small cottage, or studio, or something like that. There is electricity already, and water just outside. I'm not sure about drainage but we could get advice on that if necessary. Since we are being so honest, I need to tell you that Cathy and I are *not* happy about you returning to *The Edge of the World* to try to exist without heat, or proper food or water or anything. Anyway, we would like a resident shepherd with lambing time coming up. Would you consider moving in and helping us to convert the stable?'

Jem sat, motionless and expressionless for some seconds and both women – even Cathy – wondered if they had overstepped the mark. Then, very uncharacteristically, he jumped up and punched the air.

'Would I consider it? It would be amazing! Never will a conversion take place so swiftly – just you watch and wait. That stable and I, we have history together! It will be the best farm cottage ever!'

Chapter 33

'Are you tired?' Miles Jefferies asked pettishly, more than slightly ruffled.

Laura had hardly been able to stay awake during the interminable 'fine dining' experience at *The Pheasant*. Course followed course, each being accompanied by a pretentious commentary from the editor of the *Dale Echo*, together with suggestions for suitable accompanying wines. Although Laura enjoyed a glass of wine, she found drinking to this extent almost impossible and, after what she estimated was probably the main course, she refused further alcohol and drank only water.

'Oh, I am so sorry! How rude of me. I had a terrible night's sleep last night. I was kept awake by … by my sheepdog.'

Miles raised an eyebrow. 'Would you like some coffee? It would probably restore you to life a little.'

Laura nodded, stifling yet another wide yawn. She had hardly taken in any of the interminable monologue, lightly clothed as conversation, that her companion had effortlessly delivered. Skirting swiftly over her reason for being in Lokisdale and her work and career in London, Miles had moved fairly and squarely and with great rapidity to himself. He told with cringing false modesty how he had become editor of the paper when only thirty-five; how, with the literary contacts that his editorship had brought him, he now earned enough to sustain a large Edwardian house overlooking the reservoir and a farmhouse in Brittany *and* was able to run two cars: a Porsche Boxster and a Range Rover Evoque.

'I've brought the Porsche tonight because I thought you would appreciate being taken home in style,' he told Laura smugly and was distinctly disgruntled when she decisively refused his offer.

'My friend is picking me up at ten,' she said firmly.

During the entire evening, Laura hugged to herself the thought that, back at *Fell Farm*, the two people she realised had started to mean more to her than anyone else in the world, were working together on the stable. Despite having laboured from first light until tea time looking after the sheep and caring for Fly, who still seemed quiet and tired, Jem insisted that he was going to start that evening to clean out the building that was to be his home.

'On one condition,' Cathy said firmly, 'that we do it together! What do you expect me to do – sit indoors knitting?'

When Cathy had driven Laura away from *Fell Farm* earlier that evening, light was blazing from the squat, stone stable and Laura had felt that the last thing she wanted to do was to see Miles Jefferies. Her reluctance had been abundantly ratified: not only was the man boring, he was arrogant and offensively obvious in his attraction towards Laura. She had lost count of the number of times his eyes had slid down her figure.

Laura could have cheered when Cathy appeared at the door of *The Pheasant*, dressed in green dungarees and wellington boots, her hair tied up in an old scarf.

'When can I see you again, Laura?' Miles asked quietly, as she jumped up without preamble, forcing herself to go through the ritual of thanking him for the evening.

'Tomorrow at school,' Laura replied.

'You know what I mean, don't tease me!' Miles laughingly reprimanded her, delaying her by laying his hand firmly on her arm.

At that moment the creeping similarities between Miles Jefferies and Lewis Devrille were unmistakable. Laura flushed angrily, taking a step back in order to release his hold on her arm and his forced laughter ceased immediately.

'I am not in the habit of "teasing" decent men,' she retorted. 'My life is very busy and I am involved in a conversion project as well as my work at the moment. I will see you, and any other governors and visitors who care to interest themselves in the Creative Arts Week at St Mark's tomorrow, or later in the week. Thank you once again for dinner this evening, and goodnight.'

Laura took her coat from the waiter and smiled with relief at Cathy, linking her arm through her friend's. 'I have never been so glad to see you!' she breathed quietly. 'He so reminds me of Lewis – they could be brothers!'

'Don't worry about him! I will whisk you home in the faithful glass coach before he turns into a pumpkin!'

'You're daft.'

'I know. Wait until you see how much progress we have made this evening, Laura. You will be impressed indeed!'

Cathy stopped her car outside the stable. Unbelievably, Jem was still working, but she knew that he must have neared the end of what he was able to do without further materials. The building had been thoroughly swept and the floor scrubbed. Without the piles of hay and old sacks, Laura was surprised at how large the space actually was. The rough, whitewashed walls had been brushed clear of cobwebs and the two iron mangers had been cleaned and polished. In pride of place was a small bed, with sheets and blankets neatly folded at its foot. Cathy had even placed one of the colourful Ikea rugs brought from her flat in London alongside the bed.

Jem turned towards them, beaming. 'What do you think?'

'I love it, Jem. You've both worked wonders! But aren't you tired? I am exhausted after last night, and the mindless conversation I have been forced to listen to this evening just about finished me off! You must be shattered.'

'I've never had anywhere so comfortable to stay,' Jem stated simply. 'Back at the farm, before I went to the Friary, Father would never let us have anything bright, or soft, or comfortable. He said these things were worldly vanities and would corrupt us. I remember once my poor mother brought two matching cushions home from a craft sale at the Women's Institute in town. They were quite plain really, blue with a slight pattern of leaves. Father took them into the farmyard and set fire to them. In the Friary, my cell was about a third this size, painted white with no curtain. The beds were so hard that we used to joke that they were designed to make the brothers' backs strong for working in the Friary and the gardens. No need for orthopaedic mattresses there!'

The women looked around the sparse, almost empty space and the same thought was in both their minds: it was astonishing that this should be the most comfortable space that Jem Walker had ever had to call his own. It was shocking, and somehow very humbling, to look at the joyous, radiant man in front of them, cherishing a small stone stable as his home.

'Well,' Laura gulped down her emotions, 'even if you are not tired, I am. So goodnight Jem – we'll see you at breakfast.'

'No, please don't bother, I can get something ...'

'Absolutely and utterly not!' Cathy declared, in a voice that would brook no contradiction. She had blinked away tears at the obvious delight that their shepherd had in so little, when people who had so much continually complained. 'If you are going to live at *Fell Farm*, then you will participate in *all* our routines, and that includes food!'

'She who must be obeyed,' muttered Laura. 'There is no going against her when she is in a mood like this. It's easier to give in!'

Jem laughed. 'Willingly! I will see you both *at breakfast* tomorrow morning.'

'Oh, one further thing,' added Cathy. 'We shower before breakfast. Please use the downstairs shower. I will put extra towels in there for you. It's probably too complicated to install plumbing in here, and the house is only a few steps away.'

'I can't thank you ...'

'Well, please don't then,' Laura smiled. 'See you tomorrow.'

Chapter 34

The glimpse of his former unremittingly barren life that Jem had unwittingly given her and Cathy, made Laura determined to enrich his existence at *Fell Farm* to the very best of her ability. She arrived at St Mark's punctually the next morning and spent a few enjoyable hours working with another group of eager children, fortunately without the unwanted attentions of Miles Jefferies. At lunch time she went into town and made straight for a very old-fashioned shop that her grandmother would have called a "draper's". It was a treasure trove of fabric, towels, cushions and rugs and Laura determinedly bought the brightest, yellow daisy-strewn curtain material she could find, golden towels and white cushions with a bold daffodil motif on them. She smiled to herself, anticipating Jem's pleasure when he saw the sunburst of colour that she would deliver to him later that afternoon. Thinking of the transformation of the plain little stable and recalling Cathy's steadfast support – in this as in all things – she called into the florist and bought dahlias in her friend's favourite colours: red, purple and gold. Her face buried in the glorious riot of rich blooms, catching their slight, spicy scent, Laura came across a small gift shop, where something in the window caught her eye and she emerged several minutes later with a flat, rectangular package, tied with string.

She wasn't required at school that afternoon and, as she drove up to *Fell Farm*, Laura found that she was smiling spontaneously. All of a sudden, her life had seemed to gain a new dimension: she was living, doing things, and buying things purely and simply to give pleasure to others.

'Whoa!' Laura stopped, astonished, as she walked into the stable, hands full of shopping bags. The entire place had been whitewashed, the windows were sparkling clean, and a small electric panel heater was plugged into the socket that had previously powered heat lamps. Jem was standing in the centre of the fresh-scented, bright and welcoming space, hands on hips, smiling at her.

'What can I say to thank you?' he asked.

'There is no need: the way that this place looks now is thanks in itself.'

'Laura, there is every need. I am without words. No one has ever given me a gift like this and I still can't quite believe it. Another thing …' he hesitated, looking down at his white-speckled hands '… since I have been here at *Fell Farm*, I haven't dreamt any of the dark dreams that have haunted me almost continually since I left Lokisdale all those years ago.'

Laura sat on the white wooden chair that Cathy had unearthed from somewhere or other on the farm and looked seriously at Jem.

'I've brought you a house-warming present, to hold one of your most precious possessions. I hope you like it – I think it's the right size.

Jem unwrapped the flat, paper-wrapped parcel and uncovered a delicate picture frame, studded with small, carved white and yellow daisies to match the curtain material Laura had just bought.

'It's to hold your photograph of Josh, Jem. Do you like it?'

'I never saw anything so lovely. I am running out of thankyous, Laura.'

'I know how much you loved Josh,' Laura said quietly.

Jem nodded.

'I still do. Love doesn't just stop, it continues forever, even when the person you have loved has gone.'

Laura swallowed hard, trying to keep her emotions under control as she continued. 'And he loved you – loves you.'

'Yes. He showed it in every possible way he could.'

'So, do you think it possible that Josh was, or is, somehow trying to help you, to direct you into a new path in life, Jem? If your dreams hadn't started again, you wouldn't have returned to Lokisdale and my grandfather would have died on that night he fell, alone and in pain, rather than passing away peacefully and in comfort. *Fell Farm* would have had no shepherd ...'

'And I would never have met you – and Cathy,' Jem added, reaching out and touching her gently on the hand. 'I do think it is possible, yes. When I was at the Friary, Brother Peter used to jokingly call me 'Joseph' sometimes, because I seemed to be able to explain particularly vivid dreams which were obviously weighted with some sort of meaning beyond the obvious.'

'Joseph, as in coat-of-many-colours?'

'Yes. What is strange though, Laura, is how you seem to have become involved in what is going on in my head! When I saw you drawing the fox cub, the adult fox and the wolf, it shook me to the core. You were actually depicting the substance of one of my most disturbing dreams. I knew the wolf to be my father with his strange, amber eyes, looking with sheer hatred at my son, a vulnerable fox cub, and I felt myself to be the adult fox, poised to do anything I could to protect my child.'

'I did feel that I was being directed to produce those drawings, Jem. It seemed to me as if I was being used as the channel for someone or something to tell a story through those pictures. Although I saw a little fox cub during my childhood, curled up in exactly the way I drew him, I have never seen an adult fox at first hand and certainly never a wolf. Although I am continuing with my gentler 'modern fairy tales', I keep returning to those drawings I started for the *Fable of the Foxes* – I can't help it! I have added no further illustrations to the story yet, just embellishments to the original drawings so far, but I have a feeling that further illustrations will come – that I will be directed to produce them.'

Reflecting on what Laura had just explained, Jem sat with his head bowed slightly, thoughtfully tracing the shape of the daisies on the photo frame, while Laura quietly watched the play of emotions on her companion's face. Eventually, the silence became almost something tangible that she just had to break.

'You say that here you do not dream dark dreams, Jem?'

'No, for the first time in my life, I feel as if I am part of the ordinary world. I remember when I was at school other children would run up the hill, or down the main street, eager to reach their homes at the end of the school day. I always tried to find some pretext to stay, to delay my journey home – perhaps sharpening pencils, or tidying exercise books. I hated *The Edge of the World*! Everything there was silent and dark and full of fear. My mother drifted around the farmhouse like a ghost. I thought a lot about her in the Friary, how she had been forced to give up her first-born child and how everything she did during the day led up to the moment when I came home from school. Later, when my father came in from his farm work, his evening meal was always ready on the table – my mother was terrified of him. No conversation was allowed at meal times and we had to read in the evening. We were never allowed to go out. And then, when I lived with Ruth, it was like living with a shadow. She was never a strong character, and what we had done destroyed her.' Jem stood up and walked to the window. It had started to rain and Jem's gaze followed the little rivulets running down the small panes of glass. 'She used to sit silently for hours, her hand resting on her belly as our baby grew inside her. Her mouth worked as she bit her lip with unsaid words and unexpressed emotions. Poor woman …'

Once again, as in his dismal bedroom in *The Edge of the World*, Laura put her arms gently around him, intending to comfort him. But, unlike that first time, now Jem turned around and pulled her to him. Laura closed her eyes and leant into him and, as if it was the most natural thing in the world, Jem gently kissed her hair, then held her at arm's length.

'You and Cathy are so normal – so completely wholesome! You laugh and cook together, or go shopping, and are somehow able to put behind you the difficulties you have had in your lives. You have opened the door to the world of the living for me, Laura.'

Looking at the unspoken emotions in the depths of Jem's dark eyes, watching the still, controlled planes of his face, Laura was in turmoil. Sadness, longing, empathy for all that Jem had been through, all these feelings surged through Laura's mind, making her incapable of saying or doing anything meaningful, so she simply murmured something indistinguishable and left the stable.

That evening, immediately after supper, Jem excused himself and, with barely-controlled anticipation, went down to his cottage. Cathy had made curtains from the fabric that Laura had bought and Laura was delighted to see them drawn snugly across the small windows of the stable cottage, sending a soft, golden light out across the yard in front of the sheep barn.

She felt that, at last, she had been able to give Jem Walker the 'something more' that Cathy had challenged her to do less than a week ago: she had been able to give him his first real home. And recalling the undiluted pleasure in her shepherd's face after dinner, when he simply could not wait to return to the stable that had been converted into the most basic of homes, she smiled quietly, with infinite joy.

Chapter 35

It was Friday, and the final day of the Creative Arts Week. Laura had been relieved that, following her evening out with Miles, he had not spent any time at St Mark's, and she couldn't help thinking cynically that he had only been present on the first day of the festival so that he could figure prominently in the photographs which one of his reporters had busied herself taking.

The day started with a school Assembly and Laura groaned inwardly as she saw Miles Jefferies in the front row of chairs, directly opposite Miss Wilkins, who stood up to thank the artists graciously for the time that they had given to the school. The Headteacher had asked Laura and the other artists-in-residence to join her, sitting in a semi-circle of chairs which faced the children and adults filling the school hall, and Laura felt the same revulsion that she had experienced at *The Pheasant* when she saw that Miles' eyes were fixed more frequently on her body than on her face.

Miss Wilkins had decided to exhibit the children's work in the hall and to provide light refreshments for the parents, governors and members of the public that she had invited to attend. There was an appreciative, lively atmosphere as people bent to examine more closely turned wooden artefacts, small painted glass roundels, woven scarves and brightly illustrated stories which featured pets and larger farm animals. The Headteacher had asked the artists to place the stimuli for the children's work behind each section of the exhibition and Laura had chosen her *Tale of the Silly Sheep* and, because she judged it to be some of her best work, the drawings of the *Fable of the Foxes*.

Predictably, Miles spent most of his time bending to examine Laura's work.

'This really is of the highest quality, Laura,' he said, patronisingly.

Laura smiled politely.

'Would you consider allowing me to write an article about you and your work? You know, what inspires you, your artistic journey so far, where you live and how you spend your life in Lokisdale.'

Laura looked hard at Miles. 'Why?' she asked directly.

'Well, we always aim to showcase local talent and if there is a story behind the creativity, that's even better. I know you had a life in London and maybe we could draw on that to promote your work in Yorkshire – possibly nationally!' he declared importantly.

'Do you have a national readership then, Miles?' asked Laura disingenuously.

The editor of the *Dales Echo* had the grace to flush slightly.

'Well, not exactly, but,' raising his voice slightly to draw attention to himself, 'as I explained when we had dinner the other night, I do have national contacts.'

'All right then, I suppose so,' agreed Laura, reluctantly.

'Excellent!' Miles pronounced, rubbing his slightly plump, white hands together. 'My office, ten a.m. Monday?'

The impact of this incisive invitation was somewhat diminished by Laura asking, 'Where is your office, Miles?'

'Er, over Barclays Bank, in the middle of the High Street,' came the somewhat anti-climactic reply.

⊰◉⊱

Editor's Perspective: November 1st

A second Beatrix Potter discovered in the heart of the Dales

'You are never too old for a fairy tale!'

This is the firm opinion of Laura Jamieson, one of the latest and brightest lights to illuminate the growing Arts scene in Lokisdale. Laura had a respected career as an artist in London but has since decided to extend her artistic talents in a literary direction. She settled permanently just outside our town, Lokisbridge, when her grandfather, Geoff Jamieson, sadly died and left her Fell Farm. Geoff was well known for his outstanding farming practices and his skill in handling a sheep dog. He was a regular member of the England sheepdog trials team and won many national and international sheep dog trophies.

Laura takes after her grandfather in finding inspiration in animals, but whereas Geoff Jamieson was firmly grounded in farming life, his granddaughter weaves stories using the birds, sheep and domestic animals of the Dales, creating characters which arise from their natural animal behaviour. So, her sheep represent those human beings who follow others mindlessly, ignoring danger and risk for the sake of self-gratification; the robin which visits her garden is a nosey-parker postman, whose bright eyes pry into the lives of his neighbours; a pampered white cat is an A-lister, followed relentlessly by the paparazzi.

Laura's 'Modern Fairy Tales for Grown-Ups' are distinct descendants of Beatrix Potter's creations; but are more edgy, most definitely for adults, and directly related to twenty-first century life with its complex moral paradoxes.

Lewis Devrille's eyes narrowed as he looked at the small photograph of Laura, which accompanied the article in the *Dale Echo*. She looked radiant, vital and entirely lovely. He put down the paper sent to him by his friend Miles Jefferies and gazed out over a grey, wet London. After a few minutes' thought, he slipped his phone out of his pocket.

'Miles, how's things? Still "wasting your fragrance on the desert air"? I think it's high time I had a break in that sheep-strewn county of yours. I've got some leave overdue – how does the end of the month suit you?'

Chapter 36

'Friday's the day, Laura,' Jem announced obscurely over breakfast.

'Er, your birthday?' joked Cathy.

'No, November 5th – firework day for the ewes and tup!' Jem responded, grinning broadly. 'There is one point I wanted to run by you though, Laura. The ewes born earlier this year need to be served by a new tup – they can't run with their own father.'

'No, I don't suppose they can, Jem – I hadn't thought of that!' Laura replied. 'Could we borrow one?'

'Well, yes, I think we can,' said Jem. 'When I was down in town yesterday afternoon, I got talking to Fred Shorter, who farms up the dale from here. He has a young tup that hasn't been tried yet and he was keen to see how he would work with your flock here.'

'Are there any drawbacks?' Laura asked, frowning slightly as she always did when out of her depth.

'I don't believe so. Fred is a decent man and a good farmer. His livestock is well cared-for and respected hereabouts. I think we should take the young tup for this season.'

The young ram arrived the next day, Thursday, in a trailer. Laura and Cathy found it difficult to believe that he was barely eighteen months old, as he had the same weighty frame as 'Old Charlie'. His heavy shoulders and massive head dwarfed those of the ewes – although Cathy said she found him distinctly better-looking than his elder counterpart.

Jem settled him in one of the stables next to the sheep barn with fresh hay and a container of high-energy, molasses-based sheep nuts. He grinned as he and Laura watched him heartily munching them. 'He'll need all the energy he can muster over the next couple of weeks,' he said.

Jem and Fly separated out the young ewes, fathered by Charlie in the Spring, and penned them in a field away from the rest of the flock. Tomorrow the borrowed ram would be introduced to this small flock of ten or so young females and together he and Charlie would start, once again, the cycle of the shepherding year.

⊰◈⊱

Laura was astonished at the speed with which the rams worked. Each had been fitted with a harness, attached to which was a block of coloured raddle: Charlie had blue and the borrowed ram's was yellow. As each ram mounted a ewe, her fleece was coloured with the raddle so that Jem could see at a glance which ewes had been covered and which had not. At the end of a fortnight, all the ewes had been served and a riot of blue and yellow dotted the fields.

The tups were still attentive and Jem explained that, as long as they were interested in the ewes, they should remain with their flocks, in order to be absolutely sure that as many sheep as possible had been impregnated. 'It'll also stop the tups from getting bored, or aggressive,' he continued. 'As long as the ewes interest them, they won't think about fighting each other – which they certainly would do if they came face to face, when the pressing business of fathering the next generation wasn't in the forefront of their minds!'

Laura found it fascinating to watch the docile, incurious ewes continuing with their lives, completely oblivious of the fact that their bright blue or yellow colouring spoke to the world about their recent activities. She imagined the tiny foetuses tucked safely inside the large, warm bodies of the sheep, growing steadily despite the atrocious weather battering their mothers. She knew that she had to wait five long months before she saw the outcome of the dedicated activity of the tups, and longed for Spring to arrive once again.

Towards the end of November, Jem told Laura that he felt that the tups had completed their work. 'And we'll see just how well they have done when we get the vet to scan them to show how many lambs each ewe is carrying.'

'Matt will do that, Jem. I'm sure he won't charge.

'You don't see much of your family, Laura, do you?'

Laura shook her head. 'No. It's sad, really sad. I feel as if my parents live in a different world – of respectability and pretence, instead of reality. It drives me insane! Do you know, I have never told them about Lewis! They would make judgemental, disapproving noises and completely ignore the impact that the whole, foul episode had on me!'

'And Matt?'

'I'm really fond of him but … it's quite difficult to explain … I don't feel I *know* him. He chats away quite spontaneously, but he doesn't really *say* anything. It's a terrible thing to say about my own brother, but

I don't think I could actually describe his character to you at all!'

'I thought you said that he and Cathy became friendly a couple of months ago and that they went to York together, to clubs and places like that. Didn't Cathy chat about the time that they spent there? I bet you were secretly hoping that they would become a couple!'

Laura laughed and turned to Jem, eyes sparkling.

'Jem, you are so old-fashioned! "Become a couple" indeed! Yes, frankly I did hope that they would get together. They obviously like each other and almost seem to share some sort of secret … but "becoming a couple" has most definitely proved *not* to be on the cards! And no, Cathy didn't really say much at all about the time that they spent together in York.'

❦

It was two days later and Laura and Cathy were sleepily sitting over mugs of tea in the kitchen, trying to ignore the fact that shortly they would have to leave the warmth of the farmhouse and face the freezing fog, which lay in a thick blanket over Lokisdale. It was just seven o'clock in the morning and still pitch-black.

'Laura, get Fly out here, now please, as quick as you can!' Jem called as he flung open the kitchen door. Since her confrontation with the bone, several weeks earlier, Fly had seemed subdued and not so keen to work with the sheep or to be outside with Jem, otherwise her constant companion.

'Out you go, Fly,' urged Laura, stroking the little sheepdog, where she lay on a rag-rug in front of the Aga. Laura wasn't sure, but she didn't seem to be quite so slight – her small frame seemed to be much more amply-covered with flesh. All in all, Laura didn't think that a bad thing.

Once roused, Fly was on her feet and ready to work and by now Jem, extremely agitated, was almost dancing from foot to foot in impatience.

'What on earth is the matter?' Laura asked.

'No time to explain. Just get dressed and you will see soon enough.'

Less than five minutes later, Laura saw only too clearly the reason for Jem's concern. Both tups were together in the barn and were engaged in a fight which, to Laura's eyes, could end only in the death of one or the other. From a distance of about three metres the tups faced each other, held still for a few seconds and then, huge shoulder muscles bunched to add power to the impact, charged to meet, head-to-head. To Laura it seemed impossible that each animal could sustain such sickening blows: the crack of bone on bone was immense.

Jem held his shepherd's staff firmly and stood at right angles to the fighting animals, next to a small pen that he had constructed using sheep hurdles. He had left the hurdle on the side of the pen nearest to him ajar. Fly was by his side, tense and watchful, waiting for his command. Laura had no idea how these two mighty rams could ever be separated, and she could see by his tightly-compressed lips that Jem was worried. Then, just at the very second that the rams were about to start, once more, their charge towards each other, Jem commanded Fly to run between the animals. Laura gasped, certain that the little dog would be injured, but Jem's timing was immaculate. Fly diverted the concentration of Old Charlie, who swung around, intent on attacking the dog, whilst at the same moment, Jem swung his staff around the rear leg of the borrowed, younger tup, causing him to stagger and lose his balance. Jem then swiftly grabbed the animal by the horns and manhandled him into the pen, shutting the final hurdle and securely enclosing him. Charlie was lumbering after Fly, who adroitly dipped under the barrier at the end of the barn and ran into the field. Jem then snatched up a bucket of sheep nuts from a shelf and shook it to entice Charlie out of the main barn area and into a secure side stable.

All this had taken no more than a few minutes, but Laura felt that it had been a lifetime. She was shaking with reaction and sat on a hay bale, expecting Jem to join her. But he didn't. He vaulted over the barrier separating the barn from the near field and knelt by Fly, who was sitting, ears back, looking slightly embarrassed – if that emotion could be applied to a dog. Laura watched him stroking and talking softly to her, turning her over gently and moving his hands expertly over her stomach. Eventually, he stood up, stroked the little dog's silky head and came back into the barn. Laura saw that he was smiling broadly.

'Hope your friend's midwifery skills are up to scratch,' he commented casually, and then, hugging Laura closely, 'because in a few weeks there will be quite a few pups to be brought into the world!'

Chapter 37

'Fly?' Laura asked, incredulously.

'Yes. I thought something was wrong when she left my side whilst I was still working with her in the barn. I hadn't dismissed her and it goes against all her training, but she must have felt under threat and, well, pups come first!'

'So when did it happen, do you think?' Laura asked.

'Well, it could only be that day when she came back in trouble from eating a bone – perhaps a local dog had taken her out for an indigestible dinner!'

'Jem, be serious! How long does she have to go, do you think?'

'Well, if I'm right, about a week, maybe.'

'Can she work still, or will she need special care?'

'Oh, she'll take care of herself, Laura. You saw what happened just now. If she needs to stop, she will. We must just keep an eye on her. I tell you something, though!'

'What?' Laura asked, slightly anxiously.

'It's solved what I'm going to get you for Christmas!'

'You're not having these puppies, Fly is!'

'Yes, but I can teach you how to train one to be your own sheepdog.'

'That's assuming she hasn't mated with a Great Dane!'

Lewis Devrille looked around Miles Jefferies' office, inhaling deeply on his cigarette.

'How can you bear it, old man?' he asked. 'Why on earth are you still stuck in this dead-end town, dealing with petty news? What happened to the man who intended to work on Wall Street?'

'Well, big fish in small pond goes a long way with me, Lewis. I notice you didn't complain about your accommodation last night, nor the mode of transport this morning.'

Lewis raised his eyebrows slightly but said nothing.

'Anyway, there are real recompenses to living in the sticks. Occasionally you come across a complete gem – like Laura Jamieson, for example. Did you read that article I sent you about her? Bet you wouldn't find anything more fanciable in your London circles!'

'Actually Miles, I hate to disabuse you, but I did come across someone just as fanciable – in fact, I came across Laura herself. We lived together for about six months.'

Miles swore under his breath. 'And here she makes out she's the Virgin bloody Mary: no physical contact, keeping me at arm's length, not letting me pick her up for our date …'

'Could just be down to physical attraction. She did somewhat fall for me.'

'So why aren't you still together?'

'Got bored with her. Same old … you know.'

'Little bitch. I'll get under that whiter-than-white façade … literally … just you watch.'

And the editor of the *Dale Echo* stamped out of his cramped office and slammed the door.

Lewis smiled slowly to himself. What a fool his friend was. Now he was back on the scene, just watch Laura start to beg for what they had had together. It was only a question of time. He ground out his cigarette butt on his friend's desk, took one final, disparaging look around the shabby space, and left.

⊰∥⊱

Jem and Laura had spent a freezing morning worming the flock. Winter had certainly arrived and it had been so cold that morning that they had had to break the film of ice on the animals' water troughs. Never had Cathy's call that lunch was ready sounded so welcome, and the latest casserole that she seemed to conjure magically into being had disappeared at a startling rate – so quickly that the military precision of Cathy's timing had, for once, failed, and there was a wait of around ten minutes until the pudding was ready. Laura had flicked through her sketch book, revisiting her time in Lokisdale through her drawings. Inevitably, she came across the series of fox sketches she had produced, pausing at the picture of the cub curled upon the rocky outcrop on Jem's family farm. Thoughtfully she traced the outline of the rocks with her fingertip, remembering the heart-wrenching sight of the vulnerable little boy, clutching his wooden lorry, curls ruffled by the wind.

Cathy had just put the long-awaited steaming dish of treacle pudding on the table and Jem was in the process of helping himself to a considerable amount of it, when Laura said gently, 'Jem, you haven't been back to *The Edge of the World* for Josh's photo yet.'

202

'I know – it's just that in that forsaken place everything draws me back to the past, whereas here I can look to the future. I have been trying to gather up enough determination to make one final visit there and collect my things – well, my biscuit tin, to be precise. I think I can leave the dilapidated chair and the rather damp bedding behind.'

'I'll come with you, Jem,' Cathy smiled. 'Laura is deeply involved in some detailed drawings of Fly's rapidly expanding body. She is thinking of calling her next story *The Fable of Fly the Fat Sheepdog* ... '

'Don't be horrible, Cath!' laughed Laura. 'It's more like *The Shame of Sharing Supper with a Strange Sheepdog*.'

'I'd like that, Cathy, if you are not too busy. When would suit you?'

'Well, I'm free this afternoon.'

'Fine. The sheep are settled; weather's ok; young tup's in the field by the barn, waiting to be collected about four – just before night falls.'

'Are you sure you have had enough to eat, Jem?' Cathy asked, somewhat tongue in cheek.

'Er, most definitely, thank you. Otherwise Laura will have to fictionalise the impact of your excellent food on my waistline as *Sam the Supersized Shepherd*.'

Chapter 38

Lewis had returned to Miles' Edwardian villa to change. He had noted the name of Laura's farm from the article that his friend had sent him and had looked on his phone for its precise whereabouts. It was a cold dry afternoon and he fancied a walk: he mustn't let himself get out of shape whilst he was away from his personal trainer. On foot, his phone told him it would take him twenty-three minutes to reach *Fell Farm* so, green Hunters pulled on, and expensive tweed and leather jacket fastened, Lewis set off at a steady pace in the direction of the church and the long climb past *The Edge of the World*, to reach the low cluster of stone buildings that was *Fell Farm*.

Utterly oblivious to the sad, sometimes passionate, often forgotten, stories that the silent gravestones told, Lewis sauntered past the church and toyed with exactly how he was going to play his meeting with Laura. He thought it best if he just arrived unannounced. This would have the element of surprise and he would be able to accurately gauge how Laura was going to react towards him. He smiled slightly, showing his small white teeth, and passed his tongue over his red lips to moisten them. He was completely certain that she would, unhesitatingly, want him back. Her subservience had been complete towards the end of their relationship and she had done exactly what he demanded of her. So why should that have changed, despite the rather physical climax, due entirely to her own wilful actions? He increased his pace slightly, re-running aspects of his time with Laura and recalling a conversation that he had had with Miles the previous evening, which had increased his anticipation even further.

Miles had been boasting of his status again, trying to penetrate Lewis' impassivity. They had just finished dinner and were sitting together in Miles' study, which overlooked the reservoir.

'I can do exactly what I like in this, my own little kingdom, you know. I write my own articles, employ my own staff, play with technology to my own ends.'

'What do you mean?' Lewis had asked incuriously.

'Well,' Miles crossed the deep-piled carpet to a leather-topped filing cabinet which stood next to his desk, 'For example, see this photograph of the 'Best in Show' from last year's Agricultural Show? Using *Photoshop* I created a beast of almost mythological proportions, which the owner could use in his own promotional material … for a financial consideration, of course!'

'The possibilities are endless,' yawned Lewis.

'Well, they are, actually,' Miles said, distinctly ruffled that his friend was not in the slightest impressed by what he had just told him. 'But you can use *Photoshop* for slightly more interesting subjects than beef cattle! Look at this.'

Miles opened his computer and spent a couple of minutes in his picture files.

'What do you think of *this* image? Better than the broad backside of a bull, ha?'

Miles had used one of the many photographs that he had taken of Laura when preparing for the article in his paper and grafted it onto the body of a slender young woman, dressed in nothing but the briefest bikini, creating a hybrid that looked one hundred percent genuine. Lewis glanced briefly at this and sneered.

'Remember I had the real thing,' he told his friend. 'And it was infinitely more interesting than this botched image.'

Lewis smiled sarcastically to himself as he remembered his friend's expression – beaten, cheated, outflanked.

⊰◫⊱

As usual, Laura was completely immersed in her work. Fly was lying on her side by the wood-burning stove in the snug, her belly distinctly rounded, twitching in some deep dream. Laura was playing around with how she was going to progress the story of Fly and her puppies. She thought she would call the tale *The Fable of Fly the Fabulous* and, as she watched the little dog, from time to time she could see tiny movements as heads and paws moved around inside her womb. Laura thought that she would transpose the story to involve her grandparents and include a chance encounter with another trialling dog. In the story, her previous brilliant success as a field trial champion would be in the balance, but then, through Geoff's devoted care of Fly and her devoted care of her puppies, another champion would emerge from the litter, giving her owner an even greater chance of success in the world of sheepdog trialling. As she ran through the structure of the story, Laura smiled, anticipating the weeks and months to come when she would have every excuse to observe the growing puppies and their interaction with their mother. She was going to enjoy writing and illustrating this tale.

Laura glanced at her watch. It was only two o'clock and she wondered just how Jem was reacting to his return to *The Edge of the World*. She knew how ambivalent Jem's feelings were towards his family farm: on the one hand it reminded him of his little son and the love which they had shared; but on the other it vividly brought back to mind his bleak childhood, the cruelty of his father, and the sudden, unexplained loss of his little boy.

Over the weeks since Jem had moved into his stable cottage, Laura had realised that she was falling in love with him, deeply and completely. He was gentle and intelligent, with an unexpected sense of humour that had started to emerge, as he had gradually been able to develop into the man he had been meant to be, leaving behind the shadow of the tragic figure that circumstances had caused him to become. Jem was kind, thoughtful and unassuming, but Laura could never be completely sure whether he felt more for her, or for Cathy. She remembered the sudden warm smile that Jem had given Cathy when she had offered to accompany him to *The Edge of the World*. Did he consider her – or Cathy – as a good friend, rather than as a woman with whom he could have a relationship? The few times he had spontaneously touched her hand or hugged her, and certainly the two occasions he had lightly kissed her, had caused in Laura feelings that she had not known existed. But had this physical contact been merely friendly and an expression of his gratitude, or had it indicated a depth of feeling which matched her own? Sometimes she just longed to hold and be held by Jem, to banish the rest of the world and be utterly complete in each other. But as she watched him going about the management of the farm and the care of the animals, she was increasingly convinced that his character was blossoming simply because at last the most basic of human needs had been provided for him: security, safety, warmth and food.

Once these thoughts had started to inhabit Laura's mind, her concentration was lost. She left the snug and went into the kitchen to make herself some tea. She leant against the Aga, trying to imagine whether her friends had reached the neighbouring farm yet and unearthed the dented biscuit tin from its hiding place. She judged that they must surely be on their return journey by now and decided to take her tea upstairs to her bedroom, to catch the first glimpse of their return.

Laura put a couple of cushions on the deep stone windowsill of her bedroom, and lightly jumped up, cradling her mug in her hands as she scanned the undulating line of the drystone wall which was the boundary of *Fell Farm*. She saw a flicker of movement beyond the wall and sat up straighter to see whether it was Jem, or Cathy. Frowning against the light, she soon realised that it was neither. The figure was certainly male, but was slighter and shorter than Jem and there was something familiar in the way in which the person moved, something she could not quite put her finger upon. The man stopped and shaded his eyes, looking down the sweep of fields towards Fell Farmhouse; then hesitated for a few moments before climbing over the wall into the top field.

Concentrating completely upon how best to approach the farmhouse without drawing undue attention to himself, Lewis swiftly crossed the small field into which he had jumped, oblivious of the brooding, silent tup watching him. Glancing to left and right in order to decide on the best route down to the farmhouse, he opened the gate out of the tup field with difficulty, tried to close it again without success and so quickly abandoned this, leaving it ajar. So obsessed was he with seeing Laura that he was completely oblivious of the massive ram which had stopped grazing to slowly shadow the intruder who had dared to encroach upon his territory.

⊰⫴⊱

'No wonder you wanted to leave this place, Jem,' Cathy shivered.

They had entered the dark, foetid building by the front door and Cathy was horrified at the black mould which coated some of the walls, the filthy wooden floorboards and the complete lack of any colour or comfort.

'I just can't believe how you survived here before you moved into the stable cottage. It's probably the worst accommodation I have ever seen … and don't forget I worked in the East End of London. I've seen dark and dirty places before, but never with the complete air of oppression which seems to hang over this place!'

Jem smiled wryly. 'Glad you appreciate my ancestral home, Cathy! Just wait until you see the master bedroom!'

They went upstairs together, to the room Jem had slept in when he had returned from the Friary. It was freezing. The broken pane of glass had completely fallen out of its rotten frame and rain and sleet had driven into the room and across the bed.

'This is horrible!' pronounced Cathy. 'I'm going outside ... at least it is healthy out there. I feel as if there is some lingering disease or threat inside this house, I really do. Please be as quick as you can, Jem. I'll wait by the gate.'

Cathy turned up the collar of her fleece and wrapped her woollen scarf more closely around her neck and shoulders. She couldn't wait to leave *The Edge of the World* and felt that never had a property been more appropriately named – remembering how she and Laura had joked that *The End of the World* would have been a more appropriate name. Shivering, she ran lightly down the narrow stone staircase and out across the hall to gain the blessed relief of fresh air and light. The feeling of freedom was palpable: once again, Cathy wondered at Jem's stamina, returning to this indescribable house night after night after his return to Lokisdale earlier in the spring. Thank God they had asked him to be their shepherd and to live in the old stable! Cathy turned swiftly from the house, intending to look out across the reservoir and the majestic view beyond its dark, level surface. Facing the sweeping panorama, she closed her eyes momentarily, trying to settle her emotions. She took several deep, measured breaths before opening them again. Standing directly in front of her, by the rocks, was a small, ginger-haired boy. He looked distressed and there were unshed tears in his clear round eyes. He was agitated and shifted his weight restlessly from foot to foot, pointing behind

Cathy, back in the direction of *Fell Farm* and shaking his head.

Cathy did not hesitate. She ran back to the open farmhouse door and shouted up the stairs, 'Jem! Come down, as quickly as you can!'

Seconds later, Jem stood by her side, clutching the rusty, dented biscuit tin.

'Jem, I saw your son. I saw Josh!'

Chapter 39

Laura sat upright. There was something deeply disconcerting about a stranger who would simply jump over a boundary wall and trespass in this way. As the figure rapidly covered the distance between the small, moorland road and the farmhouse, a chilling, leaden certainty gripped Laura. It was Lewis – Lewis! How could this be? How could he ever have found where she lived and, what was more, why should he want to find her again? She recollected his final brutal rejection of her in London, *"Did I assault this woman? Are you serious? I wouldn't touch her for fear of catching something."*

He was now only minutes from the gate which led from the farm fields into the small garden which surrounded the farmhouse. She knew that the kitchen door was on the latch and that if he tried it, there was nothing to prevent him entering. It should have been a simple thing to race down the stairs and to secure the door, but Laura's limbs were leaden and shock had made the whole world appear to turn in slow motion. Eventually, she prised herself from the windowsill and descended the staircase as quickly as her frozen limbs allowed her. Just a couple of dozen more steps and she would reach the kitchen door but, as soon as this thought had crossed her mind, she saw Lewis's silhouette pass the sitting room window and she knew she was too late.

He gave a single knock, which raised Fly from her unfathomable dreams. She trotted past Laura and stood opposite the kitchen door, giving a low growl. Laura watched the latch slowly lift, despising herself for being unable to move, and seconds later, she stood face to face with Lewis. Fly's hackles rose and she lowered her head slightly, being unsure what to do as she was receiving no instruction from Laura.

'The air of this God-forsaken county agrees with you, Laura,' Lewis said, taking a step towards her.

Laura managed to stand her ground, but only just. 'What are you doing here?' she asked.

'Following your fame in the media,' Lewis smirked. 'Although it's a shame you have managed only the local press, not the national.'

'That article in the *Dale Echo*,' she murmured.

'Yes. I see that you have managed to ensnare yet another unsuspecting male. Poor Miles, we have been friends since our school days. I would have thought he could do *slightly* better than you.' Lewis scanned her body, lips slightly downturned in an expression which combined disgust with sensuality.

Laura's eyes flickered around her kitchen, warm, safe, secure, containing so many loved things – her grandmother's cast-iron casseroles standing next to the pink, heart-strewn china that Cathy had brought from her London flat, and in the middle of the lunch table a copy of the *Dalesman* that Jem had been reading before lunch. She felt the love – and almost the presence – of these people who meant so much to her, as if they were standing beside her and, at that moment, her emotional paralysis disappeared. She took a step forward, and seeing her mistress move, so did Fly.

'No one invited you here, Lewis. Please leave.'

Lewis threw back his head and laughed. 'No.'

'I will have to make you leave, then. This is my home. How *dare* you intrude like this?' Laura strode to the dresser and snatched up her phone. Instantly, Lewis was beside her, twisting her arm at an angle so that she had to release the mobile or risk having her arm broken. Experience had taught Laura that if she made any sound of distress, Lewis would be spurred on to inflict further violence, but a slight cry escaped her lips as she remembered the pain she had experienced at his hands previously. At that, Fly ran at Lewis, sinking her teeth into his thigh muscle and biting hard. Lewis swore, kicking out with his free leg at the sheepdog. He caught her full on her side and, with a yelp, she let go and, whimpering, made for her basket – to Fly, her place of absolute safety. Beside himself, with blood streaming down his leg, Lewis snatched up the first thing that he laid eyes on – a small, heavy cast-iron pan and swung it high in the air above Fly's basket. Without thinking, Laura flung herself across the body of the little sheepdog, trying to shield her from the blows that she knew were about to come. She braced herself for the first blow but, unimaginably, it never came.

There was a heavy thud as Lewis was flung against the Aga. Jem had hurtled across the kitchen and had leapt at Lewis just as he was about the bring the pan down on Laura, or Fly – it seemed as if Lewis didn't care who he hurt as long as he hurt someone.

Jem knelt on Lewis' back and twisted his arms behind him, forcing his face to the floor. 'Ring the police, Cathy. I have him secure here. Tell them that an intruder has tried to attack Laura.'

'Jem ... Jem I know this man,' Laura croaked, still embracing Fly, who was shivering.

'What? What do you mean?'

'This is Lewis ... the person I told you about. The person I knew in London.'

'Did you invite him here, Laura?' Jem was chalk-white.

'No. That stupid fool, Miles, wrote an article about me and Lewis is one of his friends. He knew where to find me.'

Jem exhaled sharply. 'Thank God for that!' he breathed. 'But we should still report him to the police.'

'Oh Jem, you don't know ... he would make everything foul, dirty. He would implicate me in some sort of situation. I just want him to leave. I love my life here with you both ... I just want to be rid of him.'

Cathy's arms were around Laura and Fly – calming Laura, whilst expertly assessing Fly's condition.

Jem released Lewis's arms and hauled him to his feet. 'Get out,' he growled. 'And if I ever see you again, you will regret to the end of your life ever having left your rat-hole in London. You sad, twisted, useless apology for a human being. All you can do is to bully women and animals weaker than you are. If you weren't so obnoxious, I would pity you. Get *out!*' And Jem kicked Lewis towards the kitchen door.

Without a word, Jem turned towards Laura, who was still crouched over Fly's basket. Cathy quietly stood up and moved to one side. He knelt beside her and wrapped his arms around her, pulling her close to him. 'You idiot! What would I have done if anything happened to you? You have given me hope, a reason to go on. What would I have done if you had been hurt or ... or ...'

'Killed, obviously! Stop stammering your angst, Jem, and focus on the situation in hand. It didn't happen and this poor lass is in labour, so stop embracing and boil some water!' Cathy, in full nursing sister mode, stroked Fly's head with one hand whilst examining her gently with the other.

Chapter 40

Lewis limped as quickly as he could back along the curving drive. He had a single thought in his mind: to put as much distance as he could between himself and the farm from which he had just been ejected. He couldn't believe that he had been treated with such direct violence, because Lewis' way was more subtle. His mind games weakened his victim until minimum effort on his part brought about maximum hurt. Never had he been tackled by a hard, heavy-muscled man intent upon incapacitating him, and he was still reeling, physically and emotionally, from the encounter.

'Bloody psycho!' he muttered to himself as he left the track to walk back to the road by the shortest route – across the northern fields of *Fell Farm*.

Old Charlie, unexpectedly liberated earlier by Lewis, had grazed his way gradually down towards the farmhouse. Intent on food because his work over the last few weeks had sapped his energy and he was constantly hungry, the old ram looked up, surprised to see his rival, standing four-square directly in front of him. With no ewes to distract them, the two males eyed each other, and pawed the ground with their front hooves. Gradually, appearing to be insouciant, they approached each other, apparently intent on grazing, but then, without warning, they backed off, lowered their mighty heads and clashed together, bone ringing hollowly on bone.

Lewis could think only of his damaged pride. How *dared* that country oaf throw him to the ground and make it impossible for him to retaliate. As soon as he reached Lokisbridge, he would report him to the police. If only he had been given time and space, he could have used some of his Tai Kwando moves on him – *that* would have showed him who was boss. And that bloody mongrel biting him – that just about capped it! He'd have it put down as a dangerous dog. Head down, conscious of the throbbing pain in his thigh, Lewis, the complete urbanite, was only vaguely aware of the titanic battle taking place alongside him. Remarkable in his self-absorption, he followed the contours of the field as they meandered to the boundary wall he had climbed over earlier. But, although he was unaware of the tups, they were not unaware of him. Each animal saw an intruder, cutting across the territory that they were battling for, and each instinctively saw the intruder as a direct threat. From focussing on each other, they started to focus on Lewis, gaining ground on him as he limped slowly up the field.

Charlie outstripped him, then turned to face this strange, dark, stick-like being that had dared to enter the battleground. The young tup stood his ground, directly opposite Charlie and behind Lewis. Charlie lowered his mighty head and charged. Because he had the advantage of being higher than Lewis, he knocked him off his feet with the first blow. The younger tup then butted him where he lay. Reeling from the immense blows, Lewis staggered to his feet, but then both tups saw each other, with only this frail human separating them. Their charge was simultaneous and their skulls crashed into Lewis from opposing sides, crushing his body like an eggshell. Again and again they charged and butted until the pile of crumpled, bloodstained clothing lying on the ground was barely recognisable as a human being.

⊰⊱∥⊰⊱

Fly was not in a good state. The savage kick to her side had brought on premature labour and it was obvious that the little dog was in some pain. Jem knew that Fred Shorter, the owner of the young tup, was about to arrive any minute and he had to go and help him to load the animal into his trailer, so he reluctantly left Laura and Cathy, who was still kneeling by Fly, gently running her hands over her distended stomach.

'Laura, I'm worried. Fly has started to bleed but is showing no signs of contractions. Could you ring Matt and ask him to come as a matter of urgency, please?'

Laura hated unnecessary hurt or violence and was beside herself that her gentle little dog had been hurt through trying to protect her. She nodded and went through to the snug to phone her brother. 'He's on his way, Cathy,' she reassured her friend a couple of minutes later. 'Shall I make some tea?'

'Please. I could certainly do with some and,' looking searchingly at her friend, 'I am sure you could too!'

Both women waited silently as the kettle boiled, and watched Fly who lay still, breathing shallowly, mouth slightly open, showing worryingly pale gums.

Without warning, the silent world exploded into noise. Almost simultaneously, Fred Shorter's Land Rover and trailer and Matt's vehicle clattered into the turning area in front of the old stone barn and Jem and Matt burst in to the kitchen together, both very pale.

'I must attend to Fly, Jem. You ring the police,' instructed Matt.

'Ssh! Less noise, *please!*' Cathy demanded. 'What on earth is going on?'

'There's been an accident, Cath,' Matt told her tersely.

'Can I help ... and is it a human or animal accident?'

'Human ... and it's too late for medical help, I'm afraid. But we do need the police. Please, both of you, can you stay here and help me?'

They heard Jem's subdued tones on the phone through in the snug.

'Thanks, officer. We'll see you in a few minutes, then.'

'For God's sake, Jem, what's going on?' Laura asked.

'I will tell you later, but it is absolutely vital that you and Cathy should stay in here.'

'It's my farm. Why can't I do what I want?' Laura demanded.

'Trust me, Laura. Please promise me that on no account will you come outside. Promise, Laura!' Jem placed his hands on her shoulders, holding her eyes with his. Clearly, he was deeply agitated and completely earnest.

'OK, I promise,' Laura told him hesitatingly. 'But don't think this is a sign of my unquestioning obedience in future ...' she added, desperately trying to lighten the atmosphere. But Jem was beyond being shaken from his purpose or his deadly serious mood.

'Thank you,' he breathed, kissing her lightly on the forehead. 'And now I must go and speak to Fred, and to the police when they arrive.'

'Matt, what's going on?' Laura asked.

'Just leave it for the time being, Lau,' her brother replied. 'There is enough of an emergency in here.'

'What's happening with Fly?' Cathy asked. 'Is she bleeding internally?'

'She may be. Her gums are pale. Has she had an accident?'

Matt listened gravely whilst Laura gave him an abridged version of what had happened. 'Right. Let's give her ten minutes. If she starts to deliver her pups in that time we will know where we are. Otherwise, I may have to take her to the surgery.'

Matt sat on the floor, cross-legged, watching Fly closely. After a few minutes she stood up and gave a quiet grunt as a tiny black and white body appeared, which Matt expertly eased into the world.

'A beautiful dog pup,' he announced, clearing the little animal's nostrils.

'Is he breathing, Matt?' whispered Cathy.

'Not yet,' replied Matt grimly. He massaged the little white chest lightly, then stood up and swung the tiny body to and fro rhythmically. Unbelievably, after a spluttering gasp, the puppy began to breathe.

'Good girl,' Laura stroked Fly, who seemed to be showing more interest in the world in general now that this minute scrap of life had appeared in it. Matt gently placed the puppy against his mother's flank and continued to wait.

Fly gave birth to six puppies – three of which failed to breathe. They came in quick succession and Fly seemed to be a natural mother, licking and stimulating the little animals with a sure instinct, and nudging them around in her basket until her three live pups were feeding contentedly.

When he gauged that her labour was ended, Matt gave her an injection. 'She's done remarkably well, delivering her pups without assistance after suffering a trauma like that,' he told Laura and Cathy. 'She's brilliant. Just look at her!'

'She is,' agreed Laura. 'But now, Matt, please will you tell me what on earth is happening outside? Why was Jem so insistent upon Cathy and me staying in here?'

Matt paused and looked levelly at her. 'There was an accident, Laura…'

'I *know* … Jem told us that much!'

'A man was killed outside in one of your fields. He was badly mutilated and we think he was killed by the tups.'

'But how could that be, Matt? They were in separate fields!'

'Well, they weren't when I arrived! They were grazing callously by the body of the man they had just butted to death. Somehow a gate must have been left unlatched.'

'Was the dead man wearing a sort of brown and green tweed coat?' she asked.

Matt nodded. 'You know who it is then, Laura.'

Laura sat down heavily on one of the kitchen chairs. 'His name is Lewis Devrille. I knew him in London and he came to … to visit me here,' she stammered.

'Well, the police need to know that, Laura. Presumably they are still here, because Jem hasn't come back inside. I'll go and speak to them … maybe suggest that they come in and take a statement from you or whatever they need to do?' Matt half-turned to leave but, as a parting comment, turned to Cathy and said, 'We must go to York together again *soon*. Your friends over there are missing you!'

'Yes. Yes, thanks Matt.'

He left and Cathy hugged her friend, not knowing quite how the news of Lewis' death was going to impact upon Laura – she had, after all, had a relationship with this man, even though it had been a bitter and abusive one.

Laura shook her head thoughtfully. 'Talk about nemesis,' she murmured, reflectively. 'Lewis was an animal, Cathy … a violent, cruel animal without human remorse, or pity. That he should have been killed by two merciless creatures, intent upon hurting and destruction is, somehow, so very appropriate. I just can't be sorry, I can't pity him! It's a terrible thing to admit, but he was incapable of feeling regret or remorse for his actions and what I feel, overwhelmingly, is that justice has been done.'

Chapter 41

Jem, Laura and Cathy sat up late, chatting around the kitchen table and finishing a couple of bottles of wine between them. The stress of the day and its extreme drama meant that sleep was the last thing on their minds. The imagination of each was working overtime. Jem was overwhelmed with the love that he now knew he felt for Laura. When he had realised that he had been within a hair's breadth of losing her, the enormity of what that loss would mean took his breath away. The joy, the gentle companionship, her beauty and dancing intellect had moved in and through his life imperceptibly but inexorably, until he felt that, if they were taken away, then he would cease to exist. Laura felt a bizarre mixture of horror at the accident, tempered by relief that her tormentor would torture her no more; astonishment at the new family nestling in a warm corner of her kitchen; and fulfilment in her relationships with Jem and Cathy. And Cathy, with her deep empathy for the feelings of others, felt some of the emotions of both her friends.

Laura's statement to the police inspector had been crucial. She had explained how she had watched Lewis taking the shortcut down across the fields, cutting across the tup enclosure at the northern extremity of the farm. This immediately explained how the field gate had been opened, causing the two rams to encounter each other. Fred Shorter had explained how the younger tup had been loaned to *Fell Farm* and testified to Jem's outstanding shepherding skills.

It was the first time that the three friends had been able to sit down together since Jem and Cathy had returned to *The Edge of the World* to retrieve Jem's precious mementos of Josh. It was to this visit – unbelievably less than twelve hours earlier – that their conversation now turned.

Atypically, Cathy had tears in her eyes as she laid her land lightly on Jem's arm. 'Josh was beautiful, Jem. I don't know how you could bear to lose him as you did.'

Jem's eyes locked with Laura's and then he turned to smile sadly at Cathy. 'I couldn't, until I met both of you,' he responded. 'As I said this afternoon, you have given me a reason to go on living. It's hard to explain, but it was almost as if the world was unreal ... as if I was watching a screen with moving shadows on it. But coming here has made life three-dimensional again – even though I miss Josh more than I can express.'

Laura stretched out her hand to Jem and it was warmly and swiftly enclosed by his – strong and hard against her soft skin.

'Laura wondered whether Josh appears, either in my dreams or in waking life, when he is trying to warn me of danger,' Jem continued. 'He was agitated when he appeared to Cathy earlier today ...'

'Yes, poor little mite. He was stepping anxiously from foot to foot and pointing back towards here ...

just when Lewis must have been climbing over the boundary wall, Laura.'

'Jem, have you ever seen Josh in your waking life away from Lokisdale?' Laura asked.

'Since his disappearance, I've never seen Josh in my waking life ... either here or anywhere else. Sometimes recently I've seen ... or imagined I've seen ... a flicker of movement out of the corner of my eye. But apart from that I have seen him only in my dreams.'

'And here in Lokisdale we know that he has appeared just at *The Edge of the World* and by the pool in the *Crying Wood* ... places where you and he spent time together.' Laura spoke quietly – almost to herself – whilst she silently traced flower-patterns with her finger within the damp ring where her wine-glass had rested. After some time, marked only by the quiet ticking of the kitchen clock, Laura murmured, 'Jem, is he somehow trapped here?'

'Why do you say that?' Jem asked, frowning.

'Well, it's as if he can't escape, can't get very far ... I can't quite explain, Jem. It just occurred to me.'

'What did your brother friars say, Jem?' Cathy asked.

Jem smiled. 'The Guardian explained that the Bible says that 'Love never ends', and suggested that it was my love for Josh, and his for me, that brought about those vivid and heart-breaking dreams and drove my desire to return to Lokisdale, in the hope that I may see my son again in my waking life. And then one day both of us spoke to a very old friar, Brother Edwin, who had experience of exorcism. He put a different and more painful spin on the subject. He was categoric that such appearances are *not* natural and certainly not based upon love, or wishful thinking. He emphasised that when people die, they should be at rest. If a very violent or dramatic event takes place, it was possible, Edwin explained, that a sort of photograph is impressed on the environment. And sometimes the people involved can appear over the years, as the incident plays itself out again and again, in slightly varying formats. But underlying all this is the fact that, somehow, the spirit of the person which should have passed on, is stuck in this world and needs freeing.'

Jem stood up and ran his fingers through his hair. He stretched slowly, easing life back into his tired body. 'This didn't help me much, as you can imagine. I came back to Lokisdale hoping to come to terms with the past and possibly to find out more about the disappearance of my son. I long ago gave up any hope of finding him alive again,' Jem said bleakly.

To Laura, at that moment he seemed almost back to the reserved and silent man she had first known, and she realised that she would do anything to help dissipate the misery he had endured for a third of his life. Recalling her brother's remark to Cathy before he left *Fell Farm* earlier, she had an idea. 'Jem, why don't the three of us go over to York for the day? Cathy, you can spend time with Matt, or shopping … or however you wish really. Jem, we could go to the Cathedral or a museum, or just be tourists and sight-see … perhaps go to the Christmas market. Let's get away from Lokisdale for a bit! What do you say?

'An unequivocal *yes!*' replied Jem, and his smile wiped away the pain that, a few minutes earlier, had been writ large on his features.

'Cathy?' Laura checked with her friend who, surprisingly, had remained silent.

'OK. Yes, fine. When were you thinking of?'

Laura was caught off-balance at this less than enthusiastic response, and stammered, 'Er, next Saturday?'

'I'll speak to Matt,' Cathy said tersely. 'And now, I must go to bed. Goodnight.'

'What was that all about?' asked Jem.

'Oh Jem, I haven't a clue! I'm so tired, that just now my mind can't compute the complexities of my complex friend! Most of the time I think I understand her perfectly, but, occasionally, it's like talking to a stranger! There seem to be whole areas of her personality that are hidden from the world.'

Jem nodded. 'I feel that too, Laura, and I can't explain it either. And I'm tired as well. I feel that if I don't go to bed soon, I will make even less sense than I usually do! So, goodnight my ... goodnight, Laura.'

Jem pulled Laura to him and she was conscious of his clean, outdoor, grass-and-heather scent. Lightly at first, and then more urgently, Jem kissed her eyes, her forehead, and her lips. She was conscious of a gentleness overlaying an immensely strong, powerful masculinity, which, as a gentle man, he kept firmly under control. Finally, he pulled away and looked at her for some moments, before saying quietly, 'I must go, Laura'. Then, turning on his heel, he swiftly left, closing the door without a sound, so as not to awaken the sleeping puppies and their mother.

Chapter 42

The next morning at breakfast Cathy was once again her usual warm, capable self. 'I've rung Matt,' she said 'and he suggests that he should drive and that we should all travel together.'

'Great!' Laura affirmed, but then added, 'Cathy, you didn't seem too keen on the idea of Jem and me coming with you ...'

'Just worried about Fly and the pups, lovely girl. We need to get a pup-sitter!'

'Well, don't suggest my dear mother! She would probably write a poem in iambic pentameter about the joys of canine motherhood! I think Fly would be safer by herself!'

'I was thinking of Sandra Wilkins, actually,' Cathy mused. 'She is competent and caring and is genuinely fond of children and small animals. Should I ask her tomorrow?'

'Yes please,' said Laura.

The following Saturday was one of those precious, early-December days that are bright, cold and clear.

Matt arrived at *Fell Farm* in his Land Rover at ten o'clock, shortly after Sandra Wilkins had arrived. The Headteacher had spent several minutes on her knees by the new family, stroking Fly and marvelling at the tiny black and white puppies.

'They sound like a small swarm of bees,' she laughed. 'I've always been too busy to have a dog as a pet and there's so much I never realised! How insistently they feed and how extraordinary that they make these buzzing, murmuring sounds when they're young! Have you written down instructions for me, Laura?'

'No, but it's pretty straightforward,' Laura explained. 'Fly sleeps or feeds her puppies most of the time, just emerging from her basket to eat and drink and occasionally go outside. She is having three meals a day whilst she is feeding her family, she's had breakfast, and I will give her supper. If you could just feed her at midday, that would be great, Sandra. I've left the food you will need in her bowl in the utility room. As far as going outside is concerned, she will just stand by the door to let you know when she needs to take a trip into one of the fields. I really can't thank you enough.'

'Completely my pleasure,' confirmed the Headteacher. 'I have foregone marriage and motherhood for my little 'darlings' and it will be vicariously fulfilling to spend today with these lovely little scraps. Go on … off you go and enjoy yourselves!'

'There is homemade soup and some rolls and …'

'For goodness sake, go!' laughed Sandra Wilkins.

⊰⊱||⊰⊱

York looked spectacular in its extravagant winter dress. Historical buildings, decorated with Christmas trees, and windows decked with baubles and fairy lights, glowed against the cold, blue winter sky. Tranquil and somehow remote from the hubbub that surrounded it, the ancient Minster soared high above the bustling city, whilst at its foot clustered the Christmas market stalls, brimming with bright, hand-made gifts, hot food and fragrant mulled wine, assaulting the senses and replicating a centuries-old pattern of mid-winter celebration.

On the drive over from the Dales, the occasional flake of snow had fallen from an unlikely blue sky, and this raised the mood and anticipation in the packed Land Rover, as the friends chatted easily about Christmas, sheep, and how they were going to spend their time in the historical heart of their beloved county.

Much to Laura's astonishment, Jem had never visited York before, and she reflected once again on the contrast between his very limited experience of the usual range of life events, and his profound emotional and spiritual understanding.

'Can't say the cathedral appeals to me overmuch,' Matt pronounced as he slammed the driver's door shut, gazing sceptically at the ancient stone edifice.

'Well, you and Cathy do your own thing, Matt,' said Laura. 'Jem has never been to York and we are both interested in the building. It's so *old!* Just think … it has looked over the city for about fifteen hundred years. The changes it must have seen are mind-blowing.'

'I didn't know buildings have eyes,' teased her brother, 'And I would have thought that Jem would have had enough experience of ecclesiastical buildings to last him a lifetime!'

'Oh, you know what I mean … don't be obtuse, Matt! Anyway, we will make our way over there and then have a look around the market, I think. Shall we catch up for lunch?'

'Matt and I were thinking of meeting up with a couple of friends from *Gigi's* … it's a bistro we have eaten at a few times. Hope you don't mind …' Cathy smiled at Laura then turned to link her arm through Matt's. 'Catch up with you about four, then?'

'Fine, yes. See you back here.'

'There she goes again, my chameleon friend,' sighed Laura, frowning slightly, as they watched Matt and Cathy walk away in the opposite direction to the cathedral, until they were lost from sight.

⊰⊱⊰

As Jem and Laura closed the heavy, wooden door of the Minster behind them, the silence was a blessed relief from the noise and bustle of the crowds jostling each other in and around the Christmas market stalls. Jem hated a situation where his usual long stride was impeded by people or obstacles, and Laura had come to love the peace of the wide moors and valleys surrounding her farm. The noise and self-absorption of the festivity-fuelled people and the mix of smells from burgers, hot-dogs, mulled wine and coffee had become overwhelming. Instinctively, as the pure, other-worldly space embraced them, they both inhaled deeply, catching the indescribably evocative perfume of incense, whilst feeling the intense chill of the soaring stone columns and shadowy space above them. In stark contrast to the press of people outside, the cathedral was practically empty, and they silently slipped into seats about half-way down the nave, wishing to absorb the timeless atmosphere. Sitting together without speaking, it struck Laura how, silent or speaking, she was entirely at ease with Jem, as he seemed to be with her. She recalled, as if it was from another life – which she supposed it was – the insistent pressure to talk which was always present in London, even if one had nothing to say, and it struck her how this seemed to be a symbol of the emptiness of existence there. People were always speaking, but saying nothing; always rushing from place to place, but never mindful of where they actually were. She closed her eyes in sheer thankfulness that this empty life was hers no longer and, revelling in the tranquillity of the Minster which wrapped around her, she folded her hands quietly on her lap. A few seconds later, she felt Jem's hard, warm hand rest lightly on hers before enclosing them.

'Shall we start to explore?' he asked, and Laura nodded.

As a living social document, York Minster was spectacular. Countless generations of people had visualised Heaven, and had portrayed stories from the Bible in stained glass windows and stone statues which had spoken to those in the congregation who could not read. Fascinated, Laura pointed out with an artist's eye the way in which the raising of Jairus' daughter must have taken from life, because of the features and expressions of the characters. There sat the child, tousled and sleepy, puzzled yet delighted to be a part once more of the living world. Her mother, almost beside herself with joy, embraced her little girl with her work-worn hands as if she would never let her go again. And, solemn and dignified, there stood Jairus, by his dress and bearing a burgher of the city. Tombs ranged from highly ornate Victorian memorials to rough slabs of limestone, hewn over a millennium earlier to commemorate the great and the good who had fallen in battle, defending this, their home city. Silently and thoughtfully, Laura and Jem looked and paused, reflected and touched lightly, empathising with the great pageant of humanity that had passed through this mighty space.

Finally they came to the Undercroft, which housed a small museum and, occasionally, held exhibitions particularly appropriate to the current season of the Church year.

'"A Christmas Carol"' read Laura. '"Why Ghost Stories are told at Christmas time". What do you think, Jem? Would you like to go in?'

Jem paused for an instant, then responded, 'Why not?'

The setting for the exhibition was particularly appropriate, as the Undercroft was the most ancient part of the Minster, even showing part of the foundations of the building. It was dimly lit, with large, printed and decorated panels set at angles to left and right as one entered the arched stone space. They started to read the first display panel:

Non-Christian Background

Before the establishment of the Christian religion, before the introduction of electric light, or even oil lamps, in the depths of the dark, challenging winter, humankind told stories which reflected the time of the year when life seemed at its lowest ebb. Sitting around blazing fires, with perhaps tallow-dips, or candles to augment the light a little, people wove their tales. The most obvious themes were of ghosts, beloved ones who had departed this earthly life but were determined to stay close to those they loved by manifesting themselves in the form that they had had on earth. The ending of these stories was, almost inevitably, the liberation of the spirit from its earthly prison, enabling it to reach the freedom of eternity. But always the key to bringing about that freedom had to be discovered within the course of the story.

'Laura, I can't stand this. Do you mind if we go outside again?' Jem was white to the lips and, hardly waiting for her response, he turned on his heel and walked swiftly up the stone steps, taking them two at a time, back into the main body of the cathedral. He walked a little way from the entrance to the Undercroft, then sat, head in hands, on a stone pillar support.

'Jem, I'm so sorry … How stupid of me to suggest visiting an exhibition about ghosts when only yesterday …'

'It's not your fault, Laura. You had no idea of the format the exhibition would take. But sometimes I feel that I just can't take any more of this agonising uncertainty about Josh! Over the last few months my suspicion that somehow his spirit needs to be released has turned to certainty … but I haven't the slightest idea how to begin the process. Am I going to live like this for the rest of my life? Not knowing where he is, not knowing how to help him …'

'Jem, I don't know. I can't answer your questions, but I can be sure of one thing. Whatever happens, I will be there to help and support you … if you wish, I mean.'

Laura enclosed his ice-cold hands in her own small, warm ones and he spoke to her with a passionate intensity which made her raise her gaze to meet his.

'If I wish? Laura, you must realise that without you, quite simply, I have no reason to live. I wake in the morning thinking of you and you are my last thought at night. I thought I loved Ruth, but I was such a child emotionally and she was the first woman I had remotely had any feelings for. Compared to how I feel for you, my feelings for Ruth were as a candle flame is to the sun, and I shall feel guilty about my relationship with that poor woman until the day I die. I loved my Josh, but love for a child is so different from what I feel for you. Don't you know I love you, Laura? I have loved you for months.'

Chapter 43

Laura felt more alive than she had ever felt before, abnormally full of energy, as if she could run, and jump and dance forever, and all because Jem loved her and she returned his love in equal measure. As they walked out of the incense-scented, mystical space together, arm closely linked through arm, they passed a large carved stone conch shell containing water which had been blessed by the clergy. Laura had not said anything at all since Jem had told her how he felt, because she was unsure how to express her feelings. Seeing the water, however, she paused and took hold of Jem's right hand, unfurling the fingers which had curled around hers automatically. She dipped her index finger into the water and wrote on Jem's palm: *I love you, Jem.* Then she kissed his palm and, with lips still wet from the holy water, she kissed him and smiled into his eyes. He straightened out his hand to read the words in the soft glow of the candlelight and, seeing what she had written, an expression of incredulity crossed his face, soon turning to one of complete joy.

They wandered out into the busy Christmas streets, cocooned in their own safe, secure world, oblivious of the bustle and the noise. Although it was only two o'clock, already an almost imperceptible chill was creeping into the winter air, and gradually the people attending the Christmas market were drifting home to their warm firesides, to soup and tea and comfort.

Still with minimal speech, they browsed the rapidly-emptying stalls. Both realised suddenly just how hungry they were – their breakfast some six hours earlier now seemed an eternity ago. Grinning, Jem bought two small bottles of champagne from grapes surprisingly 'grown in the heart of Yorkshire', then added two pork pies, a wedge of Wensleydale cheese and some fresh rolls.

'We'll find somewhere sheltered to eat this sophisticated lunch,' he laughed, 'but first I need to make another purchase.'

Laura knew that he was searching for something specific, but was still unsure as to what this could be. They passed stall after stall, selling paintings of pets, photographs of some of the most memorable sights in Yorkshire, and jewellery stalls. The thought had crossed Laura's mind that Jem possibly intended to buy her a ring of some description and, smiling, she realised that if it proclaimed that she belonged to him, she would wear the plastic ring from a milk container with indescribable pride.

Jem stopped at a stall marked 'Treasures from Whitby'. Almost as if he knew exactly what he was looking for, Jem gently picked up a necklace made from silver and mother of pearl. Two circles lay side by side on a delicate silver chain. On one circle was inscribed: Man's name; and on the other: Woman's name.

'Are only circles available?' asked Jem.

'No sir, there are flowers, or stars, or hearts…'

'How about sheep?'

'Er, yes, I could do sheep,' the stallholder confirmed, grinning broadly.

'Brilliant! Then we need two sheep: one called Jem and one called Laura. Would it be possible to pick them up later today … say in about an hour and a half?'

'Certainly, sir,' came the affable reply.

Laughing, clutching the paper bag of pies, champagne, cheese and rolls, Jem led Laura towards a large carousel, glowing gold, scarlet and blue, set up against the sheltering flank of the ancient Minster. Music blared from the highly-decorated piece of fairground equipment, the size of which dwarfed the haphazard black and white jettied mediaeval houses, which clustered around and behind it.

'At least we can sit down for our celebration picnic!' Jem grinned, paying the man who stood at the central controls. 'And what does madam fancy as her steed? A white horse, or a huge black chicken?'

'Er, no contest really … ' Laura giggled, mounting the white carved horse with red, flaring nostrils, whose painted mane had been worn by the countless hands which had touched, or clutched it, over the decades.

Jem sat alongside Laura, mounted on the alternative – a large, black chicken, with a pointed beak, red eyes and huge yellow feet.

'Mm, handsome!' he declared, sitting astride the strange-looking beast and deftly opening the small bottles of champagne.

Looking at him, grinning broadly astride the evil-looking bird, Laura once again marvelled at the change in the man she loved. The withdrawn, highly-controlled individual she had first challenged in the yard at *Fell Farm* had become a relaxed, tanned and fit-looking man, who looked at her with open and undisguised love. Laura felt a deep flush of sheer pleasure mounting to her cheeks.

The music started and the carved animals rose and fell as the merry-go-round circled. The Minster, the stalls and the decorated, mediaeval shops and houses passed and re-passed in a series of living tableaux, as Jem and Laura laughed and sipped their champagne, and munched their impromptu lunch.

'That's Cathy, surely!' cried Laura on one of the circuits.

'Where?'

'Over there by the mediaeval gateway ... look, it *is* her ... But who's she with, Jem? It's not Matt, it's a woman, I think.'

The white horse rose and the brief tableau was lost, succeeded by Minster, stalls and shops again. Laura eagerly rose on her carved stirrups, wanting to call and wave to her friend, but the moment had been lost and she sighed, 'Oh Jem, she's gone again!'

Jem said nothing – merely giving a non-committal sound of assent. He had seen Cathy and her companion when his mount had fallen as Laura's had risen, obliterating for her the view of her friend. Jem had seen the two women holding hands, smiling into each other's eyes, and then, under a bunch of holly and mistletoe hung on the jutting first floor of an apothecary's house, he had seen them kiss, quietly and passionately, apparently lost in each other.

Chapter 44

Miles was determined that he would write Lewis' obituary. He knew that Lewis had no family, and any friends that Lewis had in London were unknown to him. Miles had long ago stopped frequenting the sophisticated, expensive venues that Lewis haunted and he realised that, actually, he now knew very little about his wealthy, enigmatic college friend.

Miles gave much thought to how he should represent the accident that had caused Lewis' death. He ground his teeth as he recalled that Fred Shorter, Chair of the Farmers' Union in Lokisdale, was a strong supporter of the work that Jem Walker and that bitch, Laura Jamieson, had done at *Fell Farm*. Over and above this, Fred was besotted by the memory of Laura's grandfather, whose shepherding skills and ability to train and run sheepdogs had become legendary in the area, and he was determined to keep these memories alive, even establishing the *Geoff Jamieson Trials Trophy*. Miles decided that he would have to steer a careful course: maybe just the slightest hint at carelessness; maybe vague allusions to the relationship that Lewis had had with Laura.

The result was published four weeks after Lewis' death, only when the coroner's meticulous work had been completed. Every aspect of the death of this visitor from London had been checked and re-checked. It would be so easy for the press to over-sensationalise the accident, with a consequential negative impact upon the tourist trade in the small Dales town, which ensured that tea and souvenir shops could thrive.

The inhabitants of Lokisdale opened their *Dale Echo* on that particular Friday with considerable interest. On the front page was a particularly glamorous photograph of Lewis, smiling, champagne glass in hand and resplendent in evening dress at one of the last private exhibitions that he had hosted in London. Under the photo, the article that followed was headed:

Talented art patron dies at Lokisdale farm.

Never let life be taken for granted! A short month ago, Lewis Devrille, well-known in London circles for his patronage of undiscovered artists and his keen eye for talent, died in a most tragic accident. Two tups, that should have been separated by walls and gates, somehow came together and butted this talented genius to death.

Readers may remember that several months ago, the editor wrote an article on the exciting discovery of artistic talent living here in Lokisdale, and shared with readers details of the professional background of Geoff Jamieson's grand-daughter, Laura. This young woman frequented the same artistic circles as did Lewis Devrille in London and it is tantalising to ask whether they knew each other before Laura decided to return to her place of birth here in Lokisdale. Was it just coincidence that Lewis Devrille should have met his untimely end on Fell Farm land, previously the home of that well-known local character, Geoff Jamieson, and now run by his grand-daughter? We may never learn the truth about this.

What readers will not know is that the editor and Lewis Devrille were friends of long-standing. We met in London during our college days and maintained a stimulating friendship through the decades as each of us pursued his own path to success.

What a waste of life and talent this dreadful accident brought about! Let us trust that closer attention to supervision of potentially dangerous animals, and suitably qualified farmers and their staff, may prevent a re-occurrence of such a dreadful tragedy!

Would this do, or had he gone too far, Miles had asked himself as he had penned it? But a combination of perverse loyalty to his dead friend and the desire to punish Laura for her clear lack of interest in him, spurred Miles on to take the risk and to publish.

⊰⊱||⊰⊱

Laura and Cathy pored over the article as they finished their breakfast and Laura flushed as she read the innuendos and half-accusations that Miles had woven into the obituary.

'What are people going to think of me?' she asked Cathy.

'Well, more to the point, how are people going to react against Miles? This is very nearly libel, Laura. You could always take the advice of the police, or a solicitor, if you are concerned.'

Laura jumped to her feet and paced the kitchen floor, avoiding Fly, puppies and feeding bowls adroitly. 'What would my grandfather have done?' she asked passionately.

'Sadly, I didn't know him well enough, Laura. Is that a hypothetical question?'

Laura continued to pace the floor, arms folded tightly, but eventually stopped opposite an embroidered picture worked by her grandmother, Lily, and framed by her proud husband. It showed a version of *Fell Farm*, with a tall, broad shepherd – clearly meant to depict her beloved husband, Geoff Jamieson – standing in front of the main door, crook in hand. By his feet sat a black and white sheepdog, a forerunner of Fly no doubt, and dotted around the green fields rising behind the farm house were white sheep grazing in the sunshine. Chickens pecked around Geoff's feet and a cat preened herself on the stone wall to his left. Lily had embroidered the words:

> *I shall lift up mine eyes unto the hills*
> *From whence cometh my help.*
> *My help cometh from the Lord*
> *Who made Heaven and Earth.*

The beautifully-executed work demonstrated the values which Geoff and Lily had lived by: honesty, forthrightness, integrity and kindness. Seeing it was, for Laura, like meeting once again her beloved grandparents.

'I know exactly what my grandfather would have done,' Laura declared firmly. 'He would have dismissed this article as cheap trash and told Miles Jefferies exactly what he thought of him. Geoff Jamieson made his world strong through doing the best he could for others, through telling the truth and through exposing lies. I will do the same.'

An icy gust of wind ruffled the pages of the *Dale Echo* as Jem entered the kitchen, muffled in hat, thick scarf and thermal gloves. He whipped off his outdoor clothes and laid them on the Aga, swiftly crossing the kitchen to kiss Laura lightly on the lips.

'It is *freezing* out there,' he said, rather unnecessarily. 'Is there any coffee left?'

'For you, of course,' Cathy replied, grinning broadly at him.

'Can I go and sit in your cottage, Jem?' Laura asked. 'Have you noticed that fieldfares have started to peck about outside the sheep barn? I would love to do some sketches of them. You don't see them often enough, and I can watch them really closely from your window.'

'I have, yes,' responded Jem, 'and of course you can, Laura. What tale are they going to feature in: *Bird-explorers from the North? Raiders of the lost Arctic?*'

Despite herself, Laura gave a little smile. 'Not sure, but I need my own space for a while, Jem. I've just read this.' She gestured to the crumpled, discarded newspaper. 'It's so untruthful. Cathy will explain to you.'

Jem moved to the window to watch Laura walk down the gentle slope from the farmhouse to the stable cottage with a look of such complete loving absorption on his face that Cathy had to turn away. It made her feel so lonely – even desolate. He remained, gazing at where Laura had been, for some time after she had disappeared from sight, deep in thought.

Eventually, Cathy decided that she had to disturb his reverie. 'Miles Jefferies has written an obituary for

Lewis Devrille that verges on the libellous as far as we are all concerned, Jem,' she explained, handing over the *Dales Echo*, which she had smoothed out and folded back to reveal the article.

'That idiot seems too much like his friend for comfort!' Jem exclaimed angrily, when he had finished reading. 'No wonder Laura was upset … it's gratuitously unpleasant and the implied criticism of us all is so obvious!'

Cathy bustled about, tidying the breakfast things and starting to wash up, chatting inconsequentially about the dinner she was intending to prepare that evening, lessons she had been supporting at school, and the weather. Usually, Jem couldn't wait to down his tea or coffee and return to the work that was always waiting for him on the farm, but she was aware that this morning he was lingering. He asked for a second mug of coffee and gazed at the swirling brown liquid thoughtfully as he slowly poured in milk from a jug.

'Cathy, I need to talk to you. Can you please come and sit down with me?'

'Of course,' Cathy replied brightly, whipping off her apron and joining him at the table.

'Last Saturday in York,' Jem began, noticing that, as soon as he had mentioned their visit, Cathy stiffened, 'I saw you with a woman friend, just by the Minster …'

Cathy pushed the chair abruptly back from the table and walked over to the Aga, leaning against it, arms folded and head down.

'Her name is Arjana, meaning "paradise" in her mother tongue', she said, finally lifting her gaze to Jem's. 'She's intelligent, funny and exciting, and we can lose ourselves in each other. I met her at the LGBQT club Matt introduced me to. You know he's gay too?'

Jem shook his head. 'You haven't told Laura you're gay, have you Cathy?'

'No. How could I? Immediately she would think that I only saved her life because I think she is beautiful and unique and, almost from the first moment I saw her, thin, starving and totally vulnerable, I loved her. How can I tell her now? We have built a life together here, Jem. She has told me again and again that I am her best friend. A revelation like this would alter everything.'

'I think you underestimate Laura, Cathy. She loves you too … as a friend. There are so many different sorts of love: sexual, spiritual, friendship-love and,' Jem took a deep breath, 'the love a parent has for a child. If you share this with Laura, I can't imagine that she is so shallow that she will not want you to be in her life any more. Think about it. Can you see Laura behaving like this?'

'Let me try to explain, Jem. Unless you are celibate, being a lesbian means that you can find yourself in such a promiscuous world, where *anyone* of the same inclination becomes acceptable and I can't stand that sort of situation. When I was in London, although nothing was said, I suspected that my sexuality counted against me when those NHS cut-backs were made. Nurses with far less experience than I had were not made redundant; but they were heterosexual – 'safe' as far as management was concerned. I don't love Arjana, Jem, but I enjoy her company. I need companionship and to get away from the insecure and superficial world which constantly seeks attention from women who share the same sexuality as I do. How would you feel if you had to be celibate, year after year, longing for the relationship that would fulfil you?'

'Cathy, I was a monk for ten years …'

'Yes,' Cathy choked back tears and added, somewhat illogically, 'but you had a relationship before that, and now you have Laura! Don't you think that I long for the sort of looks Laura gives to you, Jem? She adores you. You are the centre of her world and ever since I met her eighteen months ago, she has been the centre of mine, but she has no idea of my feelings for her! To her I am just the faithful friend, the carer who cooks and talks to her and goes shopping and … and all the thousand and one little things that make up a life together. All except one, the most important one, the sort of love that lights up every day with joy because of the anticipation that you may be able to spend an hour, a single hour, with the person who makes life worthwhile for you.'

Cathy was in tears now and they flowed unchecked as she gulped and stammered her way through what had been, for her, the most difficult words she had ever spoken. Jem crossed the kitchen and opened his arms.

'Come here, Cathy,' he said gently, and was surprised and delighted when she did so, hugging him back hard and sobbing quietly as he stroked her hair. Eventually, Jem released her and held her a little distance from him.

'Cathy, you have to tell her. You must! Above all things, Laura is honest. You know how strongly she upholds the integrity and honesty of her grandfather. The longer you keep this from her, the more you will distance her. Believe me, I know her.'

Chapter 45

Jem was worried. The weather forecast over the past week or so had been threatening severe weather direct from Siberia. He knew only too well that the freezing temperatures and snow flurries which they had met on their way back from York the previous Saturday were as nothing compared to the white-outs that could occur with frightening rapidity in this high, bleak, uncompromising landscape. He had suggested to Laura that they should buy in additional supplies of hay to feed the animals in case they had to bring them indoors during the severe weather. Thank God, thought Jem, these had arrived the previous week, the heavy wagon negotiating the tight turn and the winding drive of *Fell Farm* with difficulty. He looked up with satisfaction to the loft above the sheep barn, piled high with fragrant, golden hay in which dried meadow flowers lingered, still holding memories of the far-distant summer days.

A week before Christmas, Laura and Cathy had, also at Jem's suggestion, bought in all the food that they would need for at least a fortnight, should the bitterly-cold, snow-laden weather threatened by the weather forecasters arrive.

And Jem was right. On Christmas Eve morning Laura went downstairs into darkness as all the ground floor windows were under the level of deep drifts of the snow which had fallen during the night. She flicked on the kitchen light, discovering to her great relief that the farm still had an electricity supply. Her first thought was of Jem, outside in his cottage and she opened the front door of *Fell Farm* intending to run down to stable cottage and check to see if all was well. Astonishingly, however, she opened the door to a wall of snow. Utterly taken aback, she did not at first understand what, exactly, she was looking at, but, pushing at the dense, white shimmering wall, she was shocked into realising that they would have to dig their way out of the ground floor level of their farmhouse.

Laura quickly ran upstairs. 'Cathy, just look out of the window!'

Cathy, still wrapped snugly in her duvet shook her head sleepily. 'What?'

'You are such a sleepy-head. Please get up. You will never have seen anything like this!'

Fell Farm was above the snow-line in any event, but, looking out of the southern-facing windows, the women both realised that this snow-fall was exceptional. As far as they could see, the snow lay thick and white, blanketing roofs, walls and trees, and ironing out the three-dimensionality of the landscape.

Cathy, slowly dragging on her dressing gown and yawning her way to the window, was awake in an instant seeing the impact of the snowfall on the landscape. 'It's surreal, Laura!' she exclaimed, half-excited, half-anxious.

'Laura! Cathy!' Jem, waved his snow shovel from the path that he was clearing between his stable cottage and the farmhouse door. 'Get the kettle on! I'll soon be with you.'

Laura smiled and shouted back to him, 'What would I ever do without your many talents, Jem? From shepherding to snow-shovelling!'

He laughed loudly. 'It would take more than snow to separate us, Laura!'

Cathy closed her eyes momentarily, seeing the sparkle and joy behind her companion's expression as she watched the stalwart figure of Jem, swiftly yet methodically shifting the snow. 'Laura, I need to speak to you.'

'Oh Cathy, don't be so serious! We will be OK. We have food, and our ultimate secret weapon – Jem!' With this, she ran lightly downstairs and waited in anticipation on the inside of the stout, oak front door, waiting for Jem to reach them. When he did, skin ice-cold and hair and eyebrows frosted with snow crystals, she reached up and gently held his face between her hands. 'Reward!' she announced playfully, kissing his icy lips.

⊰⧓⧍⧉⊱

Laura, Jem and Cathy never forgot that Christmas: it was unique and was etched forever on their memories.

Marooned in a silent, white landscape, high above the lights and festivities of Lokisdale, the three friends, together with Fly and her fast-growing puppies, celebrated together. Just before the early dusk fell, Jem was adamant that he must, as usual, check the sheep, now snugly gathered in the large hay barn. Unwittingly mirroring her Grandmother Lily's words and actions, Laura firmly set her plate and glass aside.

'Where you go, there I go also, Jem,' she said, smiling up at him.

Muffled warmly in layers of outdoor clothing, their breath was white on the frosty air as they made their way from farmhouse to sheep barn, along the pathway through the now frozen snow that Jem had cleared earlier. They stopped outside the barn, watching the lights that were flickering on across the hushed, white slopes in farms scattered across the fells, as other shepherds too made their final rounds of the day. Smiling at the sheer beauty of the scene, and inhaling deeply, Jem reflected upon what had happened, two thousand years ago, in a stone stable, filthy and cold, like many of those stables and barns whose lights he was now looking at, clustered on the slopes and moorland of the Dales. Looking at Laura, steadfastly at his side, he smiled and, overcome with a deep comforting rightness that they were both repeating a timeless ritual, he bent and kissed her lightly on the lips, before they continued on their slow patrol of the vulnerable, gentle animals that were in their charge.

Cathy had produced a perfect Christmas celebration dinner which was on the kitchen table waiting for Laura and Jem when they returned, with numb fingers, from their rounds. Usually ready with a smile or gentle comment, Cathy was quiet and, pleading a headache, had gone to bed soon after the last crumb of desert had been eaten. Both the bitter cold outside and the desire to spend every available moment with Jem prompted Laura to insist that he should sleep inside the farmhouse that Christmas Eve.

'I'll make you up a bed in the snug,' she told him, as they washed up together.'

'But Laura, I'm still wide awake! Can't we stay up and talk? I love Christmas Eve … I prefer it to Christmas Day. It is so full of promise, of things to come, about to be born.'

'I know, Jem. I feel the same.'

They went into the snug together and sat, propped up by cushions, side by side on the floor in front of the wood-burning stove. The wind had risen and blew in gusts down the old stone chimney, making the wood glow red and the ash blow about behind the glass of the stove.

Laura fingered her necklace, idly following the shape of the mother-of-pearl sheep. Her grandfather's brass carriage clock, set on the mantelpiece between two black and white photographs of Geoff and Lily on their wedding day, chimed midnight.

'Happy Christmas, Jem!' Laura murmured, reaching forward to kiss him.

'Happy Christmas, Laura!' Jem smiled, gently stroking back the wildly-curling hair from her face and touching the sheep necklace lightly. 'Did you really think that this was your only Christmas present, my love?'

Laura looked at him, frowning quizzically. 'Well, yes, I did ... together with the intensive sheepdog training lessons, of course!'

'You lovely, silly person,' Jem murmured with infinite tenderness. Reaching into his pocket, he took out a small, gift-wrapped package. 'Laura, I love you more than I thought man could ever love woman. I love you for your mind, your spirit and your beauty. Will you marry me ... please?'

Laura was beyond surprised, and glanced automatically at the faded wedding photos of the grandparents she had loved so much. Lily was looking up at Geoff with an expression of incredulous wonder and he was gazing at her with the same intense love in his every aspect that she saw in Jem, half-sitting, half-kneeling beside her.

'I can't imagine life without you Jem. Of course I will.'

Laura carefully opened the small leather box. Inside was an oval emerald, surrounded by tiny diamonds. Jem watched nervously as she slipped it on to her finger and gave a sigh of relief as he saw that it fitted perfectly. He mentally blessed Cathy for her detective work.

'Jem, I have nothing for you!' Laura whispered.

'But you have, you modest, beautiful, talented woman … you have just given me the best present of my life!' Jem exclaimed.

Chapter 46

Miles Jefferies had booked himself into *The Pheasant* for Christmas lunch and dined alone, delicately picking his way through the obscure, gourmet menu. Oyster mushrooms, *'cooked over a charcoal fire in bone marrow broth and served with fine slices of local smoked trout'* were followed by confit of Lokisdale duck and seasonal vegetables, and then finally deconstructed Christmas pudding. The three, minute courses, if placed together, would probably not even have been equivalent to half the average helping of turkey, roast potatoes, stuffing and vegetables being served up to hungry farmers across the length and breadth of Yorkshire. But, because Miles had paid excessively for this acclaimed menu, with its matched wines, he congratulated himself that nowhere else across his home county would his Christmas meal be equalled.

Down here in the dale bottom, the snow was thinner and snow ploughs had already cleared the major roads. A taxi had taken Miles to his lunch venue and one was ordered for four o'clock to return him to his large, imposing but somewhat overdone house which overlooked the reservoir. As he sipped his coffee and vintage brandy, however, rather than feeling replete and satisfied, Miles' thoughts concerning Laura and Lewis' death were gnawing at him constantly. At St Mark's, on one of his governor monitoring visits, he had overheard Cathy quietly telling Sandra Wilkins how Jem had tackled Lewis and thrown him out. Miles couldn't pick up the entire conversation but he understood the gist of it: Laura and Jem were 'an item'. He had thought of little other than how he could get his revenge on the woman who had rejected him, but had been his friend's lover, and was now involved with her shepherd. Then gradually, gazing into the changing landscape of the huge, glowing log fire, an idea started to grow in his mind.

⊰╫╍⊱

Christmas Day was, Laura thought, the happiest day of her life. It was two o'clock when she had finally left Jem to curl up on the camp bed in front of the wood-burning stove and had crept up to her room as quietly as she could so as not to wake Cathy. She need not have concerned herself, however. Cathy was wide awake and fully conscious of the whispered conversation which had taken place downstairs in the snug, directly under the room in which she slept. She knew that something was happening and was not surprised in the least when Laura came dancing into her bedroom early the next morning, bearing tea and a present wrapped in *Emma Bridgewater* Christmas wrapping paper.

'Happy Christmas, Cathy! Happy, joyous, wonderful Christmas!'

'Can I take it something rather exciting has happened?' yawned Cathy. She felt as if she had only just dropped off to sleep when Laura had erupted into her small, neat room.

'How did you guess?'

'Well, your rather hyper behaviour is a bit of a give-away ... but let me make another guess,' glancing at the beautiful emerald ring, 'Jem has asked you to marry him.'

'Yes! Isn't it wonderful! Such a surprise, Cathy!'

'Well, maybe to you but, believe me, to no one else,' Cathy grinned then jumped out of bed to hug Laura hard.

'You so deserve each other you know. You have both had horrible, really bitter things to deal with and now life has rewarded you with each other. It doesn't often happen. Life doesn't usually offer happy endings,' she added with a wry little smile.

Like a refrain during the farming and Christmas routines that filled the day, conversation circled around and returned to the one subject which was on all their minds.

'I think May Day would be perfect for our Wedding Day,' Jem said thoughtfully. 'Lambing will be over, and that would give us enough time to book caterers and somewhere for the reception and so on. What do you think, Laura?'

'I think you are the last of the great romantics, fixing our wedding date to fit in with the cycle of the shepherding year! But we don't need to look far for a venue for the reception, Jem. I couldn't dream of celebrating anywhere other than right here at *Fell Farm*! We can hire a marquee. The small field to the south of the barn is almost perfectly flat. It would be ideal.'

'And you needn't worry about a caterer,' added Cathy. 'You are looking at her! I may need to buy another freezer, though, depending upon how many guests there are.'

Laura sat quietly for several minutes, until Jem asked her intuitively, 'What's up?'

'The church, Jem ... I would feel a bit awkward getting married so close to where Ruth is buried.'

'So would I. How do you fancy getting married in a friary?'

'What, the one where you lived?'

'Yes. The brothers there are the closest to family I have, and it's a beautiful place, sacred and remote. You will love it.'

Chapter 47

The New Year came and went, but the snow remained, blanketing the fields and walls of North Yorkshire. Maintaining the farm involved tough, relentless work and Laura knew that without Jem she could never have carried on her grandfather's farming legacy to the exacting standards which he had set. She had made up her mind that every day she would work for part of the day with Jem, doing something at least to ensure the smooth running of the farm. She cut open the binder twine on hay bales and spread the golden food in mangers for her animals, she trimmed dirty fleeces and filled up the heavy water buckets. Some of these tasks were way beyond her strength, but she was determined to live up to the name of Jamieson that had already become a legend in the dale. She had resolved to maintain the vow that she had made after Geoff Jamieson had died: that she would do her utmost to care for the farm that he and his beloved Lily had worked all their lives through to establish.

The sheep remained in the big sheep barn, complacently munching their way through the golden, flowery hay, consuming vast quantities of sheep nuts and drinking their troughs dry several times a day. There could never be a day's respite from the round of checking and feeding the sheep, cleaning their living quarters, and replenishing their food and water.

'Don't farmers ever have a holiday?' Laura asked innocently, one lunchtime. Jem had been out working all morning and was chilled to the bone when he came in for the usual hot midday meal provided by Cathy. He had just about thawed out and was now working his way through a plate full of jam roly-poly and custard, but he threw back his head and laughed out loud at Laura's naïve question.

'How can we?' he asked her. 'The sheep can't feed themselves, or see to their own overgrown hooves, or replenish their water troughs. How many holidays did your grandfather have?'

'Well, he made a point of coming to see us during the summer when we lived over near York,' Laura told him. 'We had such good times together …'

'And how do you think he did that, Laura?' asked Jem gently.

'I'm sure you'll tell me,' Laura riposted.

'By paying a farmworker that he trusted to come and care-take his farm. It's the only option.'

Laura reflected upon the times when her grandfather had visited them as she was growing up. Clearly uncomfortable in the smug market town where his son and family had settled, Geoff Jamieson had lost himself in his granddaughter. It was only when he was dying that he had told Laura how her direct gaze and the way she wrinkled her small, freckled nose when thinking, so vividly reminded him of his beloved Lily – the woman he had eventually married and had grown to love beyond his wildest imaginings.

'Grandad had so little … what must it have cost him? Paying a farmworker, coming to visit us, the little gifts he used to bring,' she gulped.

'He loved you, Laura. Men in love do strange and eccentric things! So beware!'

Jem kissed the tip of her nose, and pulled her to him. After several minutes, gently but firmly, he distanced himself from her and gazed full in her face before heading for the coat hooks in the hall outside the kitchen, where his outdoor clothes were hanging.

'I need to do a spot of wall repair to occupy my energy and my attention! The weight of the snow has dislodged stones up towards the tup field, and we don't want any more accidents!'

⊰▌▐⊱

Eventually, in early March, the snow started to thaw. Laura couldn't believe the blessed relief she felt as the spear-tips of snowdrops planted by her grandmother under the sycamore trees in the garden started to appear; then the aconites, sprinkled under the low drystone wall; followed swiftly by the bright trumpets of daffodils, which lined the drive to Fell Farm. Imperceptibly the days lengthened but, instead of Jem having more leisure time, he had less, as he intensified the regime of looking after the sheep and preparing the farm for the pandemonium which was lambing.

With three weeks to go before 1st April – the date that Jem had circled in red on the kitchen calendar – Jem received a letter.

Miles Jefferies,
The Villa,
Lokisdale, North Yorkshire

Dear Jem Walker,
I have heard many good reports about your shepherding skills and much about the role which your late father played in the spiritual community of Lokisdale. Because of my respect for you and your family, I have a pressing matter on my conscience which I would like to discuss as a matter of urgency and would deem it a pleasure if you could find time to call on me at the above address over the course of the next week.
Yours sincerely,
Miles Jefferies

Jem was no fool. He knew from Laura and Cathy that Miles Jefferies had been a friend of Lewis, and this letter puzzled him immensely. He strongly suspected that the writer of the letter intended only harm but, with Lewis dead, and with his, Jem's, future secured with Laura, he could not begin to imagine how Miles could possibly damage either Laura or himself.

❦

'Sit down, Jem,' Miles invited him smoothly, adding with token politeness, 'May I call you Jem?' Without pausing for an answer, he continued, 'What can I get you to drink? Tea or coffee, or something stronger?'

'Nothing for me, thank you. I can spare you only ten or fifteen minutes, Mr Jefferies. There is work to be done back at *Fell Farm*.'

'Ah, yes, of course, you are living with the lovely ladies of *Fell Farm* now, aren't you?'

'I'm living in a converted stable cottage on the farm, so as to be on hand to look after the sheep and deal with any emergencies.'

'Like the one that took my friend, Lewis Devrille,' quizzed Miles.

'Look Mr Jefferies, I don't know why you asked me to call on you here, but if it is to make suggestions that somehow we at *Fell Farm* were responsible for your friend's death, I'm going to go right now. There was a full investigation, and you know as well as I do that we were found to be blameless. If that's all, I will bid you good day.'

Jem stood up firmly, buttoning his jacket and taking a step towards the door of Miles' study.

'No, it wasn't actually anything to do with Lewis. As I said in my letter, it's something on my conscience. I don't know how involved you are with Laura … or Cathy … or both of them,' Miles smiled insidiously, 'but I feel it's my duty to share something with you.'

Jem remained standing and frowned. 'What do you mean?'

'Look, do sit down again. I want to show you something.' Miles crossed to the filing cabinet and took a deep breath, as if deliberating a matter of the greatest delicacy. He was a consummate actor, mainly because, in some shape, manner or form, he always acted in everyday life, having for the past twenty years or so forgotten what sincerity or honesty meant. Appearing to do so reluctantly, he drew out a slim paper file and laid it on his desk, taking out the photographs it contained. He arranged these in a fan shape on the leather surface.

'Perhaps this is an aspect of Laura Jamieson that you haven't suspected existed, Jem.' Miles spoke softly, even managing to put a catch in his voice.

Not having the slightest idea what Miles was talking about, Jem strode over to the desk and scanned the array of photos in front of him. Miles had invested many hours into the creation of this pornographic portfolio of photos, purporting to be of Laura. Using his imaging and photo editing software he had excelled himself and Jem gazed unbelievingly down at the face of the woman he loved, smiling and lovely as always, apparently engaged in a range of practices which made him feel physically sick. He continued to look, pale to the lips but eventually, eyeballing Miles, Jem asked between gritted teeth, 'And why are you showing me these ... these disgusting photographs?'

'Because Laura Jamieson seems such an ingénue, so pure and gentle that she would take in any man; and because you and your family are so respected within the community. Did you know she was Lewis' lover for about six months when she lived in London?'

'I did,' replied Jem. 'But that was in the past, and she hated herself for it. She was on the point of killing herself because of her self-loathing. Presumably these disgusting ... things,' he made a dismissive, sweeping gesture over the collection, dislodging several and sending them flying on to the floor, 'date from those times. They have no relevance now. This all took place in the past and the past is dead.'

'Ah, but that's where you're wrong, Jem. I took these photos only a few months ago, here. As governor of St Mark's, I had quite a lot of contact with Laura over the Creative Arts Week, as you can see,' he tried to make a man-to-man joke, as Jem's implacable countenance and direct stare were disturbing him.

Jem's expression did not alter. 'So you seduced her?' he asked.

'Didn't need much seducing! Old habits die hard …'

'You filthy low-life! No wonder you were friends with Lewis! Get out of my sight before I do something I will regret!' Jem grabbed the collar of Miles' shirt and tightened it, pulling the man's face closer and closer to his own before releasing him and pushing him violently away.

Jem reached the study door in three paces and flung it open violently, bending it back on its hinges. He thrust his fisted hands deep in his pockets, not trusting himself to remain with Miles Jefferies any longer. His mind was in complete turmoil and he strode back, along the bank of the River Loki, and up the steep bank which led to *The Edge of the World*, hardly taking in his surroundings. He felt as if his brain was about to explode, so fierce were the contradictory, surging thoughts it contained. On one hand he felt that he knew and trusted Laura absolutely, and in his mind's eye he saw with perfect clarity her beautiful, flower-like face. It was impossible that she could have acted like this! She had told Jem that she had loved him almost from the first time she had seen him – and this was months before that Creative Arts Week. Jem had actually been living in the stable cottage at the time when Jefferies had said the photos had been taken, and he didn't think it possible that she could have been so utterly hypocritical as to behave like an animal with such a sleaze as Miles, whilst their own relationship had been developing. It just could not be! On the other hand, there was the evidence of the disgusting, disturbing images that he had just seen. It *had been* Laura in those photographs – her face was crystal clear.

The heavy snow of the last weeks had badly damaged *The Edge of the World* and the roof now dipped dangerously in the centre, on the point of collapse, but Jem hardly registered this as he passed the dilapidated buildings, on his way back blindly to *Fell Farm*. He knew that Laura and Cathy were out looking at wedding dresses in Harrogate, and Jem raked his fingers through his hair at the bitter irony. He had totally accepted that Laura had become involved in an abusive, degraded relationship with Lewis in the past and had forgiven her unconditionally. Anyone could make mistakes – God knows, he had! But how could he possibly entertain the thought of marrying a woman who could behave in the crude way so clearly shown in the photographs, when she had professed love for him! He burst into his warm, welcoming and colourful cottage – the most beautiful place he had ever lived – and the thought of the love he had believed Laura felt for him in providing this safe and comfortable place brought stinging, bitter tears to his eyes. Someone – almost certainly Laura – had placed a vase of daffodils on the small table in front of the window. How could this be! How could she have behaved like this? He knew that there was only one option for him, otherwise he really believed that he would go mad with grief. He knew he had to get away, as quickly as he could, before Laura and Cathy returned, and so snatched a few belongings together, stuffing them into the ancient rucksack that he had brought back from the Friary on his return to Lokisdale nearly a year earlier.

Finally, he took up the picture of Josh and carefully removed it from the frame that Laura had given him with such anticipation at his pleasure. Taking one last look around the beloved, whitewashed space, the bright curtains, the Ikea rug and the soft, comfortable bed, Jem set his shoulders and left *Fell Farm*.

Chapter 48

'Jem, Jem!' Laura ran quickly down the drive from the farmhouse to the stable cottage, waving a magazine in the air. She knocked on the door and, when there was no reply, went into the cottage. The lights were off – as she noticed they had been in the sheep barn and the stables – and the small chest of drawers that they had found in a charity shop showed signs of having been ransacked.

Laura went outside the cottage again and called as loudly as she could. 'Jem, where are you? We have found *the* perfect dress ... and for Cathy too! Jem?' When all she met was silence, she turned back again to the single-roomed cottage and saw the empty picture frame, lying neatly placed on the chest of drawers, and immediately felt a tight knot of panic in her stomach. Closing the door and running back to the kitchen door, she burst in.

'Cathy, Cathy, I think Jem's gone!' She told her friend what she had found in his cottage and Cathy's expression became thoughtful and very serious.

'Let me go and investigate, Laura. I'm sure there is some perfectly normal explanation for all this. Put the kettle on and sit down ... please. I'll be as quick as I can.'

Cathy ran down to the neat stone cottage and went in, feeling that the atmosphere had subtly changed. Now, instead of warmth and happiness, there was only emptiness. Cathy could not begin to imagine what had happened. Jem and Laura had been perfectly happy together, perfectly fulfilled in each other – only that morning they had chatted and laughed, so completely in love. There was no question of Jem suddenly getting cold feet about his commitment to marry her friend, so what on earth could have caused him to snatch his few belongings and to leave?

Methodically, Cathy looked around the compact space. On a bookshelf, containing copies of *The Dalesman* from Geoff's extensive collection and several books of poetry, she caught sight of a sheet of paper, stuffed unceremoniously into the envelope in which it had arrived: it was Miles Jefferies' letter. Cathy read it and gripped it tight. She loved Laura more than anyone she had ever known – apart from her mother, perhaps – and Laura's happiness was infinitely more important to her than any self-gratification. She switched off the light and returned to the kitchen.

Laura was on her knees, stroking Fly and her puppies which were now completely mobile and engrossed with tiny chews and toys that Laura had bought for them down in Lokisbridge. She was pale and composed, cuddling the big dog pup and gaining some measure of comfort from the wriggling, hot little body. She turned to Cathy. 'I completely trust Jem. He must have been called away to some sort of emergency. I'm sure that he will be back as soon as he can.'

'Laura, I found this,' and Cathy handed the letter to her friend.

'Perhaps that is where Jem is right now!' she suggested. 'We just need to wait. I'm sure he'll be back for dinner … you know how hungry he gets!'

Cathy was none too sure about this interpretation, but decided to play along with Laura for the time being.

Inevitably, the long evening came and went and still the friends sat alone, automatically going through the routine of preparing dinner, eating very little, washing up and tidying away the dishes.

At nine o'clock Cathy stood up suddenly and announced that she was going to ring Miles Jefferies. As her friend went into the snug, Laura continued to sit, pale and quiet, by the fire in the living room. She felt numb and her brain seemed incapable of reaching beyond the fact that Jem was no longer on Fell Farm. Her thoughts circled, searching for a reason why Jem would have left suddenly, without giving a reason.

The telephone conversation was very short. Cathy returned in less than two minutes, looking angrier than Laura had ever seen her look. 'That man! He can't speak a single sentence without innuendo! Jem did visit him this afternoon, Laura. They had a "man-to-man" chat, apparently and he left, looking quite "disturbed".'

'So, what does it all mean, Cathy?'

Cathy knelt by Laura in front of the dying fire and rubbed her cold hands between her own, much warmer, ones.

'I'm not sure but, knowing Miles, he will have been up to no good whatsoever. Was there anything that he could have told Jem that Jem knew nothing about, something that could have upset Jem deeply?'

Laura miserably shook her head. 'No, the only thing that he could have told Jem about was my relationship with Lewis … no doubt Lewis enjoyed discussing every sordid aspect with his like-minded friend!'

'But Jem knew all about that anyway.'

'He did. Cathy, I will never forget the way in which he looked at me with such love and understanding when I told him about my relationship with Lewis. All he said was, "Thank God, you are human." Cathy, I don't know whether I can stand this. I didn't realise how utterly precious Jem has become to me. What if I never see him again? Never see his face, or feel his touch, or hear his reassuring words? I don't know what to do.'

Cathy said nothing, but wrapped her arms around her friend and kissed her hair lightly. 'We'll think of something Laura. We'll do something.'

Chapter 49

It was probably the bravest thing that she had ever done. After a sleepless night, when the same futile questions continued to circle unremittingly in her mind, Laura got up, put on her warmest clothes, called to Fly, who left her puppies very reluctantly, and went out to do her best to check her pregnant sheep and see if there were any obvious problems.

The large majority of the flock seemed to be fine, but Laura knew, frustratingly, that even if there had been problems, she lacked the skill to discern these. One of the largest sheep appeared to be sluggish and was lying down, not eating – always, Laura had been told by Jem, an indication that all was not well. Laura replenished the feeders with hay and sheep nuts and refilled the water troughs, then walked back to the farmhouse and rang her brother.

'Matt, hi, I'm a bit worried about one of the ewes. She's down and not eating … No, Jem's away at the moment. Do you think you could come up? … Later this morning will be perfect.'

Cathy had to go and do the weekly food shopping, something she really enjoyed because of her love of cooking, and Laura knew that she would have at least two hours before her friend returned. Matt was due sometime after that so, rather than pacing the floor, or continuing to monitor the sheep, Laura decided that she would go into the snug, light the wood-burner, and try to settle to work – something that was within her control. She took out once again the pictures of the fox cub, the adult fox and the wolf. She stared at the fine details she had drawn of the male fox's magnificent head, noticing that she had made his eyes dark and full of expression – an unconscious reflection of the shape and colour of Jem's.

Up until this point, Laura had only added detail to the sketches she had produced already, but now she found her pencil moving to the next clean page. As with the previous drawings, she felt as if she was being directed by an energy beyond her own, and once again she was becoming the channel through which a story was being told. This new drawing was a rear view of the wolf and the cub. The small, soft-pelted animal, head down, its little brush drooping sadly, was trotting alongside the loping, dark wolf which led the way from the rocks on which the cub had lain in the previous picture, downhill towards a collection of stone buildings, some of which were cottages, and one of which was clearly a chapel with tall, arched windows. In her sketch it was a bright, clear, windy day and white clouds scudded across the sky. Laura withdrew into the world she was creating and hardly registered when Cathy returned with bags full of Laura's favourite foods.

'I thought we'd have carbonara this evening … and I've got a bottle of Chianti to accompany it.'

'Lovely, Cathy, thank you,' came the subdued reply.

Cathy grimaced slightly at Laura's tone, but consciously adopted a positive posture – smiling, head held high – as she went into the snug to join her friend.

'Coffee, Laura?' she asked brightly. 'I'm having one … it's distinctly chilly out there!'

'I'm OK thanks,' Laura replied, continuing with the meticulous drawing in front of her.

Cathy tried a different tack. 'This is lovely!' she said, eyeing the picture taking shape under Cathy's pencil. 'It's your little fox cub again, isn't it?' she added unnecessarily. Laura just nodded. 'Look, love, it's no good just sitting and moping!' Cathy gently touched her friend's arm.

'What would you know about it, Cathy?' Laura asked brutally. 'Have you ever been in love? Ever wanted to spend every second of your life with someone, just looking at them, or touching them, not even having to speak? Has anyone ever been the centre of your entire world, like Jem is the centre of mine?'

Recoiling as if she had been physically hurt, Cathy withdrew her arm, but continued to try to smile at Laura encouragingly. Although every single word that Laura had flung at her could be applied to how much she loved and longed to be with Laura, all she said was, 'I'll let you get on with your work, then. I need to unpack the shopping and get lunch ready.' Cathy stood up quietly and shut the door, returning to the realm in which she was most comfortable – her kitchen.

Almost as soon as her friend had left, Laura dashed down her pencil and held her aching head in her hands. How could she have been so vitriolic to someone who was so dear to her? All Cathy ever wanted was to make life easy and fulfilling for her and she had dismissed her so cruelly. Laura walked swiftly into the kitchen and flung her arms around Cathy's shoulders, giving her a hard hug – whilst Cathy tried to hide the tears she had been wiping away surreptitiously. 'I'm so sorry, Cathy, so very, very sorry. You mean so much to me and I have just hurt you … I know I have.'

'Well, not to worry, we all say hurtful things sometimes, Laura, and I know you had very little sleep last night, which never helps. Why don't you go up to bed and try to catch a couple of hours now? I'll bring you up a light lunch … and I bought a magazine I thought you might like …'

'Not *Bride* I imagine!'

Cathy smiled at Laura's attempted joke. 'Er, no. *Gardeners World* actually!'

'But I don't like gardening, Cathy.'

For the first time that day, Cathy saw the ghost of a smile playing around her friend's lips. 'Off you go!' she urged her.

'Do you know, I think I will,' Laura replied, yawning widely. 'I probably won't sleep, but I can learn all about …' she snatched up the magazine and scanned the contents advertised on the cover '… potting up tulips! Just what a sheep farmer needs to know. I do love you, Cathy,' she said quietly, kissing her friend's cheek before opening the door to the stairs.

As she heard Laura's light steps run up to her bedroom, Cathy gently ran her fingertips across the place where Laura's lips had brushed her cheek.

'If only you did!' she whispered quietly, bending to stroke Fly and her family.

Chapter 50

When Cathy went up to Laura's bedroom a little while later, she found her sound asleep, her hand resting on a picture of bright red tulips. Cathy bent tenderly to remove the magazine and tuck Laura's hand inside the duvet, before drawing the curtains and returning to the kitchen.

'Milk fever!' Matt announced after a very thorough examination of the ewe lying in a corner of the barn with head down and a complete lack of interest in her eyes. 'I'll get this calcium into her and she will be as right as rain. I'm surprised Jem has gone away at a time like this though, Cath. He's a good shepherd and he will know that things like this can happen at the drop of a hat.'

Cathy stood by Matt in the barn, muffled in Laura's outdoor clothes and boots. 'Ah, therein lies a tale,' she sighed. 'Come and have coffee or something to eat and I will tell you all.'

⊰│├⊱

'He's a bloody nasty piece of work, that Miles Jefferies,' Matt muttered, helping himself to a second slice of fruitcake. 'Do you have any idea what he said to Jem? Presumably Jem did go and visit him?'

'We think so, yes. We were out, looking for wedding outfits in Harrogate and when we came back, Jem had gone and we found the note I showed you.' Cathy shook her head sadly. 'Laura was so happy, and now she is withdrawing into her work again. That's all right, I suppose, but I've seen this happen to her before and she almost starts to live more completely in the imaginary world that she is creating than in the real world. It's not healthy, Matt.'

'She always has, Cathy.' Matt munched ruminatively for a few minutes. 'Have you told her about your feelings for her, and about Arjana?'

'No, Matt, I haven't. There never seems to be the right time.'

'Cathy, there never will be a "right time". It's only fair to tell her.'

Cathy stood up impatiently. 'That's what Jem said. I *will* Matt, but not just at the moment, not when she is reeling from the shock of Jem just walking out.'

'What do you think could possibly have made him act like that? Do you have any idea at all?' Matt quizzed her.

'I've been thinking about that … well, thinking about very little else really … and it must have been something to do with Laura. Jem has no family any more, no friends around here. Laura is his whole world.'

'So, someone needs to play Miles at his own game,' Matt advised. 'He is such a fake, and he doesn't realise how people regard his second-rate newspaper. He'll be out of business within the next five years as half of what he writes is fiction … talk about "fake news"!

The term could aptly have been coined about the *Dale Echo* in general and its editor in particular. Think what he knows about Laura and how he has tried to act with her. You may then get an inkling of the sort of thing he may have said to Jem. I must go … and remember what I said … *tell Laura you're gay!*'

⇥‖⇤

At five o'clock there was still no sign of life from upstairs, so Cathy tiptoed into Laura's bedroom to check whether she was all right. She was and, with her arm curled under her and cheeks slightly flushed, she could almost have been taken for a child, so deep and trouble-free was her appearance. Cathy let her be.

Realising that she knew even less than Laura about the barn full of expectant ewes, nevertheless, Cathy pulled on her friend's outdoor clothing and dutifully trudged down to the sheep barn. She went through the routine that she had seen Jem and Laura complete, of replenishing straw and sheep nuts and refilling the water troughs, and looked hard at the impassive expressions of the ruminant animals. Although she could read a human symptom of illness or distress with consummate skill, the seemingly identical faces, body-shapes and expressions of the sheep were a foreign language to Cathy. Ah well, she had done her best! She would look at them again last thing at night and hopefully, Laura would be back in the land of the living in the morning. Or possibly, even, Jem might return? But that she doubted. She had an increasing conviction that something would have to be done to bring about his return and the more she thought about this, the more convinced she became that it was she who would have to do it.

She went back indoors and, unusually for her, poured herself a glass of wine. Sitting thoughtfully by the Aga, she went through again all that Matt had said concerning Miles. It was a question of analysing the symptoms and deducing their cause – just like diagnosing an illness. The evidence that she had before her was that Jem had disappeared suddenly, almost certainly after a visit to Miles; that Miles had almost certainly known about Lewis' abusive relationship with Laura; and that he had tried to ruin Jem's feelings for Laura by revealing that relationship to him. But Jem knew already. It would have had to be something new that Miles had revealed to Jem … something new … news … Matt's scathing words about Miles' "fake news" echoed in her mind. And, in a flash, she understood. The diagnosis was clear: Miles had fabricated a lie about Laura so convincing that Jem had believed it and so damning that he had found it unbearable.

Chapter 51

'Miles? Oh hi, its Cathy Munro here. How are you? ... Good. Miles, I could do with some advice and I know you are a man of experience. Would it be possible for us to meet up sometime? Tonight? Er, yes, that's brilliant ... at *The Pheasant?* I'll meet you there.'

Cathy smiled wickedly. This was going to work! Miles was delightfully predictable.

Usually, Cathy dressed in a no-nonsense way: jumpers or shirts with trousers or skirts and flat shoes. She wore minimal make-up and just brushed her short, blond hair vigorously, rather than styling it. Tonight, however, she changed her approach. Laura had a mid-calf, jade green dress which she wore with long suede boots and, once again, Cathy tiptoed into her friend's bedroom, this time slipping the garment and boots out of the wardrobe, thinking how lucky it was that she and Laura were almost the same size. She grimaced as she squeezed her feet into the high boots – she was used to comfort rather than fashion – but smiled as she surveyed the final effect. For once, she had used make-up, accentuating her wide, clear eyes and generous mouth, and her hair shone. She fixed in place small green earrings and clipped a heavy silver necklace about her slender neck. She would do nicely for the purpose in hand! Shrugging on her sheepskin jacket, Cathy locked the farmhouse door, leaving the entire household fast asleep.

As soon as she entered the pub-restaurant, Cathy knew that she had made an impact. Heads turned as she walked in gracefully, slipping off her coat to let the figure-hugging green dress make its maximum impact. She saw Miles sitting in one of two deep, winged armchairs which flanked a low table in front of the log fire. He was sipping a gin and tonic and flicking through a copy of *Country Life*.

Miles glanced up as he heard the door open, but didn't recognise Cathy at first sight. She saw his eyes widen as he did a double-take and set his glass down carefully on the table. 'Cathy, darling,' he gushed loudly. 'You look fabulous!'

Cathy bit back her natural scathing response, reflecting that Miles was putting on an act, as usual, pretending that he and she were currently, or were about to become, 'an item' and trying to draw the attention of everyone in the restaurant to the fact. 'Hi Miles,' she purred, deliberately lowering her voice in order, she hoped, to sound seductive.

'What can I get you to drink, gorgeous girl?' Miles asked, his eyes sliding up and down her body and resting too long on her small breasts.

'White wine spritzer please, Miles,' Cathy responded, thinking, as she watched him brashly approach the bar, that it was little wonder that she was a lesbian if this was the standard behaviour from the opposite sex!

Miles placed the glass in front of her, deliberately brushing her hand. 'How can I help you, Cathy?' he asked, cloying solicitude oozing from every syllable.

Cathy sighed, tossed her head petulantly, and headed straight to the supposed point of her meeting with Miles. 'I am utterly sick to death of living with that selfish *cow*, Laura Jamieson,' she breathed pettishly. 'She thinks she is so *special*, that all men are just queuing up to take her out and to take her to bed!'

Miles nodded sagely, shaking his head in mock sadness. 'I know exactly what you mean. She was absolutely all over me, you know, when I brought her here. You will remember I *did* ask you out before I asked her, but ...'

'Ah yes, that was when I first arrived here. I was *so* missing the London scene and made quite a few mistakes at the time!'

'As for my poor friend, Lewis,' Miles continued, sighing deeply 'she led him such a dance in London, you know. Disgusting! And now she clearly has her talons into that poor half-witted shepherd she is co-habiting with. What does he have that I don't?'

Cathy shook her head, murmuring, 'Indeed!'

Miles continued: 'Ha, but he was a monk, wasn't he, for years? Probably got desperate and, since she was readily available ... well, he is a man after all!'

'But, you know, Miles, he has left. Just disappeared!'

Miles threw back his head and laughed, draining his drink. 'Another?' he asked Cathy, indicating her hardly-drunk spritzer.

'I'm fine at the moment, thank you. I've got to think of my figure,' Cathy murmured, stroking her slender waist and flat stomach and watching the predictable effect that the gesture had on the editor of the *Dales Echo*. 'You go ahead though, Miles. I know how hard you work and you so deserve some down-time.'

Miles beamed at Cathy and ordered another large gin and tonic. What a girl! Now *she* was what he called a proper, red-blooded woman. Knows how to make a man *feel* like a man. Bit different to her so-called innocent friend! 'So how can I help you, dear girl?' he asked solicitously when he had returned to their table.

'I need to move. To find a little house that I can call my own, where I can be myself,' Cathy responded dramatically. 'Stuck up there on the moors, with no one to talk to, no female friends to chat to, it's so boring. Don't forget I lived in London for years! There was always something to do there, somewhere to go, exhibitions, galleries … it was wonderful!' she sighed.

'If you wish we could go and view some properties together tomorrow,' Miles suggested eagerly. 'As you can imagine, I do have friends in the real-estate world … perhaps we could even see houses not officially yet on the market.'

Cathy leant forwards and laid her capable square hand as gently as she could on his plump, white, well-manicured one. 'Really?' she widened her eyes deliberately. 'Would you do that for me?'

'Of course!' Miles croaked. This evening was going so well, beyond his wildest expectations.

'Perhaps we could make that spoiled cow Laura leave Lokisdale?' Cathy said. 'But, if Jem comes back, she will stay …'

Miles once again drained his glass. He was so bewitched by the vision of beauty and womanliness before him that he was now drinking automatically, without thinking of his drive home, or the consequences of drink-driving. In fact, he was thinking of nothing but the wide blue eyes, the pale gold hair and the moist, delicate pink mouth of the woman who sat opposite him. 'Can I get you another drink?' he asked again.

'As I said, must look after my figure, Miles,' Cathy simpered, once again stroking her trim stomach. Miles' eyes drifted down to the curve of her waist and hips, to her firm thighs and shapely calves and stood up abruptly.

'Well, I'll just have another, if you don't mind,' he said, swaying a little on his feet.

Miles sat down with his third double gin and stared thoughtfully into the glass. 'Cathy, I can guarantee that that fool Jem will never return.'

Cathy said nothing, but looked enquiringly at her companion, inclining her head slightly to one side in studied, gentle inquisitiveness.

'I wrote to Jem and asked him to come and see me. I … er … felt that he needed to know what a predatory female he was getting involved with. The things Lewis had told me … well, I couldn't possibly repeat them to someone like you.' Once again, Miles' eyes slid down Cathy's figure and rested about thirty centimetres below her neck. I showed him some *very interesting* photos … fakes of course, but we live in a fake world anyway … Laura's pretty little head grafted onto the most compromising of bodies … young ladies without any pretence to respectability. Told him a story about her falling for me during the Creative Arts Week and me taking those pictures when she and I were enjoying ourselves together at my house. What a fool! He lapped it up!'

Cathy's nails dug hard into her palms – what a complete bastard this man was! But she had to maintain her composure. 'What a fantastic idea! How on earth did you do that?'

'Oh, just a little bit of IT magic … nothing for you to concern your pretty little head about.'

'I think you are amazing, Miles! You really have put both of them in their places! I wish I could have just a teeny glimpse of what you did though … what a laugh that would be!'

'Well, how about coming home with me tonight … this evening?' Miles asked.

Cathy did a rapid calculation. He had had three double gins – if she could inveigle him into drinking further amounts when they reached his house, then she thought she could very easily manage the outcome of any visit there. 'That might be nice,' she smiled. 'Maybe I could allow myself something else to drink once we get back to your place. You don't have champagne, do you?' Cathy recalled her mother warning her about the effects of mixing 'grape and grain'. She was no aficionado of alcoholic drinks, but she knew champagne came from grapes, and she thought gin came from some sort of grain.

'But, *of course*, my dear. Special case of Dom Perignon arrived only last week from my suppliers. I have a couple of bottles in the chiller.'

'Well, if you're sure …'

'Follow me, Cathy. I'll show you the way.' And, laughing at his own perceived wit, Miles bade a loud farewell to the barman and the world in general and made his slightly unsteady way to his Porsche.

Chapter 52

Cathy was concerned as she followed the gun-metal grey Porsche in front of her. Miles forgot to signal, cornered on the wrong side of the road and shot far too fast over a hump-backed bridge. In all honesty, potential risk to the driver of the vehicle was not uppermost in her mind, but she was deeply concerned about the danger he presented to other road users in his present state: regrettably it was too late to be able to do anything about that. Selfishly she also wanted to ensure that he arrived at his home in one piece to show her the 'fake photos' that had driven Jem away. Perhaps she had underestimated just how much alcohol Miles had actually consumed.

Eventually, having initially overshot the turning to his driveway, they arrived at Miles' large, pretentious house and Cathy breathed a deep sigh of relief. She emerged from her car in as ladylike a manner as she could, bearing in mind the height of the heels she was wearing and the fit of the dress. How Laura could dress like this and feel comfortable, she really did not understand. 'I love your car, Miles,' she cooed, trying desperately to remember all the outdated romantic films she had ever watched and attempting to inject just the right amount of coyness into her tone.

'We must go for a spin in it together sometime, Cathy,' he slurred. 'And now, as they used to say, "Come and see my etchings" … although this time they are photographs, of course,' he ended lamely.

Cringing, Cathy preceded him into the large, square hall of his Edwardian villa. As she had expected, everywhere there was a tasteless show of wealth. The delicacy of the Aubusson rug jarred with the robust leather porter's chair, and the walls were hung with several stereotypical portraits from the eighteenth century. It was a stylist's nightmare.

'Make yourself comfortable in my study,' invited Miles. 'I'll get the champers.'

Oh God, thought Cathy, how long was this evening going to have to last before her companion became insensible and she could get her hands on the photographs! The man spoke like something out of a 1930's movie and she was astonished that such an anachronism as Miles Jefferies could continue to exist.

She heard a loud 'pop', followed by a curse, before Miles returned with a large silver ice-bucket in which nestled a bottle of Dom Perignon 2006. The impact that Miles had intended to create was rather marred by a damp patch which spread down his yellow Jaeger sweater and over his trousers – presumably the reason for the muttered oath in the kitchen.

'Now, let's just get cosy shall we?' he suggested, leading Cathy to a buttoned leather sofa in front of the wood-burning stove.

'Shall we just increase the anticipation a tad by enjoying a glass or two of champagne first, Miles dearest?' Cathy whispered – she hoped, seductively.

An inane smile spread across Miles Jefferies features. He'd done it! He'd bagged her!

Desperately racking her brains for a topic that would keep Miles entertained, Cathy decided that she would ask him about himself. He was so self-obsessed that she fervently hoped he would talk until he passed out.

Half an hour passed, during which almost all the champagne had disappeared and Miles had rambled on about his business successes and his sexual prowess. Cathy sipped minimal amounts and, as Miles became progressively more drunk, he lost the ability to control the amount he consumed. The very last thing that Cathy intended to happen was for Miles to be in a position to seduce her that evening, but it was a very fine balance between rendering him incapable of seduction, but ensuring that he was sufficiently conscious to show her the photographs. Finally, Cathy judged that the right moment had arrived. Miles' eyelids were drooping slightly, when Cathy laid her hand on his arm and said:

'I almost forget … do let's see those clever photographs you showed to that fool Jem Walker!'

'Ah yes, of course!' Miles attempted to stand up, but swayed back into the sofa. 'Another time perhaps, Cathy darling!'

'No, Miles,' she pouted. 'You promised. I want to see them now.' And this most straightforward, no-nonsense woman, did her best to adopt the facial expression of a spoiled child. She must have succeeded, because Miles managed to stand this time and zig-zagged over to his filing cabinet, extracting the thin cardboard file.

'Here we are. Take a look at these!' invited Miles, clumsily removing the photos and dropping several on the floor. Cathy, with iron control, crossed the study and looked at the pornographic array spread out in front of her. They were utterly disgusting; and her overwhelming thought was that, however the moron who was swaying next to her had created these fakes, the vulnerable women whose bodies were grafted onto Laura's face and head had once actually been subjected to these degraded practices.

'Perhaps I could take a few moments and look through these to ... to get some ideas,' Cathy snatched at a reason to remain standing with the photographs whilst, hopefully, her companion would make his drunken way back to the sofa. She was right.

'I'm, er, a bit tired, Cathy ... hard day at the office. Need to muster my strength for later,' Miles grinned foolishly and staggered back to the fireside seat.

Cathy's timing was exquisite. Within two minutes he was fast asleep, head back, mouth open and snoring loudly.

After carefully collecting the photos, Cathy returned them to their file, which she placed under her arm. She walked quietly to the hall where her coat hung and shrugged it on. Turning off the light and closing the door behind her, she quickly crossed the courtyard, got into her car and drove off, leaving Miles to his erotic, delusional dreams.

Chapter 53

When she got home it was gone eleven o'clock and she was surprised to see the lights of the farmhouse blazing out across the dark countryside.

'Where have you *been*, Cathy?' Laura was pacing to and fro in the kitchen, her hands cupped around a mug of tea. She looked alert and totally wakeful, which was more than could be said for Cathy, who felt distinctly jaded after her unaccustomed consumption of champagne, the tedium of her role-playing with Miles and the boots which really had become extremely uncomfortable. 'I've been worried *sick!*' Laura continued. 'I thought that you might have left me too!'

'Don't be daft,' Cathy answered rather grumpily. 'I'll just make myself a very strong black coffee, then I'll give you an account of my evening, which was certainly interesting.'

'You're wearing my dress and boots,' commented Laura, distinctly puzzled by now.

'I know. And although very attractive, you are welcome to them!' laughed Cathy. 'I'll return them to their rightful place and go and put on my positively *unattractive*, but very comfortable, dressing gown.'

An hour later, the friends were still laughing over Cathy's vivid account of the evening.

'You're a complete genius, Cathy!' Laura commented. 'But how are you going to face Miles in the future? You are bound to come across him at St Mark's.'

'I'll deny everything. He was so drunk he won't remember most of what went on, and he can hardly claim back the fraudulent photos!'

Whilst Laura was examining the contents of the manila file, her lips had tightened. 'How *dare* he do that!' she exclaimed angrily. 'It goes beyond the worst identity fraud!'

'I know. But take solace. Miles Jefferies' pride is his most precious possession. Tonight it has been smashed to pieces.' Cathy paused, thinking carefully about where she should take the conversation next. The burning issue of her sexuality was becoming a real concern to her, as she recognised the truth of the warnings given to her by Matt and Jem about further delay alienating Laura. But, once again, to Cathy the time just did not seem right so, instead, she told Laura the next step in her plan.

'I'm going to drive over to the Franciscan Friary that Jem belonged to tomorrow, Laura. I have a feeling that he may well have returned there. Poor man, where else does he have to go? *The Edge of the World* looks to be on the point of collapse. He has no family, and he told me once that the Guardian, the person in charge of the Friary, referred to the community as Jem's adoptive family. I think he is there … and he needs to realise that these horrible photographs are fakes.'

'But what concrete proof is there that they *are* fakes, Cathy? How can we make him believe us?'

'You would never make a detective,' chided Cathy lovingly. 'You have forgotten your birthmark. That is pretty conclusive proof that the bodies in the photographs cannot be yours!'

Chapter 54

'Brother Jeremiah, you know the rules of the community – you can only fast for two days. This is the beginning of the third day and I know that you are unswervingly obedient. Have some toast or a little porridge and a cup of tea, to break your fast gently.'

Jem was kneeling in prayer in the chapel where the brothers worshipped together. He opened his eyes briefly, to glance at the Guardian, only to close them again without speaking. After a few minutes, he became aware that the Guardian had quietly knelt by him, joining him in this silent prayer vigil. After about half an hour, Jem felt a warm hand under his forearm, urging him to stand.

'Come with me, Jeremiah.'

It was an instruction, not a request. Brother Peter led Jem into his small, austere office, where he undertook the administration of the order. The stone Friary was always cool, but at this time of the year it was cold and a fire had been lit in the arched stone fireplace. Apart from the laptop on Brother Peter's desk, the scene could have been at any point in the history of the Franciscan Order, when an older, wiser brother had taken a vulnerable member of the order under his wing to advise or correct.

'Jem, the only words that you have spoken since you came back have been "Can I come home?" My role is to support and help everyone. I cannot fulfil my role if you do not share with me what has happened, what is troubling you.'

Brother Peter watched a powerful range of emotions cross the pale, tired face of the young man in front of him. Used to the long silences of meditation and contemplation, he continued to sit and pray silently, waiting until Jem was ready to speak.

Eventually, having mustered his thoughts and got his emotions reasonably under control, Jem said bleakly, 'I fell in love with a woman whom I believed to be outstanding … brave, honest and beautiful. But I was told things which made a mockery of the love I have for her and I had to leave. This is the only real home I have.'

'Tell me more, brother.'

And Jem did. The Guardian sat, impassive and unshockable. He understood only too well the weaknesses of humankind, but equally he was a shrewd judge of character. What Jem had told him just did not make sense. 'If this woman, Laura, was honest enough to tell you the truth about her previous relationship, why would she have not told you about an affair that she was conducting with another man? Surely she had done the most difficult thing. She did not have to tell you about her past.'

'I know, Brother Peter, that puzzles me too.'

'And of the two people, this Miles Jefferies and Laura, what evidence do you have about the character of each? Which one of these two would you naturally trust?'

'Laura, without question.' Jem responded to Brother Peter's question, but thereafter continued to sit in silence.

The older man, too, sat deep in thought. 'I believe that there is more to this than we think. I will reflect upon what you have told me. But I repeat, you must eat. I will go with you to the refectory and sit whilst you do exactly that.'

As always, the Guardian gave wise counsel. As Jem sipped the hot tea and slowly ate a small bowl of porridge, he realised that his fast had, in effect, disabled his thought-process. In not being able to think cogently, some of the agonising pain of his loss of Laura had been blunted. Now, as his faculties were gradually returning to him, anguished thoughts started once again to crowd his mind. Ten years earlier, after he had lost his dearly-loved little boy, Jem had thought that his heart was broken for ever. When he had met Laura, it was as if sunshine, joy and laughter had suddenly started to flood afresh into his life and he believed that the darkness of his loss was finally going to become bearable. Now, sitting in the refectory of the Friary, when he closed his eyes, he could see Laura's loving glance, almost hear her gentle voice and feel the delicate touch of her slender hands on his body. He simply did not know how he could bear losing Laura, losing the second person that he had loved with all his being.

The men sat together without speaking. Jem knew that he was taking up too much of the Guardian's precious time and was about to stand up and apologise for this when an elderly friar bustled into the room.

'Brother Jeremiah, you have a visitor. I have shown her into our reception room.'

Jem leapt up. His first thought was that it was Laura and, despite everything, he could not wait to see her. His second, less comfortable, was that he had no idea how to begin to speak to her.

Sensing his quandary Brother Peter said kindly, 'I will come with you, brother.'

⊰╫╠⊱

Cathy had been surprised when she had driven down the long entrance driveway to the Friary. She had imagined a bleak, austere place, with no gardens or softness surrounding it, but instead she drove through a tunnel of arching trees which would, when in leaf, provide a cool, green shade and a fitting entrance to this place of peace and consolation. At the end of the drive lay rectangles of neatly-dug garden in front of a mellow stone building, whilst pots of daffodils and crocus announced that Spring was just around the corner.

She had been warmly welcomed and taken into a comfortable sitting area, where there were magazines piled on a low table, next to a vase of tulips.

'Cathy!' Jem cried, as he saw her sitting, composed as usual, flicking through a copy of *Country Living*.

Two long steps took him across the room and he gave Cathy a warm hug. After a few seconds, Cathy distanced herself from him, keeping him at her arms' length and holding his gaze with her own. Emotions and questions spilled out of her. 'Jem, I need to talk to you. I'm so glad I have found you ... we have been so worried! Why did you leave so suddenly? Was it something to do with Miles Jefferies? The whole thing with those pernicious photos was a complete lie. I got the photos from him and I have absolute proof that they are fakes.'

'Shall I leave you alone?' asked Brother Peter kindly.

'No, I would be grateful if you could stay, if that's all right?' Cathy said hesitantly, unsure of the protocols in a religious institution.

The men sat down and Cathy told them the outline of the story, sparing them the fine detail of her cringingly embarrassing evening with Miles.

Jem's relief was heartbreakingly apparent. Although his face and demeanour relaxed steadily as Cathy spoke, tears ran unchecked as he accepted immediately and completely the simple truth. 'Cathy, I have made such a mistake! Can I come back to *Fell Farm* with you right now? Will Laura ever be able to forgive me?'

Chapter 55

Laura did not expect Cathy to be back until at least late afternoon and so had decided to undertake the hardest physical work that she could to counteract her agitation and restlessness. In the depths of the sheep barn, she shook out bale after bale of fresh bedding straw, filled the feeders with sheep nuts and carried fresh drinking water to her flock. When she heard the unmistakable sound of Cathy's car engine, she unceremoniously dropped the bag of food, tore out of the building and up the drive to meet her friend. For good or bad, Laura was desperate to hear news of Jem.

Cathy slowed her vehicle right down and then came to an abrupt halt as the passenger door was flung open and Jem jumped out. He flew down the few remaining metres of the long, curving driveway and whipped Laura into his arms, crushing her to him. Tears clouded Cathy's vision, making the two bodies of her friends appear to be one single body, a fitting symbol of their unity, she reflected poignantly.

'I've done my best with the sheep,' Laura muttered, where she was held against Jem's rough cloak. 'But a couple of ewes look different today …'

'I'll look in a minute,' Jem told her. 'I just can't let you go yet. Can you ever forgive me for doubting you, Laura?'

'Yes,' she replied, pulling herself gently from his embrace to look him in the face. 'I have always hated that birthmark ... but not anymore.' Jem bent to kiss her, then stroked her hair back from her face in the habitual gesture that she had come to love.

'Come on,' he said 'let's go and look at those ewes.' And, hand in hand, they walked together down the drive.

⇥⟩‖⟨⇤

The ewes that 'looked different' were, in fact, in labour and marked the beginning of three weeks of unremitting work. Jem followed the shepherd's custom of checking the sheep at midnight, then setting his alarm for three and six in the morning. Invariably the most popular hour for sheep to lamb was at 3.00 am. And maybe, reflected Jem, yawning widely where he lay on the floor of the barn, assisting a young ewe with her first lamb, it was a natural instinct to give birth when most of the world lay quiet and the momentous task of producing new life could continue undisturbed.

Jem had warned Laura that lambing was a tumultuous time and that she and Cathy would have to shoulder the burden of wedding preparations whilst he cared for their flock.

'Do you know, Cathy,' sighed Laura one bright April morning, 'I feel as if my life is a bit like the sky today – untroubled, for the first time in years. All the complexities of Jem's and my past have been brought out into the open and aired and it is less than two weeks before Jem and I are married. I'm so happy, Cathy! No more secrets to blight the future!'

Cathy was in the middle of working out quantities of food for the wedding buffet. She had ordered a small marquee, because there were only going to be a couple of dozen guests, and catering for this number would be a breeze! She had made the three tiers of the wedding cake already and palmiers and sausage rolls were safely stored in the freezer. She was sitting tapping her teeth with a pencil and occasionally making a note on the list in front of her.

Laura's words dropped like stones into the carefree happiness of the day. It had to be done – right now. 'Laura, I'm gay,' she announced in a monotone.

'Sorry ... you mean happy? You don't sound it!' Laura bantered.

Cathy took a long steadying breath. 'I mean I'm a lesbian.'

Laura looked at her friend sitting with tightly-compressed lips, white as a sheet, regarding her steadily from under her long fair eyelashes. It was clear that she was deadly serious and a thousand thoughts jostled together in Laura's mind. She had heard that a drowning person sees the whole of their life pass before their eyes before they die and she underwent a similar experience now in terms of her relationship with Cathy. She remembered the quiet, composed figure, muffled in a warm scarf who had saved her life on that bitter November evening and the way in which she had spontaneously offered Laura a home. She recalled how Cathy had lost her job, sold her flat and moved to Yorkshire to share Laura's life at *Fell Farm*, investing the small profit from the proceeds of the sale for both their benefits and sharing her little car. She thought of the love and care which Cathy had extended to her ever since the moment they had met – cooking, shopping, making countless hot drinks, encouraging her, laughing with her – and then, most recently, how she had gone against everything she was to obtain the pornographic pictures from Miles Jefferies. Looking at Cathy now, Laura could see that she expected to be rejected, and she realised with crystal clarity that every single thing that she said and did next were of paramount importance – she had to get this just right.

But actually, it was the easiest thing in the world. Just as Jem's spontaneous reaction to Laura's revelation about her relationship with Lewis had been one of relief and love, Laura now jumped up and knelt by Cathy's side. 'And you think that this will change our friendship, Cathy? How could it? We are closer than sisters. I have grown to love, respect and admire you more than any other woman I have ever known. Now, really, there are no secrets left … are there?' Cathy covered her face with her hands and quietly sobbed behind them. 'I thought you would ask me to leave … and I didn't know what I would do. I just love looking after you. You ask if there are any more secrets and there is one further thing you don't know but you will have to ask your brother about that.'

Cathy clasped Laura's hand between her square, capable ones and Laura was taken back to that night on Waterloo Bridge, when those same hands had led her from that place of misery and desperation to where she was now.

Jem came into the kitchen, ready for his mid-morning coffee, and smiled broadly as he saw the two women embracing closely and warmly. In an unconscious replay of Cathy's words when, months earlier, Laura had revealed her relationship with Lewis to Jem, he exclaimed with relief, 'Well, thank God for that!'

Chapter 56

May Day dawned bright and warm as Laura flung open her bedroom windows, breathing in deeply the sweet, fragrant air. It was far too early for the world at large to start its business of living, and the sweeping landscape was empty and startlingly beautiful. Not surprisingly, Laura had slept only fitfully, anticipating this, the start of the rest of her life. She hugged herself with the thought that, only metres away, was the stable cottage and the man around whom her entire life now centred. She need only close her eyes to see his sensitive, strong face, his dark eyes and thick, soft hair and, in less than six hours, she would be his wife.

It was hopeless trying to go back to sleep, so Laura slipped on jeans and a sweater and walked quietly along the landing, downstairs and out of the farmhouse. She strode swiftly along the drive, diverting into the stream field to pick handfuls of delicate harebells and ox-eye daisies which dotted the grass with their bold, silver-white explosions of colour.

It took less than twenty minutes to pass *The Edge of the World*, now roofless, and then follow the twisting moorland road down to where the church lay on the outskirts of the town. Feeling completely at peace with the past, Laura opened the lych-gate and went to her grandfather's grave. She shook out the dead flowers that she had placed there a week earlier and replaced them with the harebells and daisies gathered from the land he loved and had tended all his life. She kissed her hand and then pressed it against the cold stone of his headstone, whispering, 'I love you, Grandad. Be happy for me today.' Laura then made her way to the overgrown plot, marked by a leaning wooden cross, which marked the place where Ruth lay. She carefully placed the rest of the flowers in the jam jar that rested in a hollow in the turf. Tears came to her eyes as she thought of the woman who had borne Jem's child and had died – so young – to remain here alone for all eternity. At that moment she felt impelled to make a promise and, echoing the gesture she had seen Jem make, almost a year earlier, she knelt in the dew and placed her hand on the earth.

'If I can, I will do everything in my power to help Jem find your son and lay him here with you. I will do my best to make sure you are not alone anymore.'

⟢❦⟣

Cathy decorated her car with more of the daisies and quantities of white ribbon. On the parcel shelf rested a bouquet of seven cream roses, tied with lavender-blue ribbon. Jem had been forbidden by Cathy to leave the stable cottage until Matt came to collect him. It was challenging to keep bride and groom apart when they lived less than fifty metres distant from each other, but Cathy was determined to do her best to try! With less than an hour before they had to leave for the Friary, Cathy knocked lightly on Laura's bedroom door.

'Come in, Cathy … no need to knock!' Laura called.

'I have champagne for the bride, and a little for the best woman!' she announced, entering the room, and then, almost in the same breath, 'Oh, Laura!'

Laura was beautiful, and everyone who saw her was touched by this beauty, but today, on her wedding day, Laura was lit with joy from within and never had the term 'radiant' been more apt. She had twisted her thick hair up and back from her face and it cascaded richly around a circlet of cream roses and down across her neck and shoulders. The wedding dress that she had chosen with Cathy was exquisite – vintage cream lace which fell simply over the slender curves of her body. Cathy carefully placed the tray of champagne and glasses on the wide window sill and took both Laura's hands in her own.

'You look unforgettable,' she said simply. 'You are the most beautiful woman I have ever seen.'

'You look lovely yourself, Cathy,' Laura responded, thinking that the elegant, knee-length, plain cream dress and jacket suited her friend perfectly.

'Well, since I am 'best woman' for both of you, I have to try to look the part! Here's to the next generation of farmers at *Fell Farm*!' toasted Cathy.

'Amen to that,' blushed her friend.

⊰∥⊱

Jem stood in front of the altar facing the Guardian who, having formerly been ordained as parish priest, was able to conduct the ceremony. They chatted with the ease that comes from many years of working together in the same community, and Brother Peter thanked God for the change that had been wrought in the man standing with him now. A decade earlier, a devastated, bereaved boy had arrived at the Friary, full of loss and misery, desperately seeking a meaning to the rest of his life. But now a confident, mature man stood in front of him, a gentle smile playing about his lips, utterly fulfilled by another human being. The power of love was immense, reflected the Guardian, but all he said was, 'I have longed to see you like this, brother. Your wife-to-be must be an extraordinary woman indeed.'

Then, glancing up, Brother Peter saw that the bride and her 'best woman' had arrived. Laura looked ethereal – almost exalted – and as he watched her graceful progress down the central aisle of the chapel, he turned to Jem and whispered, 'I was right, she is most extraordinary.'

Chapter 57

'There is a distinct theme going on here, Michael,' Orla observed as Cathy, her silk dress covered by a capacious apron sporting a pattern of many white sheep and a single black one, brought in the magnificent, three-tier wedding cake. Instead of the traditional bride and groom standing on the top tier, she had created a tiny flock of miniature Swaledale ewes, grazing on a small patch of green field. Inevitably, the entrance of this masterpiece caused the guests to applaud heartily.

The wedding reception had been a resounding success. As with everything she did, the food that Cathy had produced was superb. Her table arrangements were perfect – plain and simple, using wild meadow flowers that she had picked that morning, as soon as the dew had dried on their petals, from *Fell Farm* fields. The formal speeches had been made and guests were now feeling happy, relaxed and mellow.

But, in sharp contrast to the other smiling guests, Michael Jamieson was distinctly subdued. He had had the most difficult conversation of his life with his son the previous evening and was still fighting to come to terms with it. In contrast, Matt lounged, drink held casually in his hand, chatting to a group of his friends next to the table which held the bottles of wine, champagne in ice buckets, small bottles of local-brewed beer and elderflower cordial.

'I just know he's going to make some sort of announcement,' Michael muttered through gritted teeth to his wife.

'Well, that's down to him. Homosexuality was deeply prized in Classical times, you know, Mike, think of Plato …'

'Actually, thinking of Matt and our family's position in this tightly-knit community is more pressing just at the moment,' groaned her husband.

Matt's father was right. Lifting his half-full champagne glass, Matt stood up, smiling broadly. He was a popular figure in Lokisdale – a highly sociable man with a keen sense of humour and an excellent vet. Everyone expected an amusing story from him now – something to round off one of the most perfect wedding celebrations that the people sitting in the marquee had ever attended. Perhaps Matt would share reminiscences from his childhood with his sister, Laura. Perhaps he would praise the skills and common sense of Cathy, the outstanding 'best woman'. The broad, weathered faces of the Dales' farmers registered comfortable anticipation as they settled their bulks back into the chairs which Cathy had decorated with bows and flowers, cradling their drinks in large, work-worn hands.

'I ask you all to raise your glasses to my sister, Laura, who has come home in many senses of the word, to find and to claim the love of her life. We wish you every joy, lovely girl!'

Farmers and their neatly-attired wives stood and acknowledged the toast made by the vibrant, laughing brother of the bride. But then Matt gestured impatiently for the guests to sit down again.

'And now, on this happiest of occasions, I would like to make a small announcement of my own. Edward ... Ed ... and I will also be getting married later in the year. So please raise your glasses again – this time to my partner and to our future together!' He smiled broadly at the striking dark-haired man sitting next to him.

It would be unfair to say that Lokisdale had not moved with the times, but to the cross-section of traditional hill-farmers represented in that gathering, invited because of their long-standing connection with Geoff Jamieson, such an announcement still came as a shock. The toast was not immediately unanimous and mutterings could be heard across the marquee: 'takes a bit of getting my head around, does that ...'; 'Eh, what old Geoff would think of his lad, standing up and saying that, bold as brass ...'

Jem was more than a little angry at this discordant note being introduced into a day that had, to this point, been unequivocally perfect. He decided therefore to steer the remains of the celebrations fairly and squarely back to Laura, his wife – the words still sounded unreal as he rehearsed them to himself – and to Cathy, without whom the whole celebration just would not have happened – in more ways than one. To his irritation, he saw that Matt's clumsy announcement had affected both women: Laura had lost the lovely flush of happiness that she had carried all day; and Cathy had become tense and apprehensive, as if she expected Matt to extend his announcement to her also. Jem was no orator, but he was going to give it his best shot.

'Indeed, warmest congratulations to you both,' he started, generously. 'I know I have given my formal speech earlier this afternoon, but it is now getting late and there are just a few extra things I would like to say. First of all,' Jem turned to the long table containing the old Dales farmers, 'because I know that your farming duties will be calling you back home before very long, I wanted especially to thank you all for coming at this very busy time of the year. And I wanted to say to you all that I envy the common thread that has brought you all here today: your friendship with Geoff Jamieson. I will regret forever the fact that I was never given the opportunity to get to know my wife's grandfather, but in her I see the ethic of hard work and dedication to her farm and to her livestock that Geoff left as his legacy here in Lokisdale. So, please raise your glasses in another toast – to Geoff Jamieson.'

This was more like it, thought the assembled farmers. They didn't know much about young Walker – his father had been a right strange sort – but as they had arrived, they had looked with expert eyes at the state of *Fell Farm* and its flock and couldn't fault them. With a chorus of gruff 'Hear, hears', they got to their feet and drained their glasses.

'But I have not quite finished yet,' added Jem, as he saw this particular farming contingent getting ready to leave. 'I have thanked Cathy already for her exemplary carrying out of her role as 'best woman', so I will say no more on that score. However, I would now like to thank her on two further counts. First, for her amazing cooking – before I became shepherd here, I was quite slight – and secondly, and by far the most important thing, for her staunch friendship for Laura. Together the friends have supported each other through many difficulties, and that is the sure test of friendship that will last a lifetime. Cathy is a unique and very special human being. You will not find a cook, or a friend, to surpass her in Lokisdale! So, once again, please raise your glasses to Cathy Munro, friend extraordinaire!'

Cathy was completely overcome at Jem's unexpected speech, and bent to pick up a glass, hoping to disguise the tears which had come unbidden to her eyes. Once again there was a whole-hearted chorus of 'To Cathy!' and, for a second time, several of the guests started to make preparations to leave. But Jem was in his stride and had not finished yet.

'Finally, and then you really will be free to return to your sheep, I would like you to join me in a toast to Geoff's granddaughter, my wife, Laura Walker. I am more comfortable with sheep now than with literature, but when I was younger, I read this in a poem:

'She is all states, all princes I,
Nothing else is ...'

'My Laura, my beautiful, kind, gentle wife means, literally, the whole world to me and I am the happiest of men to have been able to marry her. Please raise your glasses in our very final toast of the day. To Laura Walker!'

Women looked at their husbands, swaying slightly on large feet spread wide apart, with florid faces and spreading waistlines. And equally men regarded their wives, upon whose faces life had written a variety of characteristics, including the less attractive traits of bitterness, envy and selfishness. But finally, the gaze of all rested on the man and woman who had just married: Jem tall, broad and strong, every aspect of his expression showing his love for his wife; and Laura, delicate as a flower, opening fully in the warmth of her husband's love.

Jem had obliterated Matt's thoughtless announcement.

⋈

Much, much later, Laura turned to her husband in the room that from now on they would share. The curtains were drawn back and the windows to the south were open wide to the warm night air. Silver stars had started to speckle the cobalt blue of the early summer sky and only the occasional deep bleat of a ewe calling her lambs to her broke the peace and silence of the night. Laura stood before Jem in an ivory-silk nightgown secured only by the briefest of straps over her white shoulders. The only colour on her body, apart from her riotous auburn hair, was the strawberry-coloured birthmark low on her left breast.

'Who was the poet you quoted those words from, Jem?' she asked, reaching up to stroke back his dark hair from his eyes.

'John Donne,' replied Jem. 'He wrote other memorable words too, when I imagine he was in a position not a million miles adrift from the one we are in just now, since the poem is called '*To His Mistress, Going to Bed.*'

'What are they, Jem?' Laura asked.

'Describing his imminent discovery of the woman he loved, Donne wrote:

"Oh my America,
My New Found Land,"'

Her husband smiled and gently released the fine straps that held her nightdress.

⊰∥⊱

At the edge of the reservoir, a small child splashed at the still water, watching the reflection of the moonlight on its mirror-like surface split and shimmer. Then, clutching his wooden lorry close to his chest, he turned without a sound and made his way reluctantly back towards *The Edge of the World*.

Chapter 58

Over the next months, Jem and Laura started to establish the deep bonds – with each other and with the majestic, uncompromising land that is Yorkshire – that last a lifetime, and beyond. Generation after generation has dug deep, literally and emotionally, to survive the harsh winters; the heart-breaking death of stock; and the tough and resisting landscape. On *Fell Farm*, Laura was completely fulfilled in Jem and he in her, just as Lily and Geoff Jamieson had completed and fulfilled each other; and Geoff's father and mother before him and so on, right back until the first foundation stone was laid on the windswept, rocky tract of land that was to become the Jamiesons' farm.

June came and went and the Dales were in the grip of one of the driest summers that folk could remember. Panting sheep sought shade against the cool drystone walls which bounded their fields, and lambs lifted their faces in bliss to the sun, with eyes closed and ears back. Every window and door in the farmhouse was wide open and Fly and her pups – now almost as large as their mother – came and went freely. Jem was doing some basic sheepdog training with the young dogs, restraining them on a long lead whilst introducing them to the concept of circling around the sheep and bringing them back to him. Of the three, the dog showed most natural ability. He was intense and focussed and, watching him starting to work, head down, ears flattened, stalking forward, fixing the ewes with the 'eye' that he had inherited from his talented mother, Laura laughed.

'Jem, do you remember how fat he was when he was a tiny pup? He always made sure that he was the first to feed from Fly and the last to leave her. He almost looked spherical! I never thought that he would move like this … although I always admired his single-minded determination.'

'Aye, bold and determined. No wonder you called him Geoff!'

Laura remembered her husband's quizzical response when she had claimed the puppy for her own and declared her intention to name him after her grandfather.

'"Geoff!"' Jem had laughed, kissing his wife. 'If you do get involved in the world of sheepdog trialling, I don't know what the other competitors, not to mention the judges, will make of the name. You'll find other dogs called Glen, Sweep, Ben, Cap or Moss, and dozens of others … but I doubt whether you'll come across another Geoff!'

'He's going to be my dog, so I don't care whether the name is unusual or not,' Laura had said firmly, and so calls of 'Geoff' as well as 'Fly' now echoed around the fields of *Fell Farm*.

Jem had decided to name the other two young females at the same time, and they were called, somewhat more traditionally, Meg and Gael. Jem had found homes for these two but had been asked to complete their basic training before they went to their new farms. With a mother like Fly, their reputation went before them.

The grass was thick in the fields; the lambs, now separated from their mothers, were growing well; and once again the time had come in the shepherding year for a few months of relative peace, allowing Jem to concentrate on the young dogs when he wasn't involved in the never-ending routine of farm maintenance.

Jem kept his promise to Laura and tried to teach her the basics of sheep dog handling, but Laura found it very difficult to follow the strict protocols of dog training. She was too fond of the dogs not to want to touch and fondle them whilst they were supposed to be working.

'Oh well *done*, Geoff!' she would exclaim when he successfully followed a command that either she or Jem had given, and the small animal would leave his sheep and return to her, head low, ears laid back with pleasure and with tail wagging.

'Darling, he will never learn to stand with his sheep and take control of them if you inveigle him back like that,' Jem explained, chuckling despite himself.

'But he's done well and needs encouragement!' protested Laura.

'But only after you've told him to stop – when you say "That'll do, Geoff". Why don't you go and do some more work in the snug whilst I continue the session with this lot?'

'Are you telling me that I am a useless sheepdog handler, Jem Walker?'

'Well, let's put it like this. You can illustrate and write books much better than you can handle a dog,' Jem laughed, as he took her in his arms and slipped the sheepdog whistle from around her neck.

Laura had, quite simply, never been so happy in her entire life, not even when, as a little girl, she had clutched the large, safe hand of her grandfather. She was able to work with an untroubled mind and the quality of her *Modern Fairy Tales* reflected her mood of positivity and optimism: young animals at the start of their lives were involved in humorous situations, rather than embroiled in the shadowy, threatening, even violent worlds that Laura had written of only a year earlier.

Both Jem's and Laura's lives had changed beyond recognition and, probably for the first time ever, each felt able to relax, to stop following the driven, focussed existence that they had led up to that point. Often they spent the long, hot hours of the late afternoon swimming in the pool in *The Crying Wood*. Sometimes it was the only way in which they could cool off after a day working in the blazing sun and they floated lazily, for once, on their backs in the water, gazing up at the hot blue sky far above the tops of the trees. Laura would always pack her sketchbook and pencil, just as she had when a child, and hooked the strap over a branch whilst they were in the water to keep the contents dry. They both felt that the pool was part of their own private world, as no one ever seemed to stray this far into the woodland – and they loved this feeling of privacy and seclusion. Although she didn't mention this to Jem, when she lay on the flat, warm rocks surrounding the water, drying her hair and body in the sunshine, Laura always scanned the dry bracken for any sign of the small boy she had seen watching Jem, almost a year ago now. Sometimes she thought she saw a flicker of a movement, a glimpse of auburn hair, but she was never completely certain.

On the eve of Laura's marriage to Jem, Cathy had insisted that she should take over the stable cottage. 'We can't possibly carry on as we have done, Laura,' she admonished her friend gently, when Laura had tried to dismiss the idea out of hand. 'You and Jem will be man and wife and the farmhouse is your territory. You are about to found the Jamieson-Walker dynasty and you need space and freedom to do it. I will make changes in stable cottage, to make it my own ... of course I will ... and I would love still to cook for you both, for as long as I remain here. Is that all right with you?'

For her answer, Laura just hugged Cathy – hard.

⊰⧓⊱

'You'll never guess what?' Cathy announced one early July day on her return from a morning's volunteering at school, dumping her shopping bag on the kitchen table.

'Miss Wilkins is going to retire?' Laura hazarded.

'No, she's far too young for retirement. It's much more salacious than that!' Cathy declared.

'She's had an affair with Miles Jefferies, who has finally decided that his broken heart can only be healed by the love of a good woman?'

'It's nothing to do with Sandra Wilkins! She wouldn't touch someone like Miles Jefferies with a barge pole!' Cathy commented – for her, quite brusquely. 'But it *is* to do with Miles Jefferies!'

'Go on then ...'

'He's run away with the vicar's wife!'

'What, that demure young woman who never says a word?' Laura asked incredulously. 'She scuttles along like a rabbit in the headlights most of the time. I don't even know her name!'

'Yep, that's the one!' Cathy answered. 'And her name is Rachel. Of course, he's been asked to leave the board of governors of St Mark's.'

'Well, pretty difficult to have an adulterer as governor of a church school,' Laura commented wryly.

'Since Miles was a community governor – someone who represents a prominent sector of the local population – Sandra suggested this morning that when the vacancy is advertised, either you or Jem should apply. I don't know what the percentages look like, but there must be a very significant number of farmers in the Lokisdale community. What do you think, Laura?'

Laura wrinkled her nose. 'I'm not a farmer, Cathy. Look at my singular failure in training Geoff! I play at being one, but farming is in Jem's blood and his bones, and he could represent the interests of the farming sector at the school much better than I could.'

'Excellent! We can mention it to him over lunch, maybe. But there is something else, Laura.'

'Well, please don't encourage me to guess what. I'll only make you cross again.'

Cathy ignored her friend's teasing. 'They are going to start making a film here in Lokisdale!'

'What … for the television? Some sort of local beauty spot tourism film, or walks with my sheepdog? Perhaps Geoff could have a starring role …'

'What is wrong with you today, Laura? You used to be such a serious-minded woman,' Cathy grinned at her. 'No. Apparently, it's by quite a well-known film director and is some sort of Gothic romance, based on the family who used to live in Loki House at the turn of the century. The curator of the museum has recently discovered a cache of old diaries in the second-hand bookshop near the bridge – you know the one I mean – and the plot is going to be based on these.'

'Seriously? Wow! That really is interesting, much more so than Miles' adulterous exploits. When do they start filming?'

'August 1st. They are holding a public meeting in the school hall next week to give details and apparently to take on 'extras' for the filming – local people who look the part I suppose.'

'Are you going, Cathy?'

'Yes, I am. Sandra tries to do everything for everyone all the time, and people constantly put more and more pressure on her – parents, governors, staff, everybody! She needs help and I am going to support her all I can. No one else seems ready or willing to do so!'

Cathy's impassioned words, together with her slightly protective tone earlier in the conversation, were the first hints that Laura had of the possibility that a relationship was developing between her friend and the Headteacher. She smiled warmly at the thought: she respected the two women deeply for their tough, caring characters, their integrity and their determination to bring about a positive change for good in society. But Laura said nothing. She simply kissed her friend on the cheek, looked her straight in the eyes and said, 'I quite understand.'

Chapter 59

The public meeting was extremely well-attended. Dalesfolk were beyond patriotic and were determined to prevent any damaging intrusion into what they considered to be their family territory. Laura and Jem had both decided to go along and sat, elbows well tucked-in, in the tightly-packed hall, facing Cathy and Sandra Wilkins who stood together at the side of the small stage. Laura had shared her thoughts with Jem and he glanced over towards the two women, trying to gauge the nature of their relationship. The contrast between the overt passion of the embrace he had witnessed in York and the infinitely more complex array of emotions he observed now was telling. One moment the two women were sharing a joke together, the next they looked seriously at each other; the gestures of one were reflected by the movements of the other; sometimes they brushed hands, or shoulders.

Jem smiled at Laura. 'I agree with you,' he said, taking her hand in his and kissing it.

On a screen at the back of the stage were the words:

That Golden Summer
(working title)
Director: Gerard Pillinger

Sandra and Cathy had provided light refreshments to follow the presentation and these were set out on long tables at the back of the hall, together with bottles of wine and squash. The atmosphere was lively and full of anticipation, as the people of Lokisdale were clearly keen to fact-find in order to fuel their gossip, and ready to enjoy the free food and drink. The lights were dimmed slightly and a tanned man, with sunglasses pushed back into his thick blond hair, and wearing a crumpled designer linen suit, sauntered on to the stage.

'Good evening,' he began in a cultured American accent. 'My name is Gerry Pillinger and I want to tell you about my next blockbuster film.'

'Modest, then,' hissed Jem out of the corner of his mouth.

Laura gave him a sharp push with her knee.

'Imagine the scene,' continued the director. 'A dark, Gothic mansion, with a half-crazed old woman living there. In the attics a secret ... a secret that will escape and shake Lokisdale to its core ...'

'What? They've managed to incarcerate Miles Jefferies and the vicar's wife up there?' Jem whispered, grinning widely.

'Stop it, Jem! Behave yourself,' Laura tried to frown but, turning to look at her husband, the only expression that came to her face reflected the love and joy that she found with him. They quietly interlaced their fingers and continued to listen to the fluent patter of the American director.

'This is the beginning of the epic that we are going to start filming in three short weeks' time. When Mr Ian Ramshead, the curator of the museum here in your beautiful Dales township, discovered the diaries written by the housekeeper of Loki House, a powerful story indeed was uncovered!'

Gerry Pillinger turned to the quiet, grey-suited man sitting in the front row of the chairs that Cathy and Sandra had arranged to face the stage, and started to applaud him. Unused to such demonstrative displays, the applause was echoed half-heartedly by only a small percentage of the audience, who didn't quite understand what was going on. Oblivious of the natural reticence of the people in front of him and the embarrassment of the museum curator, the director warmed to his theme:

'The story is set not in the town of Lokisbridge as we now see it, but in Laikinthorpe, the small community that was flooded when the reservoir was created, because that, according to the diaries, is where the events actually took place – in Loki House. We have set aside an unprecedentedly large budget to re-create Laikinthorpe back in the studios, with the help of photos and the archives of Ian Ramshead's award-winning museum.'

There was a general buzz of interest around the hall.

'We are here tonight to get you all on board. If you know anything about those times, or about the village hidden under the waters of the dam, then please come forward … my email and phone number are shown on the screen. Better still, if you want to appear in the film, then contact me without delay.'

Jem had fallen silent and, glancing at him, she knew that the mention of Laikinthorpe had brought into his mind the sadness of the past. She knew that he was reliving the short months that he had spent with Ruth in her cottage, awaiting the birth of their child. Possibly, too, the innumerable times that he had trekked down the steep bank from *The Edge of the World*, accompanying his parents to Laikinthorpe Chapel. Laura had not seen him quiet and withdrawn like this since they had been married and she felt his hurt like a physical pain in her own body. Without a word, she linked her arm though his and pulled him gently towards her to reassure and comfort him.

'I love you, Jem,' she whispered.

⊰)|⊱

'Now, you two are perfect!' exclaimed Gerard Pillinger loudly as he made his way very deliberately towards Laura and Jem. 'Maybe I could even create a bit-part for you both.'

He eyed Jem's striking height and breadth and fineness of feature and Laura's loveliness appreciatively.

'Not on the market, I'm afraid,' Jem said firmly, interposing himself between Laura and the film director. 'We're farmers and my wife is an author. We don't have the time to wander about pretending to be people we are not.'

'OK, OK,' Gerard retorted hastily, realising that he had got off on the wrong foot as far as these two were concerned. He didn't often make a misjudgement, but he had certainly not counted on the intelligence and discernment of this couple. He tried a different tack.

'Have you lived here all your life?' he asked Jem.

'Yes, and my wife was born in Yorkshire but worked in London for a while,' Jem replied guardedly.

'Aye,' one very elderly farmer, bent almost double, added. 'And Jem's father was lay-preacher in the chapel that now lies under those waves yonder! I reckon there's more secrets under there than you'll find in your diaries!'

'Thank you,' the director said, neatly turning his attention once again to Jem and Laura.

'Well, here's my card if you change your minds,' was his parting comment.

⊰≬⊱

The next two weeks were blisteringly hot with temperatures soaring to the mid-thirties and Yorkshire featured in the national news – something that only happened when catastrophe struck, Jem observed sardonically. Sub-zero temperatures, desert-like drought, mass murder, all these crude headlines attracted the attention of the nation towards Yorkshire, not its majesty, its peace and the tough warmth of its people.

Jem had been walling, up in the high northern fields of *Fell Farm*, and returned early for dinner, looking thoughtful.

'Are you OK, Jem?' Laura asked.

'The reservoir is so low that buildings are starting to show again,' he murmured bleakly. 'It takes me back to the last time I saw those walls and chimneys, Laura. It was the day I saw Josh for the last time.'

Chapter 60

Inevitably there was intense local and national media interest in the village being gradually revealed by the receding water level. People flocked to see the slowly-emerging stones, doors and windows, some incredibly still glazed and closed against the outside environment. Leafless trees and the dry-stone garden walls of Laikinthorpe were still intact and even a red telephone box, now smeared green and brown with mud and pond weed, remained by the building that had been the post office.

A few days after the meeting at the school, Laura and Cathy decided to walk up the dale, past *The Edge of the World*, to see what was happening for themselves. They strolled along quietly together, each preoccupied with her own particular thoughts, and took the unspoken decision to pause by Jem's childhood home to take in the scene from a distance. In its present state of dilapidation, the entire farm ironically presented a more acceptable image as a picturesque ruin than it had ever been as a family home. Nature with her kind hand was clothing its harsh, dark walls with ferns and saplings, with tiny mosses and minute flowers – claiming once again from the doors, hinges and nails, the wood and iron that she had provided from her abundance to construct the farmhouse, centuries earlier.

Gazing silently for some minutes at the ruins beside them and the perspective in front of them, eventually Laura remarked, 'It's astonishing, Cathy! The whole valley looks totally different. How could the people here bear such a dramatic change! It is like a village frozen in time, somehow, and even more astonishing … look!' And Laura pulled out her sketchbook from the bag slung across her shoulder. 'This is the drawing I made in *The Fable of the Foxes* of the cub and the wolf leaving the rocks over there and heading down towards Laikinthorpe. I did it months ago, before the drought, and the position and shape of the buildings is exactly right! But I had never seen them. How could this be, Cathy?'

Her friend frowned and shook her head. 'I haven't a clue, Laura,' she said thoughtfully, examining the sketch closely. 'Even the trees are in the correct positions … I can't begin to understand this. But then there is much I can't understand.'

⊰◈◈◈⊱

Once the receding reservoir levels had started to reveal the hidden buildings, the pace of their exposure appeared to accelerate and this seemed to impact directly upon Jem, whom Laura knew was increasingly restless and troubled. Sometimes she would wake in the middle of an airless night to discover that her husband was not at her side and, inevitably, she would find him standing at their bedroom window, looking north-west towards the ruined farm and the dark memories of his youth. Although he would return to bed, she was aware that he lay awake at her side, tense and preoccupied, his mind drawn unwillingly into the past.

Gerry Pillinger, of course, lapped up this unexpected natural publicity for his latest film. He and his camera crew spent hours each morning on the perimeter of the reservoir filming the streets and narrow alleys of the drowned village of Laikinthorpe. At this point, mud still lay thickly on the site and, although it was impossible to say how deep it was, it was agreed that the situation was far too treacherous to attempt to actually enter the purlieu of the community that had ceased to exist over a decade earlier. The local police had cordoned off as much of the area as was possible and put 'hazard' signs at regular intervals along the potentially accessible stretches of the village that were slowly being uncovered.

James White, Miles' rather academic sub-editor, still struggling to keep the local paper going after his editor's scandalous exit from the close-knit Yorkshire town, chose as the headlines to his article covering the steady revelation of the hidden village of Laikinthorpe, Einstein's words: '*Time is an illusion*'. Unfortunately for him, most of the readership of his paper coughed in an embarrassed and uncomprehending sort of way when reading this erudite quotation and passed swiftly on to articles about rugby or sheep-dog trialling.

In this leader article Gerry Pillinger was quoted as saying: '*This is the most remarkable stroke of luck! We are striving to re-create an authentic plan of the village of Laikinthorpe, flooded over ten years ago, and now we can check the dimensions, even the architectural details, of cottage, house, inn and chapel*

as, steadily, they are revealed to us. This movie was
certainly destined to be!'

⊰)I(⊱

Mid-August, and still the reservoir levels continued to recede as water was consumed in ever-increasing quantities by the Leeds-Bradford conurbation. Gradually the mud-covered streets of Laikinthorpe started to bake and harden in the extreme heat.

One night, which seemed even more airless than ever, Laura discovered that Jem had actually left the farmhouse and, after calling his name several times, she philosophically gave up on any chance of either him returning to her bed, or her returning to sleep. She shrugged on a thin cotton dressing-gown and went into the kitchen, making herself some tea and taking it into the snug. There were signs of the sky lightening to the east and she knew that dawn could not be far away so, sipping her drink, she slipped into her default mode and opened her sketchbook.

She smiled to herself as she flicked over the sketches she had made of Fly's puppies. Here they ran together through the farmyard and chased the chickens. She remembered how delighted she had been when Geoff had captured several tail feathers of their aggressive white cockerel with a puppy pounce. There, in her drawing, the pups lined up, heads down, tiny tails erect, trying to stalk and intimidate the sheep. And several sketches, featuring Geoff, almost a spherical ball of fur, showed the pups eating their dinner, plump paws planted firmly in their food.

But Laura knew which of her drawings she was going to work on – one to which, once again, she was drawn irresistibly. She looked at the unspeakably sad sketch of the dejected fox cub trotting alongside the huge, dominant wolf. The last image she had caught was of the pair leaving the vantage point of the rocky outcrop near *The Edge of the World*, heading down towards Laikinthorpe. Now, once again, picking up her pencil, she started to draw the next scene in the disturbing, dark story.

The wolf stood in the left of the picture, opening a heavy oak door, with long, ornate iron hinges and a round iron door handle. The door was ajar, as the massive animal pushed it with curved claws, leaning over the fox cub which looked even smaller and more vulnerable than in the previous drawings. The young animal disappeared almost entirely into the shade as he entered the building. There was a rectangular stone above the door, on which was carved some indistinct lettering.

Laura became aware of the kitchen door latch being lifted and knew that it would be Jem returning home. Seeing the light on in the snug, he took his wife in his arms in a long, hard embrace.

'I'm being haunted again by my dreams of Josh, Laura,' he sighed. 'I just had to go back to what remains of *The Edge of the World*, to see if he was there.'

'And was he, Jem?'

'No. Nothing but darkness and emptiness,' Jem responded, rubbing his exhausted eyes. He kissed Laura's hair and glanced over her head to her desk and the scattered drawings. 'You've been drawing the fox cub again,' he remarked, frowning slightly as he held her in his left arm, reaching down with his right to examine the sketches more closely. 'That's the chapel door in Laikinthorpe that I had to enter every Sunday until I was sixteen,' he sighed, straightening the sketch book, 'and every centimetre of its appearance is etched on my brain. But how do you know what it looks like, Laura?'

'Jem, I don't! As I have tried to explain, this story is being dictated to me in a series of drawings. I've never seen this before. I think there are some words, an inscription or something over the door ...'

'Yes, it says *The Wages of Sin is Death*.'

'Cheery! I've seen that before outside churches, but usually it is followed by the second part of the quotation, which seems slightly more optimistic *But the Gift of God is Eternal Life*.'

'Well, not in the case of the chapel dominated by my father,' Jem observed grimly. 'He saw only the dark side of life. Anything sinful had to be eradicated, leaving no glimmer of hope or positivity.'

'Come back to bed, Jem,' said Laura, hugging him close to her. 'We can be together for a few hours before we have to start work.'

Chapter 61

'We're going in,' Gerry Pillinger announced on the local six o'clock news.

'He sounds as if he is about to liberate a city in a war zone,' Cathy commented with distaste.

'It's just the way he speaks, Cathy,' smiled Sandra Wilkins, pouring a glass of chilled white wine for her companion. 'American rhetoric is quite extreme sometimes. At least it catches one's attention.'

'Perhaps for all the wrong reasons!'

It was Friday evening and Sandra could at last start to relax after the pressures of the week. Cathy laughed, sipping her drink and sinking further into the deep, comfortable armchair. Sandra Wilkins' house was an old mineworker's cottage, one of a terrace of only four, with long, fertile gardens stretching down to the river Loki. The afternoon sunshine flooded into the sitting room, lighting up the vases of fresh flowers picked from the brimming flowerbeds, the delicate watercolours of the sweeping Yorkshire countryside, and the large pine bookcases, tightly packed with an eclectic mixture of books.

'I love it here,' Cathy breathed, smiling at her friend.

'And I love having you here, Cathy,' the Headteacher replied warmly, smiling as she turned in her chair to face her guest.

⊰⊪⊱

The following Monday, Gerry Pillinger and his film crew stormed the sad citadel of the lost village of Laikinthorpe and trod where no one had stepped for a decade. Gerry had decreed that he needed the services of a cartographer, so that the scale and topography of the site could be correctly replicated in the film set. Enquiries were made by a member of his admin team and the nearest available person with the requisite training and skills was found to be an employee of the North Yorkshire Police. Moreover, she was local enough to be able to accompany the director and his acolytes at short notice and with minimal cost, as they carefully made their way into the desolate, mud-coated village.

Karen Milligan was an experienced and meticulous worker and methodically noted, recorded and photographed the route that the group took. From entering Laikinthorpe via South Street, they skirted the post office and blacksmith's forge, marked by the huge rusting anvil that stood outside the collapsed double doors, and finally reached the small village square. From here four narrow streets twisted away, roughly set according to the points of the compass, after which they were named, with usual Yorkshire common sense. South Street led back towards Lokisbridge, along what would originally have been the banks of the River Loki; North Street snaked away towards a large, remarkably intact stone building, which Karen took to be a chapel because of the tall, arched windows; East Street started to rise out of the village almost immediately, heading in the direction of Wensleydale; and West Street led past the massive ruins of Loki House in an almost straight line towards *The Crying Wood*.

Karen found her work for the police force fulfilling and varied. It involved mapping crime scenes, exploring the capabilities of new traffic infrastructures and dealing with public opinion concerning the placement of new centres for police operations. Her mind was orderly and thorough and she was gaining quite a reputation in the north of England for her detailed and reliable work.

Laura and Cathy found it impossible to stay away on that morning. They stood side by side, slightly apart from a fair-sized crowd of people. There were those who had originally lived in the flooded village and had been subsequently re-housed elsewhere in the dale; those who had connections with people who had lived there; and those who were quite simply curious about observing such a unique event. Laura was missing Jem. She cherished every moment of their life together as they shared everything from the ceaseless round of jobs that comes with being a shepherd, to the lively conversation that they enjoyed with Cathy over their evening meal. But above all, she rejoiced in the quiet and private time that belonged to just the two of them when they closed their bedroom door on the world at the end of a long working day. Over the past weeks Jem had often walked by himself to the northern reaches of *Fell Farm* land, snatching a few minutes to gaze at the village which had slowly but inexorably emerged from the depths of the reservoir. He looked at the mud-coated, dilapidated cottage where his son had been born, and where his son's mother had died, and he felt once again the crushing regret of having hurt another human being so much through his own actions. When Laura had told Jem that she and Cathy were driving down to the site of the uncovered village, he had been insistent that he had to remain at *Fell Farm* that afternoon in order to check the wooden flooring of the hay-loft over the sheep barn. This did need doing, but was far from urgent, and Laura suspected that Jem was not keen to see once again the condemning glances of the rehomed Dales folk, who remembered him only from the days when he had lived with Ruth in Laikinthorpe.

Laura watched the quick, expansive gestures of Gerry and his colleagues and observed how the heavy cameras wheeled by the cameramen were being expertly trained from side to side as they made their progress along the baked mud tracks. Karen made a sharp contrast to the others: business-like and slow, she followed her expressive, creative companions with minimal movement, her full attention being focussed on recording minutely-correct detail from what she observed. The film-makers walked swiftly along West Street, probably the most attractive of the four narrow routes out of the centre of Laikinthorpe because of the rising, wooded slopes beyond. But Karen strayed down North Street, along which most of the significant buildings of the village were set, making her methodical way towards the Chapel. A row of cottages stood opposite the gaunt, dark building and, narrowing her eyes, Laura wondered poignantly whether Jem and Ruth had inhabited one of these during their short and tragic time together. Vestiges of a park were set out by the Chapel, the paved paths and collections of broken sticks which could well have been shrubberies, all coated with the inevitable dried mud. Karen entered the bleak former place of worship, camera poised to photograph the interior, and the onlookers expected her to remain inside for a considerable length of time, since this was one of the major buildings in the village, and certainly the most well-preserved. But they could not have been more wrong. Within two minutes, the cartographer emerged, deep in conversation on her mobile phone. She continued to talk as she walked at a brisk pace towards her colleagues who were now returning to the village centre. The group of onlookers were far too distant to hear what Karen was saying to the film director, but her intense attitude and animated gestures were unmistakable. They also observed Gerry Pillinger run his fingers in a distracted way through his thick blond hair and shake his head as if incredulous at what he had been told. And to all present, the speed at which the entire group returned to the point of entry to Laikinthorpe marked the sudden urgency of the situation. The group passed the intrigued group of people clustering around the barriers to the village almost as if they didn't exist.

The only clue to what was happening was Gerry Pillinger's hissed imprecation. 'That's all we need, some sort of murder scene ... Seems like a kid was involved. Karen says the body was found next to a wooden toy ... a lorry or some such.'

Puzzled, looking at each other with a complete lack of understanding as to what could possibly be happening, most of the crowd had already started to disperse slowly and were out of earshot. And although many longed to go and explore for themselves, they had become aware of rapidly-approaching police sirens from the direction of the main Lokisdale road from

Harrogate and turned their attention towards these and away from the ruins of the village.

Laura was fairly sure that only she and Cathy had heard Gerry's remark. The other bystanders stood a little distant and were chatting amongst themselves. She glanced at her friend with a sudden flash of revelation. 'It's Josh, Cathy, I know it is. I'm going to look for myself. I don't care whether the police are coming or not.'

'Laura!'

But any warning or caution that Cathy was going to give her friend was never uttered, as Laura ran swiftly along the mud-baked street into Laikinthorpe, across the village square and along North Street. Ever since she had produced the drawing of the fox cub entering the shadowed world of the chapel, Laura had suspected that this would be the final drawing she would make of the complex interactions between the cub and the wolf. In her heart she knew that the cub had entered the dark building she had sketched – the chapel – and had never emerged from it.

Chapter 62

There was a tangible feeling of oppression and profound sadness as Laura entered the building, leaving behind the shimmering summer world of the living to become enclosed by the desolate world of the dead. She encountered complete silence, almost as if the sounds of the world outside had been switched off and she recoiled automatically at the indescribably depressing environment that faced her. The detested box pews, one of which had caused such an extreme feeling of revulsion in Laura when she had encountered it in Lokisdale museum, faced her in forbidding ranks. Slowly Laura took a step forward, then another, until she came to the third pew on the right. On tiptoe, she could just see over the tall wooden partition which isolated the people in the pew from the rest of the Chapel and, just as she had expected, she had finally found Josh.

The fragile, white bones lay on the wooden floor of the pew and the tiny delicate skeletal fingers were still clasped around a wooden toy – clearly a lorry, lovingly made. No vestige of paint remained – all had been washed off by the water of the reservoir over the past ten years. Although it was impossible to be sure after all this time, Laura could see no signs of a struggle, the little skeleton was peaceful, the skull on its side and the mouth quietly closed, resting against the much-loved toy. Laura was not a praying person, but at that moment a simple prayer that her grandfather had taught her in her childhood came to mind and she whispered it as she continued to look at the body of the child.

With a deep sense of closure, Laura turned to leave the Chapel and meet the police whom she was fairly sure would by now have arrived at Laikinthorpe. Blinking against the bright light flooding through the Chapel door and with tears blurring her vision, Laura stumbled as she made her way back along the central aisle.

Glancing down at her feet, she saw something that filled her with disquiet and horror, just as the slight, white bones that had belonged to Jem's son had filled her with a deep sense of sorrow and peace.

She had tripped against another body – this time a huge skeleton lying on its front, face to the side, the massive hands grasping at a heavy stone cross which had fallen full across its skull, crushing it, leaving the mouth open in final agony.

This, Laura thought with a shudder of horror, was almost certainly Nehemiah Walker, Jem's father, and it would seem that finally justice, far beyond that of this world in its intensity and appropriateness, had been dealt to one who had caused only pain and misery during his life.

⊰⫶⊱

Laura emerged from the gloom of the Chapel and blinked hard to bring the real world back into focus.

Narrowing her eyes against the bright sunlight, she saw two things happening simultaneously: on the edge of the village, the police had arrived and were taking a statement from Karen Milligan; and a little further back, towards Lokisbridge, Jem flung open the door of Cathy's car and hurtled as fast as he could towards Laikinthorpe. Her dear friend must have returned to *Fell Farm*, intuitively knowing that Laura was about to find Josh's remains and understanding that Jem's place should be with his wife, and what remained of his son, as soon as possible. As always, Cathy was the facilitator, the one who sought to bring harmony to even the most tragic situation.

'Jem, I've found Josh!' Laura cried, as her husband raced past the dispersing crowds and the police, who were laboriously erecting a barrier across the road. Jem hugged her hard.

'Where is he, Laura?' Jem panted.

'In the Chapel,' Laura replied breathlessly.

Jem took Laura's hand and they ran together back to the Chapel. 'Where is he, Laura?' Jem repeated.

'He's here, Jem,' Laura whispered, taking her husband's hand gently. 'He is beautiful, even, even as he is …'

Jem stopped, breathing heavily. He opened the box pew door reverently and knelt by the tiny white network of bones that had been his son. With infinite gentleness he stroked the tiny skull with his forefinger – clearly a gesture that he had rejoiced in again and again when his child had been alive. 'My darling boy,' he murmured, tears running freely down his face.

After initial animosity and challenge, the police had been, Laura thought, absolutely amazing. They had listened carefully to Jem and to Laura. Taking careful notes, they explained that it was paramount to establish, scientifically, the identity of the deceased persons and asked Jem whether they could take DNA samples from him. The scene told its own story. The police were sympathetic, thorough and kind and never had community policing been so well-proven, Laura reflected.

Chapter 63

Ruth's grave had been opened to receive the tiny white coffin of her son. Jem, Laura and Cathy, together with Sandra Wilkins and a scattering of elderly Lokisbridge residents, who relished a funeral because it affirmed their own continued existence, stood around the graveside. Cathy and Sandra stood together, clearly a couple, although Laura was pleased that they did not feel it necessary to constantly touch and demonstrate overtly romantic physical contact with each other.

Jem placed the battered, colourless wooden lorry on top of Josh's coffin as it was being lowered into the grave, to rest on top of that of his mother. As Jem had listened to the age-old words of comfort which the vicar had pronounced, and as he had carried the small white coffin out of the church and into the church yard to say a final goodbye to his son, elements of grief, relief, anger and insupportable sadness played across his features. He had hardly spoken a word and Laura and Cathy were unsure how he would react after the service had ended.

But now, finally, it was over. As the sparse group of people drifted away, some shaking their heads at the memories the service had aroused in them, some already thinking of the next event in their limited lives, Jem murmured quietly to Laura, 'Let's go to *The Crying Wood*, Laura. I just want some peace. I need to get away from the prying eyes of Lokisdale.'

Laura nodded and took hold of his hand, feeling that, unusually, it was ice-cold, even though the intense heat of the summer weather continued without abating. They walked slowly, hand in hand, up out of Lokisbridge on the track which rose gently towards the wood and the moor beyond.

Jem ripped off his clothes and dived into the deep pool, remaining submerged for far longer than usual as the cool, pure water washed over his face and head, seeming to calm and soothe his agitated mind. More slowly and thoughtfully Laura slipped out of her cotton skirt and top and left her sandals on the great, flat rock where she had seen Josh over a year earlier.

Jem swam and dived and swam again, floating on his back and then face-down on the water of the woodland pool. To Laura, gliding by his side and covertly watching his slightest move or display of emotion, the wait for her husband to speak to her again seemed interminable. It was late afternoon and shadows were starting to fall across the pool surface when Laura decided that it was time for her, at least, to get out and to lie in what remained of the sunshine in order to dry her body before putting her clothes back on. Eyes closed, aware only of the sound of Jem's gentle splashing in the pool, she cupped her hands protectively around her belly. She had been waiting for the right time to tell Jem her news, but the last weeks had been frenetic and Jem had been utterly preoccupied with the events as they moved to their sad conclusion.

Laura was tired. She had been deeply moved by the tragic tableau which she had discovered in the Chapel and had been trying to be fully supportive of Jem, whilst not being demanding of his time or his conversation. The sound of the water running into the pool – still unabated despite the drought – the sleepy birdsong of a robin perched on a close-by branch, and the warmth of the sunshine, combined to make Laura drowsy. On the very edge of sleep, she became aware of Jem's voice. He, too, had left the pool and was standing close beside her.

'Laura, look!'

A white bird glided down from the cliff to their right, diving and then dipping its head in the water of the pool. Clearly it was a juvenile, as it still had some pale grey feathers in its tail and wings. Almost immediately it was joined by a large, pure-white female, who started to swim close by, even brushing the young goose's wings protectively with her own. After some minutes both left the pool and spread their wings wide in the late sun, moving them gently so that water droplets, like diamonds, ran and spilled onto the rocks upon which they stood. With a glance at each other, the beautiful birds took off simultaneously, the adult female taking the lead and flying straight for the sun and the freedom of the wide blue sky. The smaller juvenile followed, slowly at first, then gathering speed as it gained confidence.

Jem and Laura watched the birds until they disappeared into the infinite brightness of the sun and their life beyond Lokisdale, and then they turned again to each other, lifting their faces to the sky from which, at last, cool drops of rain had started to fall.

Epilogue

'Cathy, Josh, come on, come this way, but be very quiet in case they are here again.'

The twins, carrying identical lunchboxes, followed Laura, their mother. They had been born just six months after their parents had watched the great white geese flying into the freedom of sky and sunshine and leaving forever the constraints of Lokisdale.

As she had watched the adult female and the weaker juvenile soar to their freedom, Laura had remembered the legend of the white geese which she and Cathy had read in the museum. In her heart she knew that at last Josh's soul was free and that Ruth, his mother, would never be alone again. But that had been five, intensely busy, overwhelmingly happy, years earlier. It seemed like a different life – it was certainly a different era for Laura and her beloved family.

The stocky, ginger-haired little boy reached down to help his slighter sister climb the rocky outcrop near to the farm that their father had recently started to develop. An elderly, grey-coated Fly stiffly followed, soon outstripped by her large, energetic son, Geoff, who bounded around the children, tongue lolling out of his wide, grinning mouth. He had proved himself a worthy successor of his brave mother and was Jem's constant companion during his long days out on the farm with his ever-growing flock.

The five-year-olds had started school at St Mark's the previous autumn and were bright and interested in learning everything and anything. They were the delight of their godmother, Sandra Wilkins, showing a combination of their father's practicality and their mother's creative abilities. At school they were encouraged by their Auntie Cathy, who now shared their Headteacher's light and airy cottage by the river. At home they were enrapt by the 'Fairy Tales' that their mother wrote and read to them.

Laura had been offered a contract by a publisher who had visited the second Creative Arts Week at St Mark's that she had participated in; and she was gradually gaining national acclaim and a substantial following. Each of the little books she produced was dedicated to one or other of her adored family: 'To Jem', 'To Josh' or 'To Cathy'.

Cathy stopped and picked up a decayed wooden sign that was lying on the grass near to the gateway into the farm.

'The ...' she began, 'egg?'

'Edge,' corrected her mother gently.

'Of the ...word?' Cathy stumbled again.

'World, darling' Laura murmured.

'The Edge of the World?' laughed Josh, shaking back his glorious auburn curls. 'What's that supposed to mean?'

'This was the farm where Daddy was born, darling,' Laura explained. 'And it was given this name because it is on a high hill and it looks like it's at the edge of the world.'

'Was there a house here then, Mummy?' continued Josh.

Laura nodded. 'It used to be over there,' she gestured, 'but it was very old and was not safe anymore.

After some really heavy snow the year before you were born, the roof collapsed and Daddy had it taken down. He used the stone to build that big barn over there, and now there is more room for all our sheep!'

'Can we picnic here please, Mummy?' Cathy asked, sitting down in a hollow on the rocks.

'Of course, my lovely girl, it's a perfect place to sit!' declared Laura. 'I saw the fox family here only yesterday, when I brought Daddy some lunch. If we are quiet, we may see them again.'

'Will they eat my sandwiches?' asked Josh in a concerned stage-whisper.

'They will if you are not as quiet as mice!' Laura replied.

The warm Easter sun shone down on the site of the old farmhouse, now cleared, clean and wholesome, and providing shelter and grazing for the flock of six hundred sheep that Jem had built up, which he now ran over the combined grazing land of Fell Farm and The Edge of the World. The children sat close together, ginger curls blowing together in the wind, eating their cheese sandwiches and fruit and whispering about the foxes that they hoped to see.

And then, unbelievably, twin cubs emerged from the gorse thicket to the left of the rocky outcrop. Perfect bodies, softly clad in amber fur, black noses twitching, they played and tumbled together on the grass, chasing each other around a boulder and pouncing on the scattered harebells that were blowing in the gentle breeze on their long, impossibly slender stems. As is the case with very young animals, they soon became exhausted and, yawning, curled up, nose to tail. Laura noticed that the mother of the cubs lay still but vigilant, in the shadow of the gorse thicket and that the dog fox, grooming his magnificent fur, guarded his family from the shade of a hawthorn tree.

Laura smiled up at Jem, who had been quietly watching his beloved family for some time from a distance, as he arrived at her side to lay his arm across her shoulders.

His children, seeing that their father had arrived, dropped their lunchboxes noisily on the rocks, scaring away the foxes. They raced towards him, laughing and shouting, rosy faces smiling and arms outstretched.

'Daddy, Daddy!' they cried. 'We've missed you forever!'

Jem looked down at his son with tears in his eyes: his son, the image of his firstborn, and at his daughter, the image of her adored mother. He knelt in the green, flower-studded spring grass of the land that had borne him and tested him and given him such indescribably precious gifts.

'And I have missed you both, and your beautiful mother ... for ever!'

His strong arms encircling all that was precious to him, he glanced up at the sky to see and hear the calling of the great white birds as they flew and circled in the sunlight, flying from the shady half-life of The Crying Wood to a life and a freedom as yet unknown.

Two small golden heads bored into his sides and his wife, wild auburn curls flying around her head like a halo, looked into his eyes and smiled.

'I love you, Jem,' she said, strongly and boldly, replicating, although she did not know it, the look and words of her grandmother Lily.

'And I love you, Laura,' Jem laughed into the sunshine, 'more than life itself.'

About the Author

Alex grew up in the North of England, and, because her father, who was a well-known jazz musician, inspired her to try anything that life threw in her path, she enjoyed an eclectic childhood, before heading off to University to study English. This philosophy has stayed with her always and is reflected in her novels, which are about ordinary people who face extraordinary situations and frequently pose the question 'What if?'

She now lives in the Yorkshire Dales with her loyal labradors and husband who has the patience of a saint when it comes to her unconventional lifestyle. Before settling into life in her beloved Yorkshire and full-time writing, she enjoyed various careers in London, and high-profile positions in education in the west country.

Alex has two highly individual grown-up daughters whose influence is threaded through much of her work. The inspiration for this book, *The Child at the Edge of the World*, was, however, Alex's few years as an unexpected shepherd on a remote farm. It was a steep learning curve, but she loved every moment and still misses the bustle of lambing and the new life everywhere.

Alex is passionate about exploring the beauty of the natural world and has been fortunate to be able to see many parts of it, inspiring her to regularly practise Tai Chi and Yoga with her like-minded friends.

If you have enjoyed *The Child at the Edge of the World*, why not try Alex's earlier books? *The Carousel of Time* and *Saving Graces* are both available from Amazon. Her next book is set in the Outer Hebrides, where she worked on an archaeological dig whilst at University: *A Seeker of Everyday Magic* should be published early next year.

www.ingramcontent.com/pod-product-compliance
Lightning Source LLC
Chambersburg PA
CBHW031315280626
47169CB00019B/1633